THE MAN WHO DIDN'T FLY

D0109496

THE MAN WHO DIDN'T FLY

MARGOT BENNETT

With an Introduction
by Martin Edwards

Introduction © 2021 by Martin Edwards
The Man Who Didn't Fly © 1955 by Polly Thelwall
"No Bath for the Browns" © 1945 by Polly Thelwall
Cover and internal design © 2021 by Sourcebooks
Front cover © The British Library Board

Sourcebooks, Poisoned Pen Press, and the colophon are
registered trademarks of Sourcebooks.

Published by Poisoned Pen Press, an imprint of Sourcebooks,
in association with the British Library
P.O. Box 4410, Naperville, Illinois 60567-4410
(630) 961-3900
sourcebooks.com

The Man Who Didn't Fly was originally published in 1955
in London, England by Eyre & Spottiswoode.
"No Bath for the Browns" was originally published in *Lilliput* magazine, November 1945.

Library of Congress Cataloging-in-Publication Data

Names: Bennett, Margot, author.
Title: The man who didn't fly / Margot Bennett.
Description: Naperville, Illinois : Poisoned Pen Press, [2021] | Series:
   British library crime classics | "Originally published: 1955. 'No Bath
   for the Browns' originally published: 1945."
Identifiers: LCCN 2020031820 | (trade paperback)
Subjects: GSAFD: Mystery fiction. | LCGFT: Novels. | Short stories.
Classification: LCC PR6003.E646 M36 2021 | DDC 823/.912--dc23
LC record available at https://lccn.loc.gov/2020031820

Printed and bound in the United States of America.
SB 10 9 8 7 6 5 4 3 2 1

CONTENTS

INTRODUCTION

The Man Who Didn't Fly, first published in 1955, is a highly successful novel by an author of distinction whose crime writing career came to a sudden and rather mysterious end when she was at the peak of her powers.

The central puzzle in the story is unorthodox. A plane is engulfed in fire and crashes in the Irish Sea. The wreckage can't be found. A pilot and three men were on board and their bodies are missing. But *four* passengers had arranged to go on the flight and *none* of them can be found. So who was the man who didn't fly, and what has happened to him?

This is such an original mystery that I don't want to say much more about the plot, for fear of spoiling readers' enjoyment. The novel was a strong contender for the very first Gold Dagger Award for best novel of the year given by the Crime Writers' Association (in those early days of the CWA, the award was known as the Crossed Red Herring Award). In the event, it was pipped by *The Little Walls*, written by Winston (*Poldark*) Graham, while Ngaio Marsh's *Scales of Justice* and Lee Howard's *Blind Date* were also shortlisted. A couple of years later, the novel was again a runner-up, this time to Charlotte Armstrong's *A Dram of Poison*, for the Mystery Writers of America's Edgar Award for best novel.

In other words, this was the first book to be shortlisted for the premier crime novel awards in both Britain and the U.S. Julian Symons included the novel in his *The Hundred Best Crime Stories*, a list compiled in 1958 for the *Sunday Times* and also published separately, in which he described Bennett as "the wittiest of recent crime novelists, but in other respects the most unpredictable." As if that were not enough of an achievement, the story was adapted for television in America in 1958, with a cast including the young William Shatner, later to find fame as Captain Kirk in *Star Trek*, trying out his version of a British accent. Given the success of the book on both sides of the Atlantic, it's sobering to consider that it has been out of print for a quarter of a century.

Margot Miller was born in Lenzie, Scotland, in 1912, and at the age of fifteen, she emigrated with her family to Australia. In the early 1930s, she spent some time in New Zealand, working on a sheep farm. Much later, she used her first-hand experience of the massive 1931 Hawke's Bay earthquake for her mainstream novel *That Summer's Earthquake*, set on a sheep farm and published in 1964. She took a job as a copywriter in Sydney, Australia, and moved back to London at the age of twenty-three, where she continued to work in advertising. During the Spanish Civil War, she went to Spain as part of the first British Medical Unit. There she met Richard Bennett, her future husband, who shared her left-wing political sympathies. The Bennetts had four children together.

Margot's first novel, *Time to Change Hats*, was published in June 1945 but very clearly set in wartime, with references to the Home Guard and a rural English village invaded by evacuees. She and her two older children had themselves been evacuated, to a village in Cornwall. Her publishers described the book as "a story of drink, a cow, and the fine art of murder." After the long years of war, they promised readers: "If you are tired of murder in the raw, here is murder in a comedy." Bennett set the tone in her dedication ("To My Creditors") as well as in the first line: "It is difficult to become a private detective; the only recognised way is to be a friend of the corpse."

The narrator is John Davies, who finds his friends disobliging until Della Mortimer responds with a note saying: "I have not been murdered, but may be. A woman called Death has been leaving visiting cards." This makes for a pleasing start to a story, and the book was well received in Britain and the U.S., although Bennett later commented, with some justice, that her attempt to "try the novelty of combining comedy with the obligatory murder" resulted in the book being too long.

Davies returned in *Away Went the Little Fish*, published the following year. This mystery displayed Bennett's developing talent, but she promptly abandoned Davies, and she did not produce another crime novel for another six years. *The Widow of Bath* was undoubtedly worth the wait. Her skills as a crime writer had matured in the interim and the story blended first-rate characterisation with a strong mystery puzzle. Bennett was, like all good writers, self-critical, and she observed that it "had an entirely plausible and novel plot, but it was low on comedy and had too many twists." This success was followed by *Farewell Crown and Good-Bye King*, a book written with the accomplishment that marks all her fiction, albeit pivoting on a plot twist that is pleasing but perhaps too easily guessed.

Bennett felt that her last two mystery novels, this one and

Someone from the Past were her best. After her near-miss with *The Man Who Didn't Fly*, in 1958 she succeeded in winning the Crossed Red Herring Award (it was renamed the Gold Dagger in 1960) with *Someone from the Past*. The next year, 1959, she was also elected to membership of the Detection Club. She had reached the pinnacle of her profession. But that, as far as crime writing was concerned, was it. Astonishingly, she never published another mystery novel, an extreme example of a crime writer going out at the top.

Instead, she concentrated mainly on writing for film and television. *Women Screenwriters: an International Guide* describes her as a writer of B-movies, only two of which were actually produced, the comedies *The Crowning Touch* and *The Man Who Liked Funerals*. She adapted *The Widow of Bath* for television and wrote scripts for popular series such as the medical soap opera *Emergency Ward 10* and *Maigret*. Her last known writing credits were in 1968. She wrote scripts for *Honey Lane*, a cockney forerunner of *EastEnders*, and a science fiction novel, *The Furious Masters*, which made less impact than her previous venture into sci-fi, *The Long Way Back*, published fourteen years earlier.

Why did this gifted and versatile author, who lived until 1980, first give up crime writing, and then apparently stop writing for publication altogether in her mid-fifties? It's a puzzle to rival anything in her books, and I'm very grateful to Veronica Maughan for casting light on Bennett's life and career. It seems that Bennett found screenwriting more lucrative than producing novels at a time when she was also raising a family, and that in the 1960s she became increasingly committed to political campaigning. She was closely associated with CND and Amnesty International and in 1964 published *The Intelligent Woman's Guide to Atomic Radiation*, a book which (like her forays into science fiction) reflected her anxieties about nuclear proliferation.

This volume includes a bonus for Bennett fans in the form of a little-known short story, "No Bath for the Browns," which first appeared in *Lilliput* in November 1945 and then in the U.S. in *The Mysterious Traveler* seven years later; I'm indebted to Jamie Sturgeon for supplying me with this information and a copy of the story.

It was thanks to Julian Symons's *Bloody Murder* that I first became aware of *The Man Who Didn't Fly*, and when I finally tracked a copy down in a library, I enjoyed reading it. Some years later, I was invited to write an introduction to a reprint published in 1993 by Chivers Press in conjunction with the CWA, and again the story entertained me. So this is, strangely, the second time I've written an introduction for a reprint of this novel—although I've tried to avoid repeating myself! My hope is that other readers will share my enthusiasm for an author who, despite a regrettably slender output, ranks high among British crime novelists of the post-war era.

—Martin Edwards
www.martinedwardsbooks.com

The Man Who Didn't Fly

At eleven in the morning the aeroplane began its westward flight across England; shining like snow under the blue sky; losing its glitter in the thick, white clouds; passing, heard but unseen, over the Welsh hills. On the shore at Aberavon, children struggling wet into jerseys; parents snatching at animated papers, cramming sandwiches back into boxes; flinched as the plane flew too low over their heads; then watched with angry, admiring eyes as it lunged into the black clouds that pressed down on the black sea. No one saw the plane again, although there were reports of a fireball that had rolled, slower than lightning, down the sky to the sea. Rescue planes searched the Irish Channel, but they might as well have looked for Lycidas.

After the accident comes the casualty list; deaths must be documented, and no man is allowed a death certificate without first dying for it.

The death of the pilot was as indisputable as the loss of the plane. The status of the passengers was more difficult to define. Neither friend, relative, enemy, insurance company, nor coroner was willing to admit that any one of the passengers was conclusively and legally dead. Four men had arranged to travel by the aeroplane; four had disappeared; only three men had arrived at the airport, only three passengers had entered the plane.

The man who didn't fly had been spared by chance or providence. He should have appeared, smiling uneasily, to describe how he had stopped to tie his shoelace and missed his bus. He was silent as though he had taken a bus to eternity. He was not only silent, he was invisible, and, worst of all for the authorities, he was any one of four people. He could be classified only as the man who didn't fly, and he created the impossible situation of leaving three deaths to be shared out among four men.

Investigation (1)

The patient enquiries began; crackling and exploding around the Wades; splashing through Moira Ferguson's stupor; rubbing like sandpaper over the indifference of bus conductors and railway porters all the way from Furlong Deep to Brickford Airport; and tenderly nursing the facts that drooped like limp seedlings in the Fairway Arms.

The man in the bar was unco-operative. That was another piece of bad luck. It was a man. A girl would have been interested in the customers who came in that morning, or at least she would have been interested in what she thought about them. She might have studied them like tea-leaves, to see if they could affect her future; observed their positions in society or their failure to resemble film stars; built up in her head a life-time of five seconds with one of them; or flattered herself that she could recognise a man who was up to no good. Girls are romantic, but sometimes before they sail into the outer space of invention they remember the shape of a nose or the colour of a tie.

The landlord was old. He had a disease of the liver that prevented him from working at anything but the study of racing form. He spent most of his life in a back room making imaginary bets on a three-column system, and keeping accounts with the precision of a nationalised industry. In five years he had made a theoretical profit of £18,640. His wife didn't allow him any money for betting, so on the few occasions when he had to take her place he became mute of malice. He sat on a low stool, his great, yellow, rectangular face hanging over the bar like a disfigured moon; occasionally pouring a drink; taking the customers' money with disgust, as though it might be radioactive; and putting the change, one coin at a time, on the counter. He was surly, and made useless by circumstances, but he had never been in trouble with the police, so they accepted him as a good citizen, and asked their questions patiently, almost genially.

He listened to what they had to say, shaking his head slowly from side to side, to indicate complete incapacity to help. When they persisted, he retired into his own world, and answered wearily, like a man who needed sleep.

"I know you feel you can't describe any of them, Mr Crewe," the detective-sergeant said. "But there must be something that you noticed. If one of them had a moustache, now. You'd have seen that?"

Crewe shook his head again.

"You mean a man sat a few yards away from you, and you didn't see his moustache?"

"I didn't."

"There you are. They were all clean-shaven. You didn't remember a moustache, and you were right."

Crewe looked bewildered.

"Now what about hats? Did any of these men, your first customers of the day, wear a hat?"

"Could of done. Or they couldn't."

"Would you be willing to say that one of them wore a hat?"

"No. And I'll tell you why. Because I didn't see. And if I did see, I didn't remember. And if I didn't remember, it was because I was thinking of something else. And if I was thinking of something else it was the three thirty at Lingfield. And if I was thinking of the three thirty at Lingfield, there's no law against it."

"Racing?" the sergeant said stiffly, as though it was an indecent word. "Well, we needn't discuss racing. What we have to do is get these men identified. They all had names. If you heard any part of their talk, you might have heard one of their names, as I would say to you, Do you sell cigarettes here, Jack?"

"My name's Raymond," Crewe said in a confused voice.

"They were called Joseph Ferguson, Maurice Reid, Harry Walters, Morgan Price."

Crewe yawned, and sat down with his stomach resting on his knees. He looked up, blinking, then shook his head again.

"We have only one photograph. It's of Joseph Ferguson." He held out the picture of a dark, square-faced man, with a large, strong nose, and a suggestion of amiable jowls. He looked like a first, or perhaps a second, generation Englishman. "Was this man here?"

"Never seen him."

"Are you prepared to say he wasn't here?"

"No, I wouldn't say that."

"Is there anything you would say? Look, Mr Crewe, the position is this. Four men arranged to meet here somewhere around ten-fifteen before going on to the airport to get on a plane that was supposed to leave at ten-forty-five. Now, I'm asking you a straight question, Mr Crewe. Did they come here?"

"There was men here. They had whisky. They drank it and had another. And there wasn't four. There was three."

"Three? Are you sure?"

"Three. You got me mixed all the time, talking about four. Three doubles and splash and the same again. One pound four shillings in the till. The wife'll tell you," he added venomously, not looking at her.

She sat beside him, indicating by twitches of nostril and eyebrow how complete was her dissociation from her husband and his stupidity.

"One pound six and eight in the till, Raymond," she said sharply.

"There was two bitters later," Crewe agreed dully.

"Two men?"

"Suppose so. Couldn't say."

"It was only three days ago, Mr Crewe."

"It was all of three days ago," Crewe agreed.

"Did these other two speak to you?"

"They ordered bitters. It's a manner of speaking."

"I'll make enquiries among our regulars," Mrs Crewe promised. She seemed to recognise the urgency of proving she was on the right side.

"As a matter of curiosity, did you hear any of the men's conversation?"

"Which men? I don't know which men you're talking about. First it's four, then it's three, now it's the two bitters."

"No, Raymond, not the two bitters. It's the three whiskies," Mrs Crewe said officiously.

"You give me time, Ethel, give me time. I know better than you what happened. There was a word about horses and Ireland, but next thing it was accidents and Australia, or it might have been South Africa, then I lost interest."

"What did they say about horses?"

"Something about racing, it might be supposed," Crewe said triumphantly, and smiled at last. "But we've agreed that's not to be discussed. It was only the Grand National," he added generously.

"Go on. What about the Grand National?"

"Some nonsense about a million people jumping the fences and ten thousand falling with every horse. No kind of sense in it at all."

"And Australia?"

"Nothing about Australia."

"Nothing?"

"Well, it might have been South Africa. It was a place like that."

"New Zealand?"

"No, not New Zealand. It was South Africa or it was Australia. I'll swear to one of them. I've an uncle in one of them and a cousin in the other, so I'm sure of my facts."

"Canada?"

"It was Australia or South Africa, and there's no one here can tell me different."

"What about it, whichever it was?"

"One of them wanted to tell a story. It might have been about horses, following the talk of the Grand National, but it wasn't. That's all."

"All?" asked the detective, bending forward, trying to

compel the stubborn mind to spurt into action like a match. "Had the man who was telling the story been in Australia or South Africa himself? Mr Crewe, this might be important. Did one of these three men say he'd been in Australia?"

"He did, always remembering it might have been South Africa. He wanted to tell a story about—what was his word?— premonitions. He had feelings about something."

"Feelings about what?"

"Ah, that's when I went back to thinking about the three-thirty at Lingfield."

"Raymond, not Lingfield again," Mrs Crewe said humbly.

"What part of Australia?" asked the detective. "Did he say, as it were, when I was in Sydney, when I was in Adelaide, when I was in Alice Springs?"

"Alice Springs?" Crewe asked, bewildered once more.

"It's a town in Australia, Raymond," his wife said quickly, with apologetic nods to the police. "If only I'd been in the bar that morning."

"You!" Crewe said contemptuously. "You'd have listened to more than was ever said. What I heard I stand by as the truth. One of them says to another that reminds me—which I couldn't see how it did—about something that happened to me once. I had a premonition, he says, or words to that effect, when I was in Australia, or South Africa, and you haven't been there, have you, he says to that other, crushing the opposition. No, says the other. But I have, says the third man, interrupting. Isn't it time we left, or something like that, but there was no getting away from the story, which I didn't listen to, however much you sigh, and make faces," he said malevolently to his wife.

He closed his eyes again, and gave very faint groaning answers to the interminable questions about cigarettes, bow ties, girth, height, complexion, and accent. Finally he heaved himself up slowly, like an overburdened camel.

"Listen, if I was Scotland Yard I'd photograph the customers on the way in and cut off a lock of their hair before I sold them a mild-and-bitter. Not being Scotland Yard or female, I got my own business to attend to and it's not and never will be other people's. Anxious as I am to help the law."

Mrs Crewe went to the door with the detectives.

"If he knows anything more, I'll get it out of him," she whispered. "And when I find the two bitters, I'll let you know."

The detective-sergeant gave her a grim smile of gratitude as he got in his car.

"If the crooks were as slow-witted as that lot," he said to his subordinate, "we'd have crime stamped out in a week."

Investigation (2)

Brickford Airport wasn't much more than a meadow cut by a tarmac path, with a few sheds clustering at one end. It had a primitive look, as though someone was about to take off in a bid to fly the English Channel. At week-ends, there were always a few little girls with dolls' prams and boys with bicycles being driven away by angry mechanics, and sometimes a picnic party taking place on the fringes. It was the headquarters of the local flying club, but it was also regularly used by several small charter planes.

Too many questions had already been asked at the airport, and when the mechanic saw Detective-Sergeant Young he dipped his head at once into the engine of a small, red, open plane that might have been made for the Wright brothers.

Sergeant Young looked sentimentally at the innocent little

plane, and sighed. "You're William Douglas?" he asked the mechanic.

The mechanic raised his white, indignant face, and nodded. "Police?" he asked fiercely. "Or from the Daily Something or Other?"

"I'm from the police."

"Right. Here it comes. I don't need any questions. I don't want any questions. I've had enough. You just listen. I saw the Ormond go. I heard Mr Lee speak to his three passengers. I heard him say: What, only three of you? And one of the passengers said: We've waited long enough. It seems he's not going to turn up. We'll have to go without him. And the three of them got in and Mr Lee walks over to me and says: I'm one short, Bill. Then he goes over to the caff to look but he comes back alone. Then he took off. This is the eleventh time I've been asked and I know the answers in my sleep."

"And did you see what the passengers looked like?"

"I did not."

"Was one of them taller or shorter than the others?"

"I couldn't tell you."

"Did they wear hats?"

"Look! So far as they walked on two legs and wore trousers I can claim to have seen them, but I'd like it to be understood I won't have words put in my mouth. I was working on a club crate at the time, as I'm trying to do now, and I didn't look up, except after I heard Mr Lee say what he said. Then I lifted my head long enough to see their backs as they went in the plane, and three is the number I saw. I watched the plane go. He was a lovely pilot, Mr Lee, and I'll never believe he lost that plane, except it was struck by lightning."

Sergeant Young listened seriously, as though he hadn't read all this at the station earlier that morning.

"A man called Joseph Ferguson chartered the plane," he said. "Tell me, Mr Douglas, would the pilot have gone without him?"

"Couldn't say. So long as the flight had been paid for. Mr Lee might not have been able to let the other passengers down."

"The flight had been paid for in advance. But Mr Lee and Joseph Ferguson had met at least once. Wouldn't it have been reasonable for Mr Lee to say: Good morning, Mr Ferguson?"

Douglas straightened himself slowly, and began to twist the spanner round in his hand. "But he didn't say it."

"Was he a brusque kind of man—inclined to be a bit short with people, I mean?"

Douglas considered the spanner, tossed it once in the air, and then dropped it in his pocket. "No. He was a friendly type. He might have been feeling a bit off because they'd kept him waiting." He looked sullenly at the sergeant, as though he was being forced into a game he didn't want to play. "There's another thing. Was what's-his-name, Ferguson, the only one of the four Mr Lee knew?"

"He'd met a man called Walters. Harry Walters."

"Right," Douglas said triumphantly. "He might have said Hello Walters, or Hello Harry, but he didn't say that either. As only one of them didn't turn up, either Ferguson or Walters must have been there."

"He just wasn't feeling sociable. So there's nothing in that idea. Thanks, anyway. Is there another mechanic here called Clewes?"

"In there." Douglas picked up his spanner and jerked it towards one of the hangars. He was a man who would have liked to make a spanner do all his talking for him.

Clewes was a fat little man, with a ring of black oil round

his lips. He looked at the sergeant sorrowfully and begged his pardon, but what could he say? He'd had no reason to pay attention at the time, but he'd heard Mr Lee say something about being one short, and he'd seen the three go in.

Sergeant Young strode gloomily over to the Customs shed. "If you ask me," he said over his shoulder to the constable, "there's no one in this place could tell the Pied Piper of Hamelin from Hopalong Cassidy."

The passport officer was bent over his desk with his tongue sticking out, like a schoolboy fighting with an examination. He was copying a list of French irregular verbs, and for all he knew or remembered of Friday morning, it seemed likely that this was his usual preoccupation.

"There was a rush," he explained. "Three or four planes went out that morning. I must have had fifteen or sixteen people through here. One of them had a beard, if that's any help."

"One of the men on the lost plane?" Sergeant Young asked in surprise.

"Oh, I don't say that. I think it was an alien, returning to Belgium. It's only that I noticed him, having a beard. For the rest, it's faces, faces, faces all the day. In any case, if the plane was for Ireland, they wouldn't pass through here at all. Have you tried the buffet?"

Sergeant Young tried the buffet. The tea-lady, who had a contrived shade of red hair, and the new small waist with the old, spreading hips, smoothed one eyebrow with her little finger, and said she'd been talking to a gentleman from Sweden at the time, and she really couldn't remember a thing, except that poor Mr Lee had looked in to ask about a passenger who wasn't there. When she mentioned Lee's name, her eyes moistened and she turned away, fumbling until she found a very dainty handkerchief.

"Mr Lee was a true gentleman," she said, snuffling. "And all your questions won't bring him back."

Investigation (3)

The short young man came through the door of the office with his head down, like a bull expecting to meet a matador. He was dark-complexioned, and although he was young, he already had wrinkles on his forehead from raising his eyebrows.

He spoke in a high voice, but all he said at first was: "How do you do. My name's Murray." Then he sat in agitated silence, while the policeman stared at his slightly crumpled light-weight suit, and the place where the button was missing from his shirt.

"I came in about Harry," he said. "Walters, I mean."

"Yes?"

Murray sat down, and elevated his head cautiously.

"Things are pretty bare in here. Much as one had imagined."

"Are they, Mr Murray?"

"Well, yes, they are. I'm not criticising, you know. All I mean is you haven't got piles of letters and so on scattered over the floor."

"Is there something you wanted to say, Mr Murray?"

"It's about Harry Walters."

"Yes?"

"I haven't come to give myself up, or anything like that. I just know him. Do you mind if I smoke? The shades of the prison house don't close around the police station? They must, of course, for some people."

He took out a blue packet, and, after some hesitation, chose a cigarette. He found a matchbox, opened it, inspected the matches, took one, and lit his cigarette. Then he began to speak at racing speed, like a cyclist swerving past obstacles on his way downhill.

"I was talking to a man in a bar who reads all the papers. I mean really all of them, and he said they'd finished proving that flying was safer than riding a tricycle round the nursery and now they wanted to know about Harry and what was I going to do? I don't want to get mixed up with newspapers, so I thought, there's the police, what about that? You see all my inclinations were to shut up and say nothing. But then I thought everyone knows I know Harry, I've known him for years and if I shut up it might lead to getting involved. Then I rang Scotland Yard. Absolutely everything I've ever read suggested Scotland Yard would be the place to ring, but they said they positively weren't touching it, and put me on to you. So here I am."

"You want to make a statement?" Inspector Lewis asked suspiciously.

"In a way I don't. Suppose I just talk, and then afterwards if I've told you anything at all, we could write down that bit and let the rest go? Because principally, you see, I don't want to be one of those witnesses that are chewed up in court and tossed over some learned friend's shoulder. I'm sorry about Harry, but I have a reputation—professional status—a wife. Then there's the other side. It's true I'm not excessively public-spirited—I mean if I saw bandits waving guns and snatching diamonds from a jeweller's window I really think I'd just let them snatch—it's a point, don't you think, if one should risk one's life to save someone else's diamonds? I've given a lot of thought to it, and I realise that bandits should be discouraged, so I'd be willing to co-operate, like shouting: 'they went that way,' but nothing more."

"Are you trying to tell me about a jewel robbery, Mr Murray?" Lewis asked, carefully polite.

"Are you trying to accuse me of something? I've never been within a mile of a jewel robbery," Murray said fiercely. "I'm trying to make you see I wouldn't be here saying what I had to say, unless I felt I had to do it. I don't want to be mixed up in this at all, but I want to say if poor Harry was the man who missed that plane, I think it's likely he was murdered."

"Why?"

Murray looked intently at his cigarette, with the concentration of a watchmaker studying a broken hairspring. He took a matchbox from his pocket, carefully tipped the ash among the matches, and shut the box.

"The truth is," he said, "I'm an editor."

"Really, sir, and what do you edit?"

"A magazine. You wouldn't have heard of it. It's called *Vista*."

"I don't have much time for reading," the inspector apologised.

Sergeant Young tilted his head towards the inspector, who nodded.

"I know it, sir. It's a poetry magazine, with novelists reviewing each other's books on the back pages."

"I say," Murray exclaimed, looking disparagingly at the sergeant. "Have you ever bought it? For money, I mean?"

"Yes, sir."

"One of the very few," Murray said. "If there were more of you, we wouldn't be closing down. People think it's easy, you know. They think it doesn't matter, having to run at a loss. Find a tame millionaire, they keep telling me. I've looked everywhere, but I think they're dying out. Some disease— have you ever heard of millionaire's myxomatosis?"

"Mr Murray, you wanted to tell us something?"

"I'm not here for the fun of it, am I? If you've read *Vista*, you must have seen some of Harry's poems."

"I can't say that I remember them."

"Well, he was a poet, and not a bad one when he got around to it. But—do you really mind if I tell this my own way? The trouble is," he said unhappily, "I can't think of any other way to tell it. Or hadn't you noticed I'm having difficulty?"

"Just go ahead, sir, your own way."

"Then it's about Harry. That's why I've come. Harry was always short of money," he said. "Other people can come back from places like Australia with gold dust clinging to the turn-ups of their trousers, but I don't think Harry had even a clean shirt when he got off the boat four months ago. He stayed with us for a few weeks, but my wife got a bit restive. Harry wasn't at all like the other people who wrote for *Vista*. I mean most poets today work for the B.B.C. and keep their trousers pressed, but Harry had a theory that poets should be poets and nothing more. So he got a bit short of money. I expect that people like yourselves, paid regularly, don't understand how awkward that can be? Is there anywhere I could put this cigarette end? An old helmet, or something of the kind?"

Lewis handed him an ashtray.

"We've heard rumours about people who haven't enough money," he said heavily.

Murray stubbed out the cigarette and lit another.

Inspector Lewis watched him carefully, an old, knowing badger, peering from his sett before emerging.

"Your friend Harry had been in Australia. Had he ever been in South Africa?"

"I don't know everything about Harry," Murray protested. "But if he ever landed in South Africa, they probably bounced him out again. Harry would never be tactful enough for a place like that. He'd think of something to annoy, like opening a black-and-white matrimonial agency."

"It's not important."

"Then I'll proceed. When Harry left us, he'd been writing some rather good verse—sentimental savagery about the middle-classes. Did you ever read one beginning: April's always been the month for worry; Bills hissing through the letterbox like snakes?"

"No," said Sergeant Young. "No, I don't remember that."

"He wrote a few like that. They were good, so I made the mistake of paying him in advance for some more. Well—I don't suppose you've ever been an editor," he said, looking thoughtfully at the inspector. "If you ever take it up, let me give you some advice. Don't pay in advance. Because Harry, having the money, really didn't have any inducement to do the work. It wasn't very much money, but he knew that if he did finish his sequence of odes to the bourgeoisie, he wouldn't get any more, so he thought he'd write something else instead. So, just when he was looking for an emotion to recall at boiling point, he met someone in a pub—a very amusing man, who'd been in and out of jail half-a-dozen times. So Harry thought: Why not be François Villon?"

Inspector Lewis's lower lip began to project like a railway signal.

"Who was this amusing man?" he asked.

"Actually, I've rather forgotten his name," Murray said.

"François Villon was a French poet, sir. He became a member of the criminal classes and some of his poetry was written from their standpoint," Sergeant Young muttered.

"Anyway, around then I thought it was my duty as editor to keep tapping Harry's shoulder, saying, What about those verses we've paid for? But Harry had sold a couple of poems, about psychology I think, to an American magazine that paid in genuine unforged dollars, so he had drinking money. We had some pretty hideous nights, I can tell you."

"Where?"

"I've rather forgotten the names of the pubs. I was at a loss most of the time. Harry would point out a character and say: Would you like to know what he brought down the ladder last night? And I would say, No, really no. Then we'd talk to the ladder-man, and all I could think of saying would be: Have you been stealing anything interesting recently? So I had to shut up and have another beer instead. Harry mixed in and I couldn't. My analysis is that they liked him because he was—innocent. He wasn't the kind of man who could possibly have been a policeman."

Murray stopped and looked at the others anxiously. "Am I giving you some kind of idea?" he asked.

"Go on, please," Inspector Lewis said.

"He wasn't wasting his time," Murray said defensively. "He picked up a lot of good stories. There was a girl, I think she was called Lily, who was staggering about with a case full of stolen watches; police whistles and burglar alarms going off like foghorns, and she stopped a policeman and told him her husband had thrown her out and could he direct her to a hostel, and he held up the traffic and took her across the road and saw her on to the right bus. Amusing, don't you think?"

"Very."

"Then there were a couple of sinister characters Harry told me had once been the reigning cracksmen of England. Go anywhere, steal anything. About two years ago they made a mammoth haul. Was there something called the Sackford Diamonds?" He looked up enquiringly.

Lewis nodded. "In June, two years ago."

"Anyway, three of them planned that, three of them carried it out, and two of them were still in the house when the third man cleared off with the lot. They've been looking for him ever since. He's well known to a lot of the boys. They say he had exquisite manners, perhaps not in those very words. And every night at closing time one of the other two brings out a photograph and pushes it under your nose. Or so Harry said. It was never pushed under mine. They offer a reward for information about him, just like the police. The point of the story is they've never stolen anything since. They can't work alone, and they don't trust each other or anyone else either. Their lives are ruined, Harry said."

"I suppose you can't exactly remember their names either?"

"I was never introduced," Murray said firmly. "I'd better come to the point. After a few nights, Harry turned up and said: 'The boys don't like you. They think you look like a plainclothes man.' I was pretty shaken, as anyone might be."

He looked appealingly at the inspector, who stared back with enormous detachment, as though he was studying him through plate glass.

"Actually, I'd already suspected I was being a social failure. I didn't much fancy having my face smashed in with a bicycle chain. So I dropped out."

"But Harry went on?"

"Yes. I didn't see him again for a couple of weeks, then he told me, in strict confidence, and I'm quite aware I'm betraying him, I feel like a louse, that he'd been asked to go out on a job with the boys. He said What if he was caught? He could do better than the ballad of Reading Gaol anyway. It was one of those railway mailbag things, but he wouldn't tell me what or when. I was very unhappy about the whole thing."

"You were unhappy," the inspector repeated with a different inflexion. "But you did nothing?"

"I didn't know the train—or even the date. I didn't know who the boys were. I could have rung Scotland Yard and said someone's thinking of robbing a mail train, soon. They'd know that already. Somebody's always thinking of robbing a mail train."

"You could have reported the activities of your friend Harry."

"That would have been going a bit far, wouldn't it?"

"So you're not opposed to robbery if it's conducted by your friends?"

"I knew this interview wasn't going to turn out well," Murray said. "But you can put away the thumb-screws. I haven't connived at any crime. I knew Harry well enough to know he could never finish anything. He didn't take part in any robbery. He missed the train."

"Intentionally?"

"It was just the way he was. He was a man who was always rushing into situations and then drifting away from them. He wasn't reliable, in any way. I don't know if he meant to miss the train. But he did. Then something happened."

"Yes?"

"The robbery was a flop. Someone informed. There were to be four men in it as well as Harry. And three of them were caught."

"And Harry missed the train?" Lewis commented. "This would be about five weeks ago?"

Murray nodded. "About that. I saw Harry the next day. He said his failure to catch the train might be misinterpreted. He said he didn't want to be François Villon anymore, and crooks were tedious company. He said he was afraid they might be tedious enough to put him in a sack and drop him over London Bridge. He said all he wanted was a quiet place where he could write."

"But not Reading Gaol?" Sergeant Young said.

"No."

"Why have you come here with this story, Mr Murray?"

"Naturally, when I heard about this disappearing passenger, I assumed Harry had had a mortal interview with one of the boys."

"Do you think he informed against them?"

"Well, you'd know, wouldn't you, not me? I couldn't tell you what Harry would do. He was an odd sort of man, but very likeable, in his odd sort of way," Murray said sadly. "May I go now?"

"Just one or two questions, if you've no objections?"

They asked him a great many questions, but at the end of it they were no wiser, and they let him go.

When he had gone they opened the windows to let the tobacco-smoke out, and then sent for the files on the train mailbag attempt, and on the Sackford Diamond robbery.

"I hope this Harry is the man who missed that plane," Lewis said. "I'd like to meet him."

Investigation (4)

Moira Ferguson sat watching the Wades being interviewed again. Her manner suggested that she was present as a judge, not as a witness. The Wades behaved more like inexpert conspirators. In the four days since the crash of the plane they had lived in a state of shock interrupted by perpetual questioning; now they were so bewildered by their own evasions that they left a little of the truth behind in each abandoned position.

Charles Wade sat now gazing in mournful appeal at his two daughters, begging them silently for permission to say more than he had said. Hester gave him a quick glance of warning, then closed her eyes. Prudence scowled at the police, then quickly substituted an icy smile. She was sixteen, and her greatest fear was that they might think her unsophisticated.

Inspector Lewis, looking peculiarly solemn and incorruptible, like a judge at an agricultural show, examined all their faces. Sergeant Young looked around the room, a shabby room in worn chintz, a room with a view across a valley where the morning shadows lay like folds of drapery. He glanced at the roses that sprawled from a blue vase.

"I'm sorry," Hester said. "They're dying. I've had no time to change the water." She looked quickly away from the roses, as though the sight of them caused her pain.

"So there's nothing you can tell me about Morgan Price. Nothing at all, except that he was about forty and had no bad habits. In fact, Mr Wade, from what you've told me, I'd say he had no habits at all," Inspector Lewis said carefully.

"He always thought he was ill when he wasn't," Prudence said in a kind of explosion.

"So he came here for his health?"

"I don't know. I'm not sure," Hester said, frowning at Prudence.

"But he lived with you as a paying guest?"

"Yes, that's true," Charles Wade said, glad of the opportunity to answer a simple question.

"How did he come to live here? And when?"

"About a year ago. We put an advertisement in a paper," Hester said shortly.

"What did it say?"

"It's not easy to be sure now. Something like Quiet house

in quiet Cotswolds. Room for paying guest. Suit artist, writer, country-lover."

"And which was Morgan Price?"

"He wasn't an artist or a writer anyway," Prudence said promptly.

"So he must have been a country-lover," the inspector suggested.

Moira gave a little twitching laugh.

"Would you describe him as a country-lover?" Inspector Lewis persisted.

"He sometimes went for walks," Hester said.

"But mostly he stayed in the house," Prudence added.

"Why did you want a writer or an artist or a country-lover?"

"A strange taste is not necessarily criminal," Hester muttered.

"Do you have any other paying guests?"

"No. Let me save you a few questions. We are rather poor. We found we had a spare room, and hoped to make a little money easily. Morgan paid his rent regularly, by cash," Hester said with some spirit.

"Did he have many friends?"

"No. I think he was shy," Hester said.

"I don't think he was shy," Prudence said.

"What do you think he was?"

"I can't explain." Prudence wriggled in an unsophisticated manner. "But when we were talking he was always listening to something else, not the conversation, so that people stopped listening to what they were saying and everyone got jumpy."

"Had he no profession, no business, no occupation?"

"Not when he was here."

"Did you think he was a strange guest, Mr Wade?"

Wade looked round for help. "I don't think so. People have

independent means, sometimes. I still know some people who have, and some of them are shy."

"And what seems strange afterwards didn't seem strange at the time," Hester added quickly.

"Can you tell me anything about his general behaviour?"

"He liked doing chess problems or at least he didn't," Prudence said. "He would set the pieces up and stare at them then knock the board away and go to the window and look out. That was the way he read books too, for about five minutes at a stretch. He was always sitting down and getting up again. And he and Harry..." She looked at Hester, then let the sentence die.

"And he what?"

"Oh, nothing."

Inspector Lewis looked at his fingernails, and Sergeant Young looked at the inspector. They appeared to communicate, for Sergeant Young drew a line in his notebook and turned the page.

"Now, what about Maurice Reid?" the inspector said. "I'm told he was a friend of the family. Is that so?"

"Yes," said Hester, almost whispering. "A friend."

"How long had you known him?"

"About nine months."

"And you'd seen a lot of him?"

"He took a cottage to be near them," Moira said contemptuously. "Joe never liked him."

"He was here the night before the plane left, Mr Wade?"

"Yes, yes. That's true. Hester, do you mind, could we have some coffee?"

The inspector was kind enough to ignore this wistful suggestion.

"How did you spend this—this last evening?"

"He had dinner here, but I went to a dance," Prudence said casually.

"Then…" Wade began. He looked in appeal at Hester.

"Then we listened to music," Hester said quickly. "Records. Bach. Do you like music, Inspector?" she asked wildly.

"I'm tone-deaf," the inspector said.

"I do," said Sergeant Young unexpectedly. He smiled at Hester. "Do you play, Miss Wade?"

"I play the violin," she said, looking at him for the first time, and appearing to be surprised that he should seem so like other human beings.

"I was once going to be a professional pianist. But I wasn't good enough. So I joined the police force." He looked cautiously at his superior, who smiled just enough to show that the sergeant was to be allowed rope to inspire confidence.

"What kind of man was Maurice Reid, Miss Wade?" Lewis asked more amiably.

"He seemed reliable and kind. He had a square, brown face. I think he had travelled a lot. He wasn't young—between thirty-five and forty, I suppose. He always seemed healthy, and almost aggressively clean." She looked gravely at the two detectives, who were brushed, scrubbed, shaved, creased, and shining, as if they had been preparing for inspection by Royalty. "He had a flat in London. Down here he had a tiny week-end cottage, and lived alone in it." She looked coldly at Moira. "To be near them, the third person plural, one supposes."

"What was his occupation?"

"Something in the city, wasn't it, Father?" she said, trying to control the trembling of his hands with a look.

"So he had money?"

"Not real money," Moira Ferguson intervened again.

Lewis turned to her. "It was your husband who chartered the plane?"

"You know it was. I've said so, often enough. He had to go to Ireland on business. He chartered it for himself and his associates, who in the end couldn't come. That's why these others flew with him—if they did. He was trying to fill up the seats. And I'll tell you now that he had an occupation. He was a company director, and his special interest was the Constellation Circuit—cinemas, you know. He at least was respected by everyone," she said in a flat voice.

"I'm sorry to ask these questions now."

She ignored the apology, and sat as still as if she had been drugged.

"Then there's Harry Walters," the inspector said.

"Harry?" Moira repeated with hatred. "He stayed with us. But there's nothing I can tell you. He's Hester's concern."

Hester stared at the floor.

"He was a poet," Prudence volunteered.

"A poet," the inspector repeated, apparently surprised. "Do you know anything about poetry, Sergeant?"

"A little, sir."

"I thought so." The inspector shut his lips and sank back in his chair.

"Did you like his poetry?" Sergeant Young asked Prudence carefully.

"I thought it was pretty feeble," she said. "I like good poetry. Browning and people like that."

"I don't care for Browning much. Did you like his poetry, Miss Wade?"

"Yes."

"And you, Mrs Ferguson?"

"I'm no judge," she said, looking away. "My husband didn't like Harry."

Lewis sat up again. "Did he ever read you his poems, Miss Wade?"

"Read? Not exactly. No, he didn't read his poems to me."

"But he sometimes quoted lines?"

Sergeant Young turned away, like a specialist whose evidence was no longer required.

"I'm anxious to help," Hester said in a low voice. "But I don't see the point of those questions."

"I'm trying to form an idea of all those four men. They were all known to you. Did you know Harry Walters well?"

"Not exactly."

"Did anyone here know him well?" He looked directly at Moira Ferguson.

"I did," Prudence said. "He was always coming here for meals. And he used to play Donegal Poker. With Morgan."

The inspector looked at the sergeant for help. "I've never heard of it, sir."

"So Harry Walters and Morgan Price were friends?"

"Not exactly."

"Is there anything that Harry Walters was, exactly?"

"Nothing that could be described in a few words. People aren't classified, like racing cars," Hester said in agitation.

"Take as many words as you like."

Hester looked desperate, and her father spoke quickly, trying to shield her from the heavy artillery, like a loyal native with a bow and arrow.

"How can we answer these questions? What can one decently say of the dead? Harry was cheerful, entertaining, kind. He was helpful, even generous, sometimes," he protested.

Inspector Lewis nodded incredulously, and turned to

Hester again. "He sounds an ideal character," he said, on a note of suggestion.

"I know how I'd describe him," Prudence muttered. "Oh, I'm sorry, Hester."

"Please say what you think, Prudence," her elder sister said contemptuously. "Inspector Lewis wants information."

"I won't say a word," Prudence said, beginning to sob. "I promise you I won't, Hester."

"This is worse than words," Hester said.

Moira laughed, implying that she could say a great deal about Harry, if she chose.

"Tell us what you want to know," Hester said.

"I'll try to explain, Miss Wade. One of these four men, all intimate friends of your family—and all known to you, Mrs Ferguson—had such powerful reasons for wanting to disappear that he took the course of pretending to die on that plane. Shall we say that he missed the plane, heard of the crash, and discovered almost instantly—the same day, if he listened to the news bulletin—that no one knew which three of the passengers had travelled? He took the chance of pretending to be one of them, and of disappearing for good. There must have been something very strange in this man's private life to make him do this. You're in a position to know something of the private lives of all these men. In the public interest, I'd like to hear what you know."

"Oh, the public interest," Prudence muttered scornfully.

"There are other points," Inspector Lewis said mildly. "There's Mrs Ferguson, here. She doesn't know if her husband is dead or alive. Some of the others might have been married—might even have fathers, or sisters, who are doing a bit of worrying now." He stopped, and gave them a minute to let their confusion deepen.

"I think, Hester," Wade began resolutely, "I think—"

"I think there's nothing more we can tell you," Hester said loudly.

"Not if one of them was connected with the criminal classes? Not if one of them was frightened? Not if one had a peculiar background, or financial troubles?"

"Nothing. Nothing more."

"There's the question of property. That's very serious. No legatee would be able to benefit, as things are now. Have you thought of that?" Inspector Lewis urged.

Moira looked grimmer than before.

"And there's the possibility of crime," the inspector said in a harsher voice. "The man who didn't fly on that plane may be dead. How are we to know unless you give us the facts?" he demanded of Hester. "Do you think that's a possibility, Miss Wade?"

"I don't know," she whispered.

"If people are murdered, it's for a reason. Was there anything in the lives of any of these four—and remember, it might have been something as simple as carrying too much money in his pocket-book—anything so out of the ordinary that it might have led him into trouble?"

He waited. No one spoke, although the silence had an intensity that suggested everyone was about to speak.

"You're all reasonable people," he said. "I'm not here to attack you. I came in the hope that with your help I might arrive at the truth." He looked again at Hester, and saw her make her decision.

"It's so difficult to explain," she said. "I don't know how to begin."

"Did anything unusual happen before they left? They were all here on Thursday night. Can you tell me anything about Thursday?"

They looked at each other, their collective memories moving slowly back into the events of Thursday, a day already buried beneath the weight of other days. They returned to it slowly, like divers exploring a submarine cave; seeing the grey form of the fish trembling in the still water; clutching at the sunken rock with both hands while their bodies streamed upwards as lightly as weed; fingering the crevices; scraping empty shells from the deep sand.

Hester shook her head. "I can't begin with Thursday. On Wednesday I met Marryatt first, Jackie came at night, and Harry—I think I must begin with Wednesday."

"Then Wednesday. Two days before the plane took off."

"Wednesday," she said wistfully. "On Wednesday morning everything seemed so peaceful. Father was painting a room…"

Wednesday (1)

Charles Wade stood on top of a step-ladder, painting a wall with wild, frightened strokes. Harry Walters lounged against the door.

"Is there any advice I could give you?" he asked. "If you worked more from the wrist, wouldn't it look less like a hair-shirt?"

"This new paint dries like glass and lasts for ever," Wade said.

"But the wall behind it won't, Father. Shouldn't you have filled in the hole first?" Hester asked.

"It's only a little hole. It could have paper pasted over it," Wade said.

Hester tapped it with her knuckles. Sand streamed out of it and down the wall. "The ruined sides of kings," she said absently.

Wade stared at her with baffled, parent's eyes.

"You're in a destructive mood, Hester. Now I'll have to fill it in. Be a good girl and get me the bag of plaster. It's in the larder."

"Two flights of stairs," Hester said. She looked at Harry, who sat down in a corner and lit a cigarette.

"And bring a bucket with some water and another bucket for mixing," her father called after her.

"You should take longer strokes with the brush," Harry said.

Wade put down the brush, picked up a rag, and began to wipe the paint off his fingers.

"Harry," he said, "personally, I couldn't like you more. But you'll accept my advice—as a friend? You'd never do as a son-in-law."

"I'm not often taken for a marrying man. Are you warning me off the premises? I thought I'd been asked to lunch?"

"Naturally, you must stay to lunch," Wade said irritably.

"Then that's all right. Unless Maurice is coming. I can't eat when he's there. He takes away my appetite."

Wade sat down on top of the step-ladder.

"Harry, you have insulted my closest friend."

"Keep your money in your socks when your closest friend is there," Harry advised.

"Harry, you say these things without meaning them. You say them in a casual way that is very annoying. You haven't any respect for people. Society..."

"Ah, yes, society," Harry said. He settled down comfortably to listen. In five minutes Wade would be far away from the subject of sons-in-law.

Hester went downstairs and into the big, square kitchen where her sister Prudence, surrounded by utensils, was muttering over a cookery book.

"I've got an absolutely wonderful idea for dinner, tomorrow's dinner, I mean, because it takes twenty-four hours to make. I've counted up, and it has nineteen different things in it. Listen, I need a bay leaf and some Cointreau. Cooking Cointreau, do you suppose? Will the pub have it? And where do I get a bay leaf?"

"Plant a tree and wait," Hester said. "It won't make dinner later than usual."

"And some thick cream," Prudence said. "Absolutely everything in this book needs thick cream. Do you think we could put in a permanent order to the farm for a pint of cream?"

"Cream's terribly expensive. Couldn't you leave it out?"

"It's not worth trying to cook for this family," Prudence said angrily. "It won't taste like anything without the bay leaf or the Cointreau or the cream."

"Harry's staying to lunch. What could we have?"

"Something out of a tin's good enough for him."

"Prudence, don't be rude, and do find something we can eat today. I wish Mrs Parsons hadn't gone."

"All that lovely boiled fish," Prudence said. "Cooking is an art," she informed her sister. "You wouldn't like to grate some onions for me?"

"I'm fetching some plaster for Father. Another bit of the house is falling down."

She went upstairs again. Wade was sitting on top of the ladder with the paint bucket, talking to Harry about Society and bees.

"Most bees are freelances, anyway," Harry said. "They don't join in all this hive nonsense. They live alone and choose their own flowers."

"How do you think the room will look, Hester?" Wade asked heavily. He picked up the brush again and began to wave it. "We must have the floor white as well. Light walls, white floor—yes, Hester, white—white furniture, white floor, dark green rugs, then the drama of red chairs. Do me a favour, Harry. Get me another tin of paint. It's in the larder downstairs."

"Prudence is in the kitchen. She's longing to see you," Hester said.

"Knife in hand?" Harry asked.

Hester waited until he had gone.

"What are you going to use this room for, Father?"

"Guests."

"Father, we don't want any more guests."

"We make ten pounds a week out of the one we have. Now, I don't want to be corrected, Hester. It's gross profit, not net. I know the difference."

"I don't think you know all the difference. I'm going back to medical school in the autumn. So you'll have to hire some staff."

"There's Prudence."

"Prudence is only sixteen. She should stay at school. But if she doesn't—she wants to go to the Academy of Dramatic Art."

"My dear daughters. Harley Street and—and the Old Vic. How proud you make me! But there's no problem here. When I get four more bedrooms into action—all double—I'll have an income of eighty pounds a week. Then I'll be able to afford cooks, butlers, anything. I wonder when Harry's coming back with that paint."

At the mention of Harry's name, Hester's expression changed. Her father looked at her in time to see the small, secret smile.

"Hester," he said sharply. "Don't have anything to do with

Harry. I warn you. He's no good." He climbed down from the ladder and began to mix plaster with water. "At his age—he must be about thirty."

"Twenty-nine, Father."

"And he has no job."

"He's a poet."

"I'd like to hear some of his poetry."

"I don't think you would, Father. It's not your kind of poetry."

"Then I wouldn't. But poet or not, he's no good. He looks like the kind of man who's been spoilt by his mother and kicked out by his father. Hester, it's an old-fashioned word, but—"

"Please don't let's have any old-fashioned words. Is that all the plaster you need?"

"A piece about the size of my thumb will do."

"All you have against Harry is that he's wandered about the world getting experience instead of going to work in an insurance office. Don't talk about him. I'm not in love with him," she said thoughtfully. "Shall I begin to clean the floor?"

"When you were a little girl you used to put your hands over your ears when I tried to tell you anything. Now you talk about plaster and floors. You simply won't take advice."

"I thought you were in a hurry to get the room ready for more guests. Though I should have thought the one we have was a warning. Morgan gives me shivers."

"Morgan is a beginning. I'm going to work this place up into an hotel. Only thing is, I need a hostess. What would you say to a stepmother?"

"I'm too old to worry. I'm twenty. I'd be out of her grasp."

"But I don't know anyone I want to marry. Why don't you stay, Hester?" he asked shyly. "Drop this idea of a career. Stay here and help me run the place. Wouldn't that be better than medical school?"

Hester maintained her pleasant smile. Inside her head, alarms sounded; pilots leapt to the fighter planes; and softer thoughts were rushed out of the battle area.

"No, Father, it wouldn't be better than medical school. I dislike housekeeping. We'd end by quarrelling, and I can't endure a good quarrel."

"Nor can I," said her father. "So you mean to desert me, Hester. When it comes to the point, family affection simply doesn't exist. You are determined to cut me out of your life, Hester, and in due course Prudence will do the same. I'll advertise for a good general maid."

"Help wanted, fourteen in family," Hester suggested. "Father, I don't want to interfere, but I'm sure this isn't a good idea about the hotel. It will be like the fruit farm and the antique shop. Couldn't we stop trying to make money before we've lost all we have?"

Wade took a little ball of plaster and spread it neatly over the hole; where it at once disappeared. "If I'm not to have your help, Hester, I don't need your advice."

"You need some more plaster, anyway," she murmured.

"There's a space behind," he said angrily. He took a handful of plaster and forced it into the hole. "It will be all right when I've filled it up."

"The wall's beginning to bulge," Hester pointed out.

"It will be all right when it's dry."

Hester walked to the window and looked across the tops of the quivering green trees down into the valley; and along the road which passed through the solemn little village; dipped to the green fields where the distant cattle seemed like black-and-white wooden toys; then twisted up through woods to the top of Furlong Hill. She wanted to tell her father how much she loved home, and Furlong Hill, and all the Cotswolds; she wanted to tell him how often she had dreamt of floating in a boat across the slow green waves of the tree-tops; she wanted to make some gesture of friendship that would wipe away all resentment.

"Don't worry too much about money," her father said.

"Money? I wasn't thinking about money," she said sadly.

"Someone has to think about it. We're not rich, you know, Hester. We haven't much. I shouldn't be doing all this work myself if we had. But at last I see light ahead. I have a plan—at least Maurice has a plan."

"Oh, Maurice," Hester said in a voice of relief.

"To tell you the truth, I've had to put a lot of work in with Maurice. He obviously knows the tree the money grows on—these people who work at something mysterious in the City usually do. I've asked his advice often enough. But he's said to me quite frankly that one rocket looks like another until it bursts, and he doesn't want me to risk my capital on a dud."

"Father, he's right. Don't gamble on the Stock Exchange. Take Maurice's advice and keep what capital is left."

"At four per cent? You know we don't get enough to pay the grocer's bill."

"But Maurice knows better than you, Father."

"Maurice has been very excited for the last week or two. I'm convinced he's on to something big." Wade hesitated, and looked shyly at Hester.

"I've cashed some securities already," he said. "What are they worth? Four hundred a year. What am I risking? Nothing."

"I know we live in hard times," Hester said. "Even so, four hundred a year isn't exactly nothing."

"But it's safe. Maurice won't let me put money in unless it's safe. Hester, we might be rich—rich enough to live on capital again. What would my little medical student say to a year in Paris—or Vienna?"

"That's not the way I see it," Hester said shortly. "Please try to keep your head, Father. You know you're not good about money."

"And what do you know about money?" Wade demanded angrily. "You're only a child, Hester. It's not my habit to take advice from children."

"Nor from anyone else. Oh, this is much worse than your idea about the hotel. I can't let you risk the little capital you have. When you lose it, what shall we do?" Hester asked in agitation. "It's three years before I qualify—and there's Prudence. I'll speak to Maurice."

"Hester, I forbid it. Maurice is reluctant enough, as it is. I absolutely forbid you to say one word to Maurice. I know what I'm doing."

"Father, the wall!" Hester said.

Wade turned round. The wall into which he had been ramming plaster was bulging dangerously. There was a noise like a rifle shot, then about two square yards of wall, borne outwards by the weight of the new plaster, crashed into the room and was buried under the sand that poured from above.

Hester looked at the ruins. "The home decorator," she said, impelled by the bitter force that nature provides to intensify the war between generations. "Oh, Father, I'm sorry," she said quickly, anxious for peace.

"It's nothing," he said. "Nothing. Only more money to be spent."

"Don't work any more now. Come down to lunch," she said uneasily.

"Lunch!" he looked at her sorrowfully, like a man who could no longer afford to eat. "Lunch. Yes, that reminds me. Be a good girl, Hester. Don't ask Harry to stay to lunch."

"He's already been asked."

"I wish you wouldn't issue these invitations without consulting me."

"But I didn't ask him. You did."

"I don't believe it. I don't believe anyone asked him. This kind of thing is always happening with him. Tell him he can't stay to lunch after all."

Hester looked at him angrily, then suddenly she saw the disappointment and weariness on his face. He stood beside the ruins of the wall, the inefficient man confronted once again with the wreck of his hopes. She went to him quickly and squeezed his hand.

"Father, even if it's falling down it's lovely to be home again. The view from this window is better—better than a week in Paris. Come and look out of the window with me. I'm so happy when I look over the treetops. Most people only see trees from underneath."

He went with her to the window.

"It's you I'm thinking of—and Prudence," he said.

"I know, Father. I'll leave you with the view and go and speak to Harry."

Harry was sitting at the bottom of the stairs.

She sat down beside him.

"Harry, I don't think it would be tactful to stay to lunch."

His face became strained and infinitely sad. He looked at her with his melancholy, appealing eyes, until she was filled with a conviction of his helplessness, and so was all the more touched when he spoke, not of himself, but of her.

"Hester, you're tired. You're trying to carry the house on

your back. It's a thing that only snails can do. If you're not a snail, the house will flatten you hard as a sixpence. Give up all this snaili-ness. Come butterflying to the pub with me."

"I thought you had no money."

"I could borrow some from Uncle Joe." His face became serious. "Well, perhaps I couldn't. Not today." He leant back, thinking.

"Your father might be willing to lend me a pound," he suggested.

"I don't think I want a drink," Hester said brusquely. She stood up. She wasn't entirely in sympathy with Harry's ideas about money. Most of her conversations with him left her in a confusion of tenderness and disapproval.

"If you don't want a drink, I do. If I'm not to have lunch, I'll wait in the drawing-room and have a sip of your father's sherry."

"No, Harry, he wouldn't like it. Oh, I do wish you had some normal conventional feelings," she said in despair.

Wednesday (2)

"Has Harry gone?" Morgan asked.

"He hasn't stayed to lunch," Hester said, looking quickly across the table at her father.

Morgan's flat, usually expressionless face, registered a brief smile, and he began to talk rapidly. He was like a clock that after days of standing unwound on a mantelpiece has suddenly been jolted enough to make it tick again. Everyone always felt relieved when Morgan spoke.

"When Harry stays to lunch," he said, "the next thing that happens is that around two in the morning I'm being asked to play Donegal Poker. You have two cards each and you take away the value of the one from the other. Then you bet a penny, or a shilling, or a pound that the difference in your cards is bigger than the difference in his. Or if you don't want to bet, you put your money in the kitty instead. And you get extra from the kitty for every point you win by. It's a gambling game," he added unnecessarily. He glanced at Wade. "If any girl decides to marry Harry, she'll have a bad time."

"This is wonderful soup, Prudence," Hester said.

"I had to grate twelve onions with my eyes shut," Prudence said. "I'd better warn you that my cooking phase is nearly over. I'm going on to dress-designing next. Why would any girl who married Harry have a bad time, Morgan?"

"Gamblers are always losing the housekeeping money," Morgan said.

"Always? Don't they sometimes win?" Prudence asked. She was still at the age when contradiction is automatic.

"Not often," Morgan said, looking around for help. His conversational phase was over, and he wanted to be left alone on the mantelpiece again.

"I thought they sometimes had syndicates and died rich," Prudence persisted.

"Not many do."

"And some gamblers make fortunes on the Stock Exchange and go to Hunt balls. It would be O.K. being married to a gambler like that. The real thing is not to generalise," Prudence said sternly.

"Harry doesn't make fortunes on the Stock Exchange. He plays Donegal Poker in the small hours," Morgan said angrily. He was usually a very quiet man, emotional only about his illnesses, but Prudence could annoy him very quickly. She was sixteen, not at all shy in her assumption that she had the solution to all human problems; and she added to this common adolescent feature a frightening competence. She could light a fire with one match and mend broken fuses.

"I don't see that Donegal Poker would ruin his wife," she now said scornfully. Morgan wasn't old enough to be treated with the dubious respect she gave her father. He was about forty, too old to count, not old enough to be allowed indulgently to revel in his imaginary illnesses, and he had a twinging smile that scraped uneasy symbols on her mind.

Wade took no part in the discussion. He was lost in a private world of monetary calculations, where the house, miraculously restored, was crammed with guests who paid large sums of money and incurred no overheads. He began to pencil figures on the tablecloth. '9 at £10 each.' Then he thought of Maurice, and looked up smiling.

"How would everyone like a little trip to Madeira this winter?" he asked genially.

Hester smiled at him unhappily, beginning to realise that her father was like a greyhound, doomed for ever to run round a circular track after an electric hare that would never be caught. She stood up, and began to gather the plates.

"The dining-room is so far from the kitchen," she said. "Couldn't we move the dishes by bicycle, Prudence?" She wasn't entirely used to the house. Her father had bought it, an astoundingly bad investment, when he had been forced to sell The Grey House to cover his losses on the fruit farm.

In the kitchen they found Harry with the soup saucepan in front of him. He was eating from it with a spoon.

"There was no sherry in any room at all," he explained. "So I thought I had better come out here to say goodbye. Who's lunching here today?"

"Morgan. He pays for his board, so we have to toss him a biscuit now and then," Hester said coldly.

Harry pushed the saucepan away. "Morgan's got so much anxiety in his heart he walks with a list to the left side. He has the merit of being very fond of the game of Donegal Poker. I'm still a hungry man, Prudence. You'll give me a spoonful from that casserole before you take it in?"

"If you help with the washing-up," Prudence said, scowling.

"We can discuss that later," Harry said easily. He emptied some of the meat from the casserole on to his soup plate.

"Morgan drinks without getting any pleasure from it," he said. "He drinks alone in his room."

"Harry, how do you know?" Hester asked.

"I've seen the empty bottles. He hides them in his wardrobe, like Hemingway."

"But how did you come to look in his wardrobe?" Hester asked, shocked.

"It's the place to find empty bottles. Why is Morgan hanging around that room your father is painting?"

"Is he?"

"When I couldn't find any sherry, I went up there again. He shot out of the room like a clay pigeon from a trap."

"We'd better take what's left of the casserole to the dining-room," Prudence said bitterly.

"If you don't want him in that room, getting in the way, I'll tell him doctors have discovered this new paint is a prime cause of T.B. That will send him off to London for an X-ray," Harry said.

Prudence hovered in the door with the casserole. "Come on, Hester."

"How long is it since anyone was in the room—the attic room?" Harry asked.

"Years, I suppose," Hester said over her shoulder.

She was worried when she went back to the dining-room,

and she found it hard not to take too obvious an interest in Morgan's face. She had never before met a secret drinker, and she looked at him now with a mixture of clinical interest and human sympathy; she saw nothing but a cold, reticent face, with features that suggested strength far more than weakness. She wanted to help him, but she was surprised when she heard herself saying:

"I want to walk to Furlong Hill this afternoon. Would you like to come, Morgan?"

"A walk?" he asked grudgingly. "I don't know. I'm not sure. Yes, yes, thank you, Hester. In about an hour?"

"Morgan is a bit queer," Prudence said when the two girls were alone in the kitchen.

"He's probably going to sit in his wardrobe with the door shut, drinking," Hester said. "I wonder where Harry is?"

When she went up to the attic she found Harry. He seemed to be tapping the walls.

"What are you doing, Harry?" she asked.

"You saw. I was tapping the walls. Looking for more weak spots."

Morgan's uneasy face appeared in the doorway. He stared at the sand and broken plaster on the floor.

"I didn't know you were going to make so thorough a job of this room," he said accusingly. "Are you going to have all the walls down?"

"Very likely," Harry said.

"If I were your father," Morgan said to Hester, "I should leave this room alone. It's too big a job for one man."

"But I'm going to help," Harry said.

Morgan wavered in the doorway, then left.

"He looks worried," Hester said.

"He does indeed," Harry said thoughtfully.

He walked up and down the room, not speaking to her, and she went to the window and looked out again over the trees.

"Do you hear a ticking?" Harry asked from behind her.

She listened. "Only my watch, I think."

"It's not that."

"I don't hear anything else." She turned round. "You're probably listening to your own watch."

"I haven't got one. I lent it to a friend. He went to South America. Lie down on the floor and listen."

"I'll get paint on my clothes."

"Lie down and put your ear to this board," Harry said. His eyes were bright and excited, his normally sad, mocking face was stern. He looked like an anarchist who at last has his hands on a bomb.

Hester lay down obediently. She wasn't sure. She heard, or thought she heard, something that might have been a ticking.

Her father opened the door and looked at them in consternation.

"Sshh!" Harry said. "We're listening to a ticking. It comes from under the floorboards."

"A ticking," Wade repeated. "You're mad, Harry."

"I'm not. The boards are ticking."

Wade tried to laugh.

"If you think it's a joke," Harry said, "lie here and listen."

Hester stood up. "What do you think it is?" she asked uncertainly.

"Death watch beetle," Harry said curtly.

"What?" Wade said in a stunned voice. He put out a hand to the wall, to support himself.

"Death watch beetle," Harry repeated with relish. "They eat their way into the middle of boards and through and through and suddenly the floor collapses, and then the ceiling underneath. They nibble their way round the walls and through the beams on the roof until the whole building shudders and turns to dust—like something found in an Egyptian tomb. Listen!"

Wade dropped on his hands and knees beside Harry and put his ear to the floor. He thought he heard the sound of ticking.

"They make the noise by banging their heads on wood," Harry explained. "It's a mating song. When the female death watch beetle hears the male banging its head on wood, it gnaws its way through the intervening timbers to reach the male. I suppose they carve themselves out a little cell. It's like the end of *Aïda*, except they have children."

"*Aïda*?" Wade asked, looking defenceless and baffled. "What has Italian opera got to do with it?" He was fond of opera, but he hadn't Harry's talent for seeing one event in terms of another.

"Oh, Father, don't look so worried," Hester said. "There's bound to be some way of getting rid of death watch beetle."

"Of course there is," Harry said briskly. "You send for—I think it's the County Sanitary Engineer. When he's confirmed it's death watch beetle he lists your house as a dangerous structure. You have to pull it down or rebuild."

"That sounds arbitrary," Hester said coldly.

"Or you can take the boards up yourself and soak them in paraffin. That often cures it."

Wade looked round the half-painted room at the crumbled wall. "I don't think I can tackle it today."

"I'll do it for you," Harry said. "Get me a hammer and chisel and a gallon of paraffin, and I'll fix it for you."

When the tools had been brought to him, he began to wrench up the boards and pour paraffin on the joists beneath.

"You look like a fire-raiser," Hester said.

"These boards aren't too bad," Harry said. "It may have spread to the floor beneath, that's all. Morgan's room is under this, isn't it?"

"Morgan wouldn't like to have his room torn up," Wade protested.

"Take him out for a walk, Hester, then he'll never know. I'll do it very neatly," Harry promised. "But I'll need some more paraffin."

"I'll send Prudence up," Wade said.

Hester lingered.

"Harry, do you know what you're doing? You're not going to do any damage, are you?" she asked unhappily.

"Damage?" He looked up with a serious, preoccupied face. She felt ashamed of her suspicions, without knowing precisely what her suspicions were.

"It's hard to know when you're being serious, Harry. You're so different from anyone I've ever met," she said despairingly. She left the room quickly before he had time to answer.

Prudence appeared with the paraffin, and stood, peering intently at the exposed joists.

"I'd like to see a death watch beetle," she said.

"They're like woodworm, only smaller. You'd need a magnifying glass."

"I'll get a magnifying glass."

"They take cover. They don't like being exposed to light. You can try, if you want to. I think I've finished this bit. I'll have a look at the room downstairs. You wouldn't like to hammer these boards back on for me?"

"Not much."

"I'll put them back later, then."

He picked up the tools and the paraffin, and walked

downstairs and nonchalantly into Morgan's room. Prudence followed.

"Does Morgan know you're going to be in his room?" she asked.

"I didn't ask his permission. Death watch beetle can't wait."

"I can," said Prudence, and sat down on the bed.

Harry looked at her briefly, then walked over to the heavy, dark, Jacobean wardrobe, and opened the door.

"See," he said, "bottles."

Prudence looked, entranced.

"Harry, I thought you weren't serious."

"People are always thinking I'm not serious, when I am. Help me roll back the carpet."

They lifted a table to the corner, then took one end each of the frayed green carpet and rolled it to the other side of the room. Harry looked quickly at the dusty boards underneath, and walked thoughtfully to the middle of the room. He bent down and tapped one board with the hammer.

"There's a lot of dust about. Get me housewife's implements, and I'll sweep it up," he said to Prudence.

She was out of the room for several minutes. When she came back, she carried a book as well as a brush. Harry had already lifted one board and was staring into the hole.

She stood beside Harry, scrutinising him, noting with distaste that his brown hair waved, that his nose was not quite straight, as if it had once been broken, that his face was round and his mouth and chin soft. She liked a man to have a hard, lean, Hollywood look. Harry was nearly handsome, but he didn't look like a man who would be put in charge of a space-ship.

"I've been reading about death watch beetles in my insect book," she said.

"Yes?" Harry stood up.

"Are you looking at me with narrowed eyes?" he asked.

"Death watch beetles court in February," she said. "You wouldn't hear them tick in August. It's people you hear ticking," she added cryptically.

"In February?" he said, grinning. "Then I've made a mistake."

"You have."

"A natural, human mistake," he said cheerfully. "So I'll put the boards back and say no more. Imagine these little creatures confining their love life to February!"

"What do you know about death watch beetles anyway?" she asked grimly.

"I used to collect them when I was a boy. Relax, Prudence, unless you're training to be a girl detective."

"Do you mean to tear up any more floorboards?"

"There wouldn't be any point in it, if I can't separate them when they're courting."

"You know there aren't any death watch beetles there," she said accusingly.

"For all I know, there may be. I regard them as not proven. I'll put the boards back."

"Harry, I don't know what you've been trying to do, but I shall tell Father. Then what will you say?"

"I shall feign madness. And I'll leave him to put the floorboards back. You'll never find out what I was trying to do. But if you keep your mouth shut, you'll discover something very interesting—about Morgan."

"About Morgan?" Prudence asked, frowning.

"Or perhaps you think he's an ordinary man with nothing queer about him?"

"He is a bit odd," Prudence said slowly. "But so are you."

"In the next two days I'm going to show you just what Morgan is. You'll have your name in the papers."

"My name in the papers!" Prudence repeated scornfully. "Exactly what do you think I am? A child of twelve?"

"All right then. You win. Tell your father. I'll give up. I'll leave Morgan to get on with it," Harry said savagely. He picked up the loose floorboard and dropped it back into place, his face drooping into melancholy. He looked down at the hammer and chisel he still held, then let them slip from his fingers. He looked like a man who had climbed nearly to the top of a pit, and was sliding down again.

"I won't speak to Father now. I'll give you two days," Prudence said in the clipped, decisive voice that English-women use to intimidate foreigners on the Golden Arrow.

Wednesday (3)

Morgan walked halfway up Furlong Hill with Hester before he was overtaken by ill-health. He clapped one hand to his side, waved a hand weakly in the air, and leant against a tree for support.

"I can't go on," he said.

"What's wrong, Morgan?"

"It's a pain at my heart, that's all. I suppose it's nothing, really."

"Have you ever had trouble with your heart before?"

"I've suspected for years that there was something wrong."

Hester looked at him thoughtfully. In the short time she had known him he had suffered from his liver, his appendix, and his tonsils. She knew nothing of how to treat a hypo-chondriac invalid.

"Are you unhappy about something, Morgan?" she asked.

"Unhappy? I feel as though I was being knifed," he said in a gasping voice.

"But is there something else troubling you, Morgan?"

He groaned. "My heart!"

She sat down beside him. "We must wait until you're better."

"Hester? Did you see some strangers in the village?"

"I didn't notice. Probably. It's August, Morgan," she said impatiently. "The village is always full of tandem bicycles or foreigners doing England in a one-day coach tour."

"Your father told me this was quiet country where strangers never came."

"It's not Father's fault that England is small and everyone has a holiday in August. Would you like to come home and rest?"

Morgan rose, wincing, and hobbled painfully down the hill. The path plunged steeply through the woods. He looked at it nervously, as though he thought it had been mined.

"The country life is wonderful," he said, groaning a little.

Hester turned her mind away from him. She saw that the blackberries had ripened early. She picked some, and ate them. She held out a handful, offering them to Morgan.

"They might be poisonous," he said. "You shouldn't go eating berries."

"I thought you said you'd been brought up in the country. Where did you live, Morgan?"

"I was born in London. My father—well, I'm too old now to talk about my father," Morgan said, hatred flashing across his face. "He wasn't a careful man about money."

"Lots of people aren't, I suppose. Think of Harry."

"Harry! I don't want to think about him. I always thought

I'd like to meet a poet. Harry isn't my idea of a poet," he said accusingly.

"Morgan, are you happy here? Are you sure you like living in the country?"

"All those fields to look at! Yes, I like it. It's quiet, you see, Hester, I've got to have quiet. My heart…" He sat down again.

"Perhaps you should go to bed when you get home. And I'll get Doctor Nelson."

"No." He stood up, and they went on.

About fifteen yards above the road, Morgan stopped and clutched Hester's wrist.

Three men were drooping along the road. They weren't at all like the strangers who usually passed through the village, bent under rucksacks or excessively tweeded. They wore jackets of a markedly Edwardian style, trousers that were tight everywhere, and narrow, pointed shoes that seemed to be giving trouble.

One of them sat down by the side of the road and began to dust his shoes with his handkerchief.

"I limp so bad," he said.

"Smell the country air," another advised bitterly. "You haven't breathed so good since you was a boy at Southend."

"Five miles to the next pub," the first said. "Turn right, turn left, turn right round, cross the field with the bulls, and I'd fight the field full of bulls to be back in Old Compton Street right now. What gave that foggy-boy the idea he was living here? Living! The country is the part of England they should dispose of, which is what I'm going to do when we get to that railway station." He limped dejectedly behind the other two.

Morgan stared after them down the road. Hester, looking at him curiously, saw that he was standing erect and breathing naturally. His heart attack appeared to be over.

"Go on, Hester. Don't wait for me. I think I'll sit around and rest for a little," he said in a strained voice.

"You're sure you're all right?" she asked doubtfully.

She was glad to leave him. She wanted to walk alone and think about Harry.

She crossed the road and went into the woods on the other side, her mind moving irresponsibly around Harry's appearance, changing his clothes, seeing that his hair was cut regularly and his shirt was always clean. She thought of the attic room as her father had planned it, with a white floor and green rugs. She furnished it with a desk and some clean paper, and set Harry to work, writing a more jocund version of "The Waste Land." In the autumn they went to Italy and lived simply in a villa within reach of Florence.

She came down on the road again and walked through the village. Poetry didn't earn much money, but there was satisfaction in being heralded at literary lunches and making experimental dashes into the poetic drama.

Moira Ferguson waved to her, and she smiled back from Stockholm, where the Nobel prizes were being distributed.

"Come in and have some tea," Moira said. "Joe's raging against Harry, and it's much nicer for him to have a new listener."

Hester made the correct social noises and then went in, although Moira Ferguson always made her feel immature and badly dressed. Joe treated her like a favourite niece, and the household was an entrancing but resistible specimen of the comfort associated exclusively with wealth.

The grey stone house had once been a farm, but the farmer had been glad to move out and build himself a red brick bungalow. The barn had been converted to a servants' flat; the dairy to a squash court; and where the pigs had lain, gasping with gluttony on the straw, was now a rose garden.

Inside the house, in the corner by the fireplace where generations of farmers had sat mourning over night frosts, east winds, spring droughts, Uncle Joe now sat worrying about the weather. It was hot, it was hot even for August, and people were staying away from the cinemas he owned.

"Do they care?" he demanded passionately of Hester. "In the winter they come begging, they stand in queues, they go to my managers with tears in their eyes, two, only two, they beg, even at seven-and-six. Now, in the bad times, they keep the half-crowns in their pockets and walk in the park instead."

"We have no money, Hester," Moira said comfortably. "Just fancy, we are ruined." She put a finger idly on the bell and a parlourmaid materialised with a tea tray.

"Moira is always thinking about money. It's the curse of the age," Joe boomed happily. "We can't afford to keep the servants, she says, but we have two, only two. We want a holiday, we go to Bermuda, Gleneagles, anywhere we like. Money, money, money, she says. We must save. She wants a new skirt. Go to Paris, I tell her. Get Dior, Balmain, one of those, to make you a skirt. No, we can't afford it, she says. Now if I wanted to play the violin, I would hire Menuhin to teach me, but not Moira. She would go to Miss Botts down the street. Money!"

"We could think about it more than we do," Moira protested idly. "We have three cars. Two cars make sense. What's the use of three?"

"It's no good keeping up appearances unless you keep up a good appearance. I can't keep up appearances with a motor bike. Moira tells me I'm having a financial crisis. I remember having a financial crisis in Persia. I left it with forty-two thousand owing. I paid back every penny, except what I owed the Persians. Money! I never think of it."

Hester accepted her tea. She wanted to turn the cup over and see if the price was written on the bottom. Joe looked at her, grinning.

"Twenty-five shillings each, about, these cups cost," he said.

"Uncle Joe, you are clever," Hester said admiringly. "How did you know what I was thinking?"

"It's a parlour trick," Moira said contemptuously. "He can always tell when people are wondering what something cost. That's the kind of thing they often wonder, in this house. They don't ask about the Shropshire Fergusons, nor even the Berlin branch of the family. It's always what it cost."

"But I wasn't thinking how much the cup cost," Hester protested. "I—I—"

"You were thinking, perhaps, I would like it to be known how good our cups were," Joe said. "You come here," he added in a voice of immense sorrow, "to see how the rich live. You are a welfare worker in reverse. But you come to the wrong place, my child. We don't live as the rich do. We are the little pigs who have built our house of paper money, and one day the wolf comes and he huffs and he puffs and he blows our house down. So inside the house we must tell ourselves we are very happy. But when the house is blown down, what can I do? Only one thing. I can drive a car. Perhaps when you are buried you look round on your way to the churchyard, and find I am driving the hearse."

Hester began to laugh. She liked Joe and the blasts of energy that came from him. Moira looked sulky and bored. It was possible she had heard the joke before.

"I wanted to ask you, Uncle Joe, is Harry really your nephew?" Hester said cautiously.

Joe swallowed his tea and crashed the cup on the table. He

was as dismal as if he were staring through a series of empty cinemas. Moira looked at him angrily.

"Harry came back to the London flat one night with Joe and said he was his nephew," she explained coolly to Hester.

"It was true. For the night, he was a relation," Joe said.

"And he was going next day. But he was very interested in music. We have a Hi-Fi in London," Moira went on. "It's too loud for the country."

"I don't even know what Hi-Fi is," Hester said.

"You have a kind of horse-trough filled with sand and a box of knobs for the gramophone records," Joe explained. "You hear every sound, even the tears rolling down the conductor's cheeks. After you have Hi-Fi, there is nothing else, absolutely nothing, but to go out and hear the concert when it's played. But Harry likes this Hi-Fi noise. He plays records every day. Carried away on the space-ship to the music of the spheres, he explains to me. But he's not carried away. He's anchored on the sofa. Why do I have this Hi-Fi, perhaps you ask? With my connections, how can I ask my friends to hear a clockwork gramophone?"

"You see, Harry spent the first few days just listening to Hi-Fi," Moira said, beginning to smile. "It seemed rude to interrupt him."

Joe scowled. "Then I begin to tell him, you'd like to go soon, Harry. This very evening, he says, but the banks are closed, can you cash a cheque? A very small cheque, Harry, I tell him. A very small cheque indeed. How much is it worth to me to get rid of Harry? Ten pounds, perhaps, I think, but he makes it twenty. He is about to go. Suddenly it is raining. His coat is at the cleaner's, he tells me, and he'll have to stay the night after all. So what happens?" He stopped, scowling at Hester.

Hester smiled sadly. She wanted to leave, but it was hard not to hear everything about Harry.

"What happens?" he repeated. "At three that morning I am playing Donegal Poker. I go to bed at six with Donegal Poker insomnia. It is true I have won, but all I have won is my own cheque back from Harry. The next day I have to see accountants, managers, lawyers—it is very difficult for me. But Harry is not difficult. He is happy. He is writing a poem. We mustn't disturb him, Moira says."

"Poetry is a wonderful occupation," Moira said angrily.

"The next afternoon, at five, he goes—with another cheque, because the banks are closed again. At eleven he is back, with friends he wants to hear our Hi-Fi. Take the Hi-Fi, Harry, I say. Take it and go."

"The next morning I find him telephoning dealers, asking what they will give for a second-hand Hi-Fi. Now I want to get angry. Moira stops me. He's a poet she says."

"He is a poet," Moira said softly. Hester looked at her with the astonished glance of a woman acknowledging an enemy. A flash of contempt for Moira's forty years crossed her face like a beam of light.

"He is a poet in words. That is now of no importance. I am a poet of money. Words! We have too many words. Word poets talk all the time of love and death. People fall in love and they die, and no amount of poetic advice has ever helped them to do either of those things more successfully. They are interested in love for a few years, and later they are afraid of death. But they are always interested in money. Everyone, everywhere is interested in money all the time. There's never been an age when people agreed so heartily to be interested all at once in the same thing. They're crazy about money, even if it's only to buy a bar of chocolate or a diamond necklace.

This is how I am a poet in money. I'm not tied down to pearls and cigars. I have imagination and daring. I'm not frightened by six figures. I make beautiful combinations with banks and factories. I have just been buying more cinemas," he added reflectively.

"A poor poem, at the moment," Moira commented.

"I was telling you about Harry," Joe said in a sombre voice. "In the end I say we are going to the country for a week. We lock up the London flat, I tell him. I am sorry, I say, but this time it's goodbye. And what happens? He comes with us to the country here. I spend the first night in the quiet of this village playing Donegal Poker. I am lucky he doesn't stay in London, break into the flat, steal my wife's jewellery."

"Which is in the bank," Moira said, yawning.

"Because he is a bad man. I warn you, Hester, he is bad. He's the kind of man who would pawn his grandmother's crutches to buy a drink for a friend."

"Thank you for the tea," Hester said in a furious voice.

"You're angry?" Moira enquired curiously. "Has Joe said something to offend you? Don't take him seriously."

"I don't think it's right to say these things about Harry," Hester said. "You shouldn't say them, Uncle Joe. It's not true. Whatever Harry is, he's honest. You just don't understand him."

"Have some more tea," Moira suggested.

"I don't understand him!" Joe repeated in amazement.

"No you don't. He's not one of the people who's interested in money. He stands for something much finer than money. He doesn't know about money, and because he doesn't worship it as you do you think he's no good. I agree with him. I despise money."

"But so do I," Joe said. "My dear child, I couldn't agree

with you more. So there's no argument. I won't quarrel with you. You know, Hester, I'm not even rich. I owe much, Inland Revenue is after me, and I leave the rest to Harry."

He looked at her anxiously. She didn't smile.

"I'm a ruined man, Hester," he said pathetically. "Television and the weather—I can't survive them. I'm going to Ireland on Friday to buy some new cinemas, try to earn a little something."

"You told me you were going to Ireland to get away from Harry," Moira said maliciously. She glanced at Hester, seeming to absorb and reflect again the knowledge that Hester was wearing last year's clothes. "I don't say I believe you. I should have thought the way you feel about Harry, something far away like India would have suited you better. A *soupçon* more cream, Hester?"

"My wife doesn't like Harry," Joe explained. "She is only afraid to dislike him because he is a poet. We are both worried when we think we think of nothing but money. So we have Hi-Fi, and go to opera."

"Opera. Wagner is divine," Moira agreed, yawning.

Joe's jowls sagged a little at the mention of Wagner.

"Verdi, Bizet, now Bizet is something," he said quickly. "Do they have Verdi and Bizet in India?" he demanded.

No one knew.

"I thought Bizet was very O.K. Then I saw that first thing of his. Enough. I didn't like it. But the Russians—Eugene Onegin? Do they have Eugene Onegin in India or Australia? Europe is all I want."

"Is Ireland Europe?" Moira asked languidly. She rose and glanced quickly in the mirror. Her complexion was the cosmetician's dream come true, as rich and soft as marshmallow, just tinged with Turkish delight.

"How are you going?" Hester asked coldly. She hadn't been deceived by the talk of opera. Joe hated Harry, and she wanted to leave his house.

"I'm flying," he said. "I've chartered a plane and it has three empty seats. Do you happen to know anyone who would like to share it?"

Wednesday (4)

Hester walked home through the woods without looking at them. There was a world inside her head, and it was filled with a dozen versions of a defenceless Harry overborne by enemies. England was a country that didn't appreciate its poets until they were playwrights, or dead, but even so, she was astonished by the malice which her father, Uncle Joe, and Morgan had shown towards Harry. She knew that what they hated was not Harry, but their own failure to be as he was. Harry, in his innocence, was like a clear pool in which they saw their own pretences. She couldn't endure any more attacks on Harry. She hesitated at the gate, and then turned away from the house and walked through the woods until she came to the ruined chapel.

The chapel was roofless and derelict, but it had the melancholy romantic air that ruins so easily adopt. Nettles sprang through the cracks in the stone floor, but beneath this lay the bones of long-dead wool merchants, so that as well as its other charms, an implication of mortality lingered inside the broken walls.

Harry was sitting on one of the fallen stones.

"I came here to think," he said in a guilty voice.

"All right. I'll leave you."

"Hester, please."

She sat down beside him.

"I've been given a lot of advice about you today, Harry. Are you so bad?"

"I'll tell you the truth. I'm no good at all. You'd do the right thing to tell me to go now. But I can't make myself go, unless you tell me. I can't move, with love of you closing over the top of my head."

He knelt beside her and she put her hand on his shoulder. "So bad, Harry?" she whispered.

"In every way. You only have to trust me, and I'll let you down."

"It's not true, Harry," she said, beginning to cry quietly. "Anyway, you're a poet."

"Yes, in a way. Yes, I am."

"So you wouldn't be the same as other people."

"I'm telling you, I'm worse than other people. You've no right to make excuses for me. And if I'm a poet I'm too lazy to be a good one."

"I don't believe it. You haven't had a chance. You've had too much worry, with nowhere to live and no money."

"Listen, Hester. I'm trying to tell you. I've had plenty of places to live, but I've been thrown out of most of them. When I was sent down from Oxford my mother couldn't bear it any longer. She threw me out too. I went to Australia. I wanted to be an old-fashioned remittance man, but she wouldn't send me the remittance."

Hester made a weak attempt to laugh.

"It's nothing to laugh about," he said angrily. "I had to work on a sheep station. It was hot."

"Hot?"

"It was so hot the snakes used to get burnt crossing the floor of my hut. It was so hot the mosquitoes turned into fireflies. The kangaroos fainted with the heat. And I was in the middle of it all, hacking away with an axe at the prickly pear, digging with a spade to reach the artesian wells fifty feet below ground—so that the sheep could get a drink. And the nearest pub was ninety-five miles away. It was filled with bearded men who had never seen rain. They carried guns. They shot anyone who tried to make a joke."

"Harry, I don't believe a word of it."

"Even now, if I see a sheep in Hyde Park, I get the bush staggers."

"I liked your Australian poetry."

"You're an angel in blue stockings."

"What did you do when you came back from Australia?"

"This and that. Angels never ask questions."

"When did you come back from Australia?"

"About four months ago."

He stood up.

"Hester, I'll have to go away. I want to tell you how I love you. I want to steal all the words of the poets and make a chain of them that will hold you for ever."

She waited. He moved away from her, and for a minute they were poised in silence, with emotions swooping between them like birds.

"I can't say anything, Hester. I was trying to write something when you came. Here it is. It's on an envelope."

He felt in his pocket, then gave her the envelope, and she read:

> *"Her strength's a language that will not speak*
> *To strength, or understand the strong who love and praise.*
> *She's marked to choose the man who's weak,*
> *Who'll ruin all her later days."*

"You understand I haven't finished it?" he asked anxiously. "A clumsy offering, but it means something. I'm not giving it to you as a love poem. It's a warning. You think now your strength is enough for two. You're making plans, you know. Soon you'll feel you have no right to marry a man who is strong. Hester, you've the air of a woman who wants martyrdom. I'm the man to give it to you."

"You don't mean all this, Harry," she said in distress.

"Be quiet. Goodness is as much a part of you as redness is of a cherry. I'm the worm that will eat the cherry away, redness and all. You think now you can change my character, tidy me up, get me a nine to five job, give me a room to work in, and watch the self-respecting income roll in one door while the works of genius roll out the other. But the cherry doesn't change the worm. It's the other way round. I'm an experienced worm. I know!"

Hester looked at him with the intensity of someone waiting for a miracle to be performed.

"You're the fourth person to tell me today how worthless you are. I don't believe it."

"Well, I've tried," he said gloomily. "I'll not try again. Just describing myself makes me see I'm only half the man I was. I can't reason any more. I met you two weeks ago, and I've been drowning ever since. My past life has come up before my eyes so often it's beginning to look like a non-stop revue. Throw me a straw before I sink for ever. Are you in love with any other man?"

"I've never been in love—except with actors and people I haven't met. That was when I was young. I've never wanted to marry anyone."

He didn't take up the offer to talk of marriage, but sat down again beside her.

"What made you come here now, Hester?"

"I came here to think, too," she said, flushing. "I'd like to be buried here."

"Now?" Harry asked. "You're in a hurry, aren't you?"

"Of course I didn't mean now. It was only a mood."

"Anyway, you couldn't, unless they made a special place for you, like Napoleon or Lenin. Just tell me how you'd like it. What about a mortician's dome in rose-coloured plastic?"

"It's nothing to laugh about," Hester said, beginning to laugh. "I was being perfectly serious. I'd like to be buried here. There are vaults at the other end. Prudence and I used to play here with the Peters boys, and they raised one of the stones and we all went down and sat beside the coffins and smoked Father's cigars. He used always to have boxes of cigars, it was before we lost our money. Prudence was the youngest, much, but she was the only one who wasn't sick."

"You were all sick in the vault?" Harry enquired with interest.

"Oh, no," Hester said in a shocked voice. "Even the Peters boys wouldn't have done a thing like that."

"Is this a roundabout way of telling me I have a rival called Peters?"

"I've told you. I've never been in love. I don't know what it's like to be in love," she said stiffly.

"I don't know what it's like for a girl. It makes a man want to smoke. Have you a cigarette on you, Hester?"

"I bought some for Father this afternoon." She took a packet of cigarettes from her bag, and gave it to him. He lit one, and absently put the packet, with his own matches, in his trouser pocket.

She considered the action.

"You can give me a cigarette case for my birthday next

month. I like cigarette cases and watches—they give a man something to pawn in time of need," he said easily. "Let's get back and have some tea, shall we?"

They walked back together, without exchanging a word of love. They went quietly in by the back door to the kitchen.

Harry sat down, with a sigh.

"Put on the kettle, there's a good girl," he said. "Hester, you'll do me a favour? If Morgan talks of changing his room, you'll tell me?"

She stopped, with the teapot in her hand.

"But why?"

"One of my peculiar ideas. I'm always having them. I'll offer you something in exchange. Don't trust Maurice."

"I thought it was Morgan who interested you," Hester said.

"Morgan is a special case. Do you know something, Hester? Your father is a man who lures catastrophes. He's what you might call accident-prone, but his accidents are all economic. I think Maurice is going to be one of them."

Hester poured the tea. "I wish people just for one day would stop warning me against other people," she said drearily. "If you want to know, I don't believe anything you say about Maurice. He's—he's splendid. He's the best friend we have."

The door opened, and Morgan's pale face, looking bonier than ever, appeared.

"Harry," he said grimly, and came into the room. "Harry, I want a word with you."

Harry put his cup down. "Is it going to be an ugly word?" he asked regretfully.

Morgan advanced. "Have you been in my room?"

"And what would I be doing there?"

"I told you he was no good, Hester," Morgan shouted. "I don't know what he was doing in my room. If he came to pilfer, he did a clumsy job."

"You should know," Harry said. He was beginning to grin in an excited way, like a nervous sniper marking down his target.

"You've been searching my room."

"If you accuse me of searching your room, you're accusing yourself of having something to hide," Harry said in a reasonable voice.

"Get up and I'll hit you," Morgan invited.

"Then I'd better keep sitting."

Morgan stepped forward and caught Harry by the back of the neck. He forced his head down, then stooped and caught the back legs of the chair and jerked them up. Harry sprawled on to the floor. Morgan stood over him, waiting. For a second he looked almost happy, like a ghost seeing a joke.

"Get out of this house," he said.

"It's not your house, Morgan. You can't order him out of it," Hester said.

Harry stood up slowly, and the other two watched him, waiting for the reprisals.

Harry stepped forward and sat down on the nearest chair.

"Shall we continue the conversation, Morgan?" he asked.

Morgan was walking forward when Hester stepped in front of Harry.

"No, Morgan," she cried.

Wade came bristling through the door.

"What's all this, what is it, Hester?"

"Shall I tell him?" Harry asked insolently.

"We'll settle this later," Morgan said, muted and polite, like a hangman discussing business with the prison governor.

Harry looked quickly at Hester and her father.

"It's only a little row in napkins and a blue bonnet," he said airily. "It may never grow up at all. By dinner-time it will have shrunk back to an embryo."

Wade coughed, and looked at his feet. He was a man of natural goodwill, who could have been very happy if everyone else had been the same. He could handle all the inhabitants of the ideal world, but reality often left him pained and confused.

"Harry, we can't, honestly we can't have that kind of row here."

"Did I start it then?" Harry appealed to Hester.

"I don't know," she said angrily.

"You'll see. By dinner-time Morgan and I will have our arms round each other's necks, exchanging tips for tomorrow's races, although it's a strange thing I've never been able to care if a horse has three legs or runs on roller skates."

Wade looked at him hopelessly.

"Harry, I hate to say it, but I haven't asked you to dinner. Maurice is coming over tonight. I wanted to have a private talk with him."

"Then I'll go back and dine with Uncle Joe," Harry said without embarrassment, "I've been neglecting him a bit, lately." He turned to Hester with his face drooping into melancholy again. "Goodbye, Hester."

"I'll walk as far as the village with you," Wade said. "I've run out of cigarettes."

"Don't bother to go down for a little thing like that," Harry said quickly. "Here!" He felt in his pocket and brought out a packet of cigarettes. "Have these. You can give me them back some other day."

Wednesday (5)

Harry found Moira lying in sulky idleness on a chaise longue by the sunny windows. Blue lights were shining in her black hair.

He sat down on the floor beside her.

"Would you like the curtains drawn, or is your hair guaranteed fadeless?" he asked her.

"Harry, where have you been all day?"

"At the Wades'."

"It's Hester," she said sharply. "Oh, it's so unfair, I'm absolutely excruciated with boredom here when you're away. Just because she's younger you'd stay with her all day for a single smile. But I'm left to smile alone."

"I wouldn't stay with anyone all day for a smile," Harry said coldly. "I have to eat somewhere until I sell another poem. Uncle Joe's making it difficult here."

"If you're in love with Hester, perhaps I'll make it difficult too," she said.

"Very well, I'll go and stay with the Wades. They've done everything but ask me."

"Oh, no, Harry. Everyone here is so boring. Apart from you and the Wades we don't see anyone who isn't disgustingly rich. They're all so offensive about money, pretending it doesn't matter, as if it had been conferred on them like a divine privilege. They don't see any fun in having lapis lazuli dashboards on their cars, and that kind of thing, but Joe says some of them are just as shaky as we are, even the brewers. I mean the small brewers—we don't know any of the old brewing aristocracy." She lay back, sighing.

"You don't happen to know a small brewer who'd want to finance me as a poet? They used to like that kind of thing."

"I'm certain they don't like it now. If you were a college you might get endowed. Harry, Joe's being very queer."

"In some new way?"

"He's going to Ireland."

"Why?"

"He says he wants to buy some new cinemas, but his real purpose is to get away from you. He says perhaps he'll buy a farm in Ireland and stay there until you go away. He says you're giving him a nervous breakdown and he can't bear another week of it. He's so keen to go that although Aer Lingus is booked up because of the Horse Show, he's chartering a plane. He was taking a couple of directors with him, but now their wives are ill or they're having alcoholic cures or something and they can't go. He ought to cancel the plane, but he's trying to find someone else to share it, and even if he can't, he's going alone. I think that's extravagant. It has four seats."

"He'll be able to put his feet up. Have you any cigarettes in the house, Moira?"

"There's a box somewhere. Oh no, there isn't."

Harry stood up and walked restlessly to the mantelpiece. "Would you like to ring for some?" he suggested.

"I can't. I'm sorry, Harry, I can't. Joe says as he only smokes cigars and would never let a cigarette touch his lips, and I don't smoke at all, we're not to keep cigarettes in the house. He says you smoke them all. Harry, he's getting restless. He doesn't want you to stay."

"I'm getting restless, too," Harry said. He sat down beside Moira and took her hand in his. "I'm getting worried about Joe. Suppose he had guests in the house who weren't me, what's he going to do about keeping up appearances? Shareholders won't appreciate the rose garden when they want to smoke."

Moira looked down thoughtfully. "You have wonderful hands, Harry. Lovely long fingers with the most exciting vibrations. But you should use a nail brush. He's keeping some cigarettes in his bedroom for emergencies."

Harry stood up. "What drawer?"

"I don't know. I should try the top one, in the dressing-chest with the handkerchiefs."

While Harry was upstairs, she lay back, frowning, then arranging the softly flowered dress over her knees.

He came down holding a box. "I like a handmade cigarette," he said. "Good old Joe." He leant against the mantelpiece, opening the box.

She stood up in a graceful, swirling movement, and walked towards him with short, rather plodding steps, as though she was crossing an expanse of suet pudding.

"Shall I get you a light?"

She stood beside him, and he put his arms round her and kissed her. When he let her go, he was grinning.

"Why have you gone so hard?" he asked.

"It's from Paris. The corset's built into the dress."

"You feel like a piece of machinery. It's like embracing a robot," he said.

"These damned dress designers. They never think of practical details," she said angrily.

"If you could think of a practical detail for a moment—is Joe really trying to get rid of me? Or is he trying to get rid of you?"

"Me? Joe trying to get rid of me. Harry, why should he?"

"Is he taking you to Ireland?"

"No."

"Is he taking me to Ireland?"

"No."

"So he's going to leave us alone together, in this house. Do you suppose he'd be happy about that unless he wanted trouble? I can see the way it will be," Harry said, his eyes beginning to shine. "He'll only pretend to go away. He'll come back suddenly, in the small hours. It's the classic situation, except that he may come by helicopter. Is he a *very* jealous man? Do you think he wants a chance to kill me, or is he only after divorce?"

"Oh, Harry!"

"If he goes away, we'll have to be very careful. The only safe thing would be to have nothing to do with each other. Unless you want to be divorced?"

"Do I?" she said. She stood and thought, until her face forecast all the lines and bitterness of middle-age. She saw herself less brutally than the observer, not for a moment imagining that the pool was already drying up and that the thirsty traveller would pass it without a glance. She knew that soon she might have to rise from the pool and clutch the traveller and hold him while his eyes turned away.

"Perhaps I don't. I'm used to dear old Joe," she said. "But, Harry, how awful if he's really plotting against me!" She began to cry a little. He wiped her eyes with a pale blue silk handkerchief.

She stopped crying.

"That's Joe's handkerchief," she said.

"I know. When I was getting the cigarettes, I remembered I was out of handkerchiefs. I did put some out for your old crab of a housekeeper to wash. But they never came back. I suppose she got them mixed up with Joe's. So I took a couple of his. While we're on the subject, Moira, I suppose you couldn't trouble your feminine head about what happened to my other shirt?"

"She came to me—but we were talking about divorce."

"Go on about the shirt."

"She asked if she was to wash it or throw it out. Joe was there. He said, *en passant*, throw it out." She laughed, a little nervously.

"Well, really, Moira!" Harry said in an outraged voice that made her laugh harder.

"But look at what I'm wearing!" he said, and took off his coat. She looked at the torn and dirty shirt underneath and laughed so much that she had to totter to the chaise longue and sink down, tortured by laughter.

Harry looked down at his shirt and laughed uncertainly.

"All right, then, let's talk about divorce," he said.

She made wild motions with her hands.

"Stop it, Harry, you're killing me," she said, choking.

There was a loud knocking at the door. She tried uselessly to control herself.

Joe walked into the room, looking fixedly at the floor.

"I knocked," he said. "In my own house, I knocked." He stood looking down with exaggerated meekness. "I was afraid of what I might see. You will be able to explain, Harry, what has been happening in this room?"

"I was talking about laundry," Harry said, putting on his jacket. "It made Moira laugh."

"It's true, Joe," Moira said. She was panting, and her face was streaked with tears of laughter.

"I haven't laughed so much for years," she said apologetically.

"Thank you, Moira, you have exposed the results of marriage. Harry, if you could make me laugh so much, I might keep you in this house for ever, but for me you are not a joke. You are so unamusing that I thought of hitting you. I have something to tell you. I am going to Dublin. I am going for a few days' rest."

"The last time I was in Dublin I didn't go to bed for forty-eight hours," Harry said reminiscently. "Moira says you're chartering a plane. Why don't you both go?" he asked in a generous manner.

"And leave you alone in this house? No, Harry."

"I wouldn't be quite alone. There are the servants."

"I don't want them corrupted. In any case, Moira is not coming with me. I wouldn't want you to stay alone in the house, with her. The neighbours would talk."

"I could stop their lying mouths with gin and tonic," Harry suggested.

Joe very markedly didn't smile.

"Have a cigarette?" Harry said, holding out the box.

"I don't smoke cigarettes, Harry. I am going to Ireland on Friday. Would you like to pack now?"

"If I can find my clean shirts," Harry said. He looked at Joe, measuring him. "Anyway, this is Wednesday. I don't have to pack until tomorrow. I have to make arrangements," he said in a reasonable voice.

"All this time you have had to make arrangements, Harry. Now we do not wait for the arrangements. You understand."

"Right," Harry said briskly. "Shall we have a farewell drink?"

Wednesday (6)

Hester and Prudence were in the kitchen, preparing dinner. It had to be a special meal, because Maurice was coming, and a man of many virtues should be honoured.

The whole family, in a way, depended on Maurice. He was the man who knew what to plant in the garden; when to ask the low-spirited out for a drink; how to do the maths homework. He looked reliable as a Rolls-Royce and steady as a lighthouse. Above all, he seemed to like the Wades enormously. He certainly deserved a good dinner, Hester thought, but it was a pity that good dinners involved cutting up so many things into such small pieces.

"Next dice the raw, fat pork," Hester said gloomily. "Do you think it would be better if I used a razor blade? I'm getting blisters. Mix it with the remainder of the diced meat. Chop carrots and shallots very fine. Now remove skins and seeds of eight small tomatoes. Chop pulp of small aubergine previously fried very lightly. Have you previously fried it, Prudence?"

Prudence didn't look round. "You'll have to do that. Don't forget the olive oil and the garlic. I'll murder you if you overdo the garlic."

Hester sighed. "Isn't there some simpler way of preparing food, Prudence?"

"When we have simpler meals, you can make them by yourself," Prudence said. "There's no satisfaction in throwing some fish into a frying pan. If a meal can't be a poem, it isn't worth cooking. When we've finished this, we'll feel like artists. Please cut those carrots a bit smaller. What should we feel if we'd been content to fry a piece of bacon?"

"That we'd provided food with less expense of time," Hester said. "You can't be a perfectionist in everything, Prudence. Life isn't like that. You'll find out."

"I'll find what I choose to find. Did I tell you I was taking up clothes next? If life was nothing but grim essentials, I'd be content to dress for ever in a white blouse and a school skirt. Oh horror horror horror! I think I may go in first for a terribly elegant simplicity and then branch out into *dernier cri* clothes. That reminds me, Hester. Those tight bodices and full skirts you're always wearing make you look awfully like a student, and an art student, at that. I suppose when you're a doctor you'll wear tailored suits all the time."

"You sound exactly like a schoolgirl who glues pictures of Paris models inside her science notebook," Hester said coldly.

"Ah, the elder sister line," Prudence said, sighing. "I warn you, Hester, in a few years you'll come to me for advice. I'll give you some now, if you like, while you stir the sauce. Don't have anything to do with Harry. He's not good enough for you. If you marry him, you'll spend half your life looking through a wire grating."

"Wire grating?"

"Visitors' day at prison."

"You're an insufferable adolescent, Prudence, and I hope your damned dinner burns," Hester said angrily.

"Oh, Hester, I'm only saying it because you're so good you can't see when other people are bad. Please go on stirring the sauce. I'm beating the egg-whites and I can't stop. Maurice is coming to dinner. I do want it to be perfect. You think you can change Harry, but I know you can't," Prudence said, beginning to cry.

"You're dropping tears in the soufflé. You'll spoil it," Hester said. "I'll go in and see if Mrs Timber set the table before she left."

She took off her apron and went to the dining-room, thinking sadly how much easier life was in term-time, when she lived alone. She had a bed-sitting-room in a dingy house in an undistinguished street and there, whatever else happened, she was free from economic pretences. At home her father still dreamt of the easy past when he had sat in the manor house like a benevolent ornament; and even Prudence felt it was a social necessity to provide elaborate meals cooked with butter when they could afford to eat only bread and margarine. With the slightest encouragement her father would have insisted on dressing for dinner. She didn't see this as going down with the flag flying: it was more like struggling to live underwater in a sunken ship. The pressure was too great; the quarrels were inevitable.

She heard a tapping on the dining-room window. Harry was outside, making expressive faces. She opened the windows and let him in.

"Hester," he said, "I couldn't keep away. I get pulled to you like the tides following the moon." He held out his arms to her. She didn't respond.

"You'll have noticed that the ocean follows the moon for eternity but it never gets much closer," he said. "Do you suppose it's content with that?"

She moved dreamily towards him and he caught her wrist with one hand. She heard a step outside the door and pulled her hand away. She moved quickly to the table and began to rearrange the knives and forks with excessive concentration like a child who had almost been caught smoking.

Prudence came in, sniffing the atmosphere suspiciously. "Harry! I thought you'd gone home hours ago."

"Home?" he said harshly. "You mean Uncle Joe's? Don't worry, Prudence, I'm going away again."

"You must stay to dinner," Hester said doubtfully.

"Oh, Hester! Father would be furious."

"You needn't worry about me," Harry said heavily. "I'll wait. I needn't eat. Tell me a room that's empty. I'll wait there. Maybe I could sit in the bathroom if no one plans to have a bath at dinner-time. That's what I'll do. I'll take a book and sit on the edge of the bath."

"Prudence, there's no pepper left in this thing. Will you get some more?" Hester said.

"We can bring it in later." Prudence lingered by the door, glowering at Harry.

"Please, Prudence. I want it now," Hester said angrily.

"Oh, if you're going to make a scene about pepper," Prudence said, "I'll oblige by leaving the room. But I'm coming back right away with your pepper."

They watched her march out.

"Harry, what is it? What's wrong?"

"Only that Uncle Joe is turning me out. He thinks I'm not his nephew after all. But that's nothing. I came here about you."

"Me?" Hester asked in amazement, as though it had never occurred to her that Harry was more than an acquaintance.

"I had an attack of conscience. I'm not used to it—I feel very queer. What I thought was it would be all right if your father wasn't your father. I don't believe in interfering with the course of nature. But I know what Maurice is. He's practically got it embroidered on his shirt. Hester, he's a crook of the simplest kind. Can't you see it?"

"Why don't you attack him to his face?" she asked contemptuously.

"Because he's not attacking me," Harry said in a reasonable voice. "Look, I've met a dozen Maurices. He could sell a horse a sack of paper oats for its lunch, and steal the shoes off its feet while it was counting out the change. Your father—"

"Leave my father out of this."

"He won't leave himself out. He's a glutton for money. He's the kind of man who's doomed to spend his life exchanging wallets with strangers as a sign of confidence. Maurice won't hit your father on the head to get his money. He'll just stand still, and your father will ram it into his pockets. All Maurice has to do is look excited, as if he was on to something big, and your father will be standing on his head trying to get the hook into his mouth."

"It's not true. I know Maurice. I trust him. What have you got against him?"

Harry suddenly grinned, like a man enjoying a private joke. He tried to look serious again, but the intensity had gone out of him, as though he had changed his mind about climbing to the top of a mountain. He looked round him, easy and relaxed, enjoying the view.

"Maurice is disguised as a man who would remember to send his old Nannie peppermint creams at Christmas," he said lightly.

Hester walked out of the room. She was shaking with anger. There was nothing in her experience to explain Harry's changes of mood. Talking to him was like discussing the scenery with a fish, or a bird.

Prudence was waiting in the hall, clutching the pepper shaker. "I can hear the car!" she said in a warm voice. "It's Maurice."

"I'll go and see what's happening in the oven," Hester said. She went quickly along the hall and back to the kitchen. She needed a few minutes to practise her smile of welcome. She was already struggling to bury Harry's remarks, but they kept reappearing in her mind like the shoots from a vigorous weed. She reminded herself again how easy it was to like Maurice; what relief his company gave to her father, who needed so badly to talk about war and money with another man who understood these subjects. Maurice treated Prudence and herself with an avuncular affection that was always understanding and never presumptuous. What brought him so close to them all was his air of having the same values; of believing in the same virtues, loving the same countryside, taking the same level-headed interest in music, painting, archaeology. When they had met him first he was only an occasional visitor to the village inn, since then—and it proved how much he loved the Cotswold country—he had rented a small cottage on the far side of the village. Harry would probably never earn enough money to rent a barn. It was natural that he should resent such a solid member of society as Maurice.

Wednesday (7)

When she had helped Prudence to take in the dinner, Hester was able to look on Maurice with what she thought was the old, untroubled affection. She was surprised to find herself saying: "Did you have a Nannie, Maurice?"

"A Nannie?" He looked at her with his brows lifting, and his face shadowed by his solid, comfortable smile. "Of course I did, but why?"

"No reason at all. I just wondered if you ever saw her now?"

"She's very old. She lives in Wales. I can't tell you much about her, except that she's passionately fond of Edinburgh Rock. So I send her some at Christmas, as a weak apology for not going to Wales."

Hester made some trivial remark, and then smiled and smiled and wondered why the room was so hot. She listened in an accumulation of fear to her father's efforts to squeeze financial information from Maurice. It appeared that Maurice was determined not to discuss his business affairs, but Wade coiled his conversation around him, darting up with sudden questions, until it was revealed that Maurice was deeply inter-ested in the financing of oil wells.

"Where did you say this oil was?" Wade asked.

"I didn't say it was anywhere," Maurice protested.

"I'd like to discuss it with you, if it's not too late," Wade said greedily.

Morgan, who had been listening quietly, gave an abrupt, barking laugh, and Hester turned on him quickly, half hoping that he was daring to criticise her father, so that she could direct all her uneasy energy against him, but his face was already cold and empty.

"I wouldn't advise it," Maurice was saying. "There's an element of risk… I'm willing to take the risk myself, because it's a moral certainty, but I'm aware of the gulf that lies between a moral and a real certainty. My own money is one thing, yours is another," he said in a voice that indicated his rectitude.

"What profit are you likely to make?" Wade asked, his face yearning towards Maurice. "Did you say twenty per cent?"

"I'm just as likely to lose," Maurice said. "By the way, did I tell you I'd brought over some Bizet records you might be interested in? Hester must have told you about our jaunt together."

Wade couldn't endure the digression. "I've always admired Bizet. Did you say twenty per cent?"

"Who's Bizet?" Morgan asked.

"He's a composer," Hester said. "The one that makes people think of *Carmen*."

"*Carmen*?" Morgan repeated, looking bewildered.

"An opera."

"Opera? Yes. I see. I've never been attracted to opera. I've never been to an opera in my life, unless you'd call American musicals opera?"

"No," Maurice said judicially. "It's not to say one is better." He was always gentle with other people's views.

"I can see you're avoiding my question about twenty per cent," Wade said in a good-humoured voice. "I suspect you hope to get more."

"Perhaps."

"Much more?"

Maurice suddenly looked deeply serious. "I wouldn't like to tell you how much I hope to get. You might think I was having dreams of grandeur. I'll tell you what I'm going to do if it comes off. I'm going to leave the City, abandon the whole thing—now, don't laugh—I'm going into the furniture business. I'm tired of the shoddy stuff that's produced. I know a little about furniture, I've ideas of my own about design. I know a cabinet-maker, an old-fashioned craftsman, who's willing to join me. He has a son who's learnt to be a wood-carver. We're going to produce handmade furniture, hand-carved. This clean, empty modern line is a bit boring. We think we can produce something beautiful—and expensive." He looked round the table, smiling. "So I'll probably lose all the money I make on Australian oil."

"Ah, yes, furniture. Furniture is a big subject," Wade said, sighing. "It's Australian oil, is it?"

Morgan roused himself. "How did you find out about this oil, living so far from Australia?" he asked.

"I was taking a little trip for my health. I'd just made rather a lot of money on a take-over bid. I feel ashamed of it now. It's only a kind of piracy. But money is money. It's exciting, in a way. I went to a little place in Western Australia where they were drilling for oil. One way and another, I made contact with some of the men on the job. You know they did in fact strike oil in Western Australia a year or two ago? That was a different company, nothing to do with me, but it made what had been just a dream a little closer to reality. So now..." He broke off with a laugh, not looking at Wade, who was leaning forward with his eyes shining.

Hester looked at her father. She wanted to get up and shake him. Instead she spoke politely to Morgan.

"Have you ever been in Australia, Morgan?"

He shook his head. "I've been in South Africa," he offered.

"Now?" Wade asked Maurice eagerly. "Go on."

"I didn't like South Africa," Morgan said, and returned to his own thoughts.

"Do you know, I did rather like South Africa," Maurice said easily. "I haven't been there for years—I know they have their racial troubles, very regrettable, I couldn't approve less, but perhaps it was the tension that made it seem so exciting. It's like a game of chess, you know—White to play and mate in three moves—but Black has most of the pieces."

"South Africa is a problem," Wade said, sighing. "What were you saying about a contact in Western Australia?"

"A man called Garvin. By an extraordinary coincidence, he went to my prep school. What he said was that someone was going to get rich if he struck oil, and he didn't mind if it was me. He sent me a cable today." Maurice felt in his pocket and produced a form. He tossed it to Wade. It was on Cable and Wireless paper, and said, "Happy Birthday, Sam."

"What does it mean?" Wade asked.

"Code," Maurice said succinctly, and took it back. "It means they've struck, and the news will be out on Friday."

"Isn't it a bit dishonest of your friend Sam?" Prudence asked sternly. She had been very quiet all through dinner, listening and learning.

"Yes, it is, Prudence," Maurice said. "The whole arrangement is open to criticism. I'd like to pose as an ethical man, but money isn't entirely an ethical object. That's why I want to get out of the City for good, and into furniture."

"Furniture!" Wade said impatiently, remembering perhaps

the money he had lost on antiques. He moved the food around his plate, then put down his knife and fork. When the meal was over he could go into another room and talk to Maurice alone.

"No one seems hungry tonight," he said. "Would it be too much trouble for my daughters to bring coffee to Maurice and me in the little room? While we discuss the mystery of money."

"There's a soufflé," Prudence said in a threatening voice.

"Oh, no, not a soufflé. Not a soufflé tonight," Wade said. "We'll have the coffee now. The soufflé will do another time. There will be all the less to cook tomorrow. I have to consider the cook, now that she's my daughter," he added, smiling to Maurice.

Prudence looked stricken. "The soufflé will do tomorrow!" she repeated. "Father, you're—I mean you don't know what you're saying."

"It will be all the better tomorrow. We can have it cold," he said with a pleasant smile.

"I'll rush out and buy a refrigerator," Hester suggested.

Prudence blinked several times, then recovered. "Where's *Vogue*?" she asked dramatically. "Where's *Harper's Bazaar*? I'm going to begin on clothes now."

"I'll make the coffee," Hester said quickly.

She stood up, then bent her head forward, listening.

"I thought I heard a noise upstairs."

Everyone listened.

"I think you're right," Maurice said.

"It's that damned Harry, searching my room again!" Morgan shouted.

"But he's not in the house," Wade said.

"Yes, he is. He's in the bathroom," Hester said.

"He's not, he's up in my room," Morgan said, surrendering himself entirely to rage.

They all began to move out of the room. In the hall they met Harry, coming, not from the bathroom, but the kitchen.

"Did you hear something?" he asked blandly. "Because I thought I did."

They went upstairs, moving far more cautiously now that they feared the existence of a real burglar.

Morgan, followed by the others, rushed into his bedroom. There was no one to be seen. Maurice ran along the passage and opened another door. It was Wade's room. He hesitated briefly, then pounced at the far side of the bed.

"I've got him," he cried, looking in some bewilderment at what he'd got.

It was a small, fair youth in green trousers and a yellow pullover. He stood with his face sunk on his chest while the others crowded into the room.

"Ring for the police, Morgan," Wade said, but when he looked around, Morgan wasn't to be seen. "Then, Hester, will you ring?"

"Don't call in the police, Guv'nor," the boy whined. "It's m'first job, and I've stolen nothing. Why don't you kick me round the room? You'd like to give it to me, wouldn't you? Go on, give me a good kicking."

He made an appealing gesture of martyrdom. Wade shrank away.

"Ring for the police," Maurice, the voice of society, repeated.

The boy still stared at his toes. "I'd never have done it, except I thought I'd pick up a watch or a fur coat. I've no money and no job and m'mother's ill. I'm a waiter, see, I was away ill and lost m'job and m'mother's in hospital. I'd be working if I had the chance. All I need is a chance, see, and I'd work as well as anyone." He stood drooping before them, one of the system's rejected serfs.

Harry laughed. Wade looked at him reproachfully. Harry was always striking the wrong note.

"Give him a job," Harry said cheerfully. "You need help in the house, don't you?"

"I'll go straight," the boy said eagerly. "Honest, Guv'nor, it's m'first time up a ladder and it'll be m'last. If I had a job and some money…"

"Perhaps I could find you work with someone else," Wade suggested weakly.

"It's up to you," Maurice said crisply. "I've no patience with his kind. I'd ring the police and be done with it." The Wades didn't sympathise with this intolerant attitude, but by some strange process it made Maurice seem more admirable than ever—a man whose support for society and the law was automatic and unyielding.

Wade hesitated. "Do you think he's speaking the truth?" he asked weakly. "Hester?"

"I don't know. The police—I'm sure we ought to tell the police. No. Couldn't we just let him go?" She thought for a minute, then assumed responsibility, as she always would. "Give him a job," she said firmly. "We must give him a job, Father. I see that now."

Prudence had been standing aside, delighted by the drama.

"If it means someone will wash the dishes, by all means give him a job," she said in a splendidly bored voice.

"Give him a job," Harry agreed. "He might be an honest man. You've got the fact that he broke into the house to encourage you."

Wade looked unhappy. "We'll talk it over," he said.

"I'll take the poor fellow into the kitchen and give him a cup of tea," Harry offered, in a concerned voice.

Hester, following the others downstairs, thought she heard her name as the echo of a whisper. She turned. About two inches of Morgan's face was visible through his partially-open door.

She went back.

"Hester," he said, and groaned.

"If you're not well, Morgan, why don't you lie down?" she suggested.

He put a handkerchief to his lips. He seemed too ill to speak.

"Are you in pain? Where is it?" She guided him towards his bed.

He slumped abruptly, like a man on the verge of unconsciousness. She wasn't sure that she could feel any sympathy for him, but she tried. He must be a very miserable man if his only pleasure lay in pretending to be ill.

"I think it's here," he said, touching his heart fearfully. "And other times it's in the small of my back."

"I think you had better lie down until you have decided," she said patiently.

"Hester, have you sent for the police?"

She sighed. "No, we've decided to let him work here for a little. He might change, if he was given a little human sympathy."

"First Harry, then a ladder boy! I wonder what your father will collect next? Hester, I've been feeling very bad. Do you think a change of air would do me good?"

"It would depend on the air," Hester said.

"Didn't you say that Ferguson had chartered a plane to go to Ireland?"

"Yes."

"And he's looking for someone to share it with him?"

"He's looking for three people."

"But all the formalities are over already? I wouldn't have to meet anyone? I mean if I decided to go."

"I suppose you'd have to meet the Customs authorities, like everyone else. But do you want to go to Dublin?"

"It would make a change. Yes, I'd like to go. Just for a few days. I'd come back, you know."

She stood with her hand on the door, bored and uneasy, anxious to help, anxious not to be asked to help too much.

"Why don't you go and see Uncle Joe about it now?"

"I'm not well enough to walk all that way."

"You could telephone."

"I don't want to see Harry. He's downstairs."

"Harry's in the kitchen with the burglar, so far as I know."

"Hester, do me a favour. Keep them in there while I telephone. For ten minutes. Only for ten minutes, Hester. I don't want them hanging about, listening and worrying me."

"All right," she said reluctantly. "Just for ten minutes." She disliked being involved in even elementary conspiracies.

Wednesday (8)

When Hester went into the kitchen Harry was sitting with his feet on the table, talking to the blond burglar, who looked wispy and immature, like an exploited child, as he stood labouring by the sink. He had taken off his yellow jersey and was exposed in a flowered shirt, reminiscent both of the fashions advertised for Florida and of the waistcoats worn by young bloods in the bound volumes of nineteenth-century *Punch*. Hester felt mournfully responsible even for his taste in clothes and his lavishly-styled hair. She knew it was Society that made juveniles into delinquents; she represented Society; it was her fault that he had attempted to steal.

"He's called Jackie," Harry told her. "He always washed the dishes for his Mum. That's why he's so good at it."

"What's your other name?" Hester asked gently.

"Daw, Miss."

"Change it," Harry advised seriously. "There are other names that go with Jack. Try Sprat, or Cade. What about Built? This is the house that Jack Built. Or Broke? This is the house that Jack Broke into. Do you remember the story, Hester? This is the What that lay in the House that Jack broke into. This is the Who that tried to get the What that lay in the House that Jack Broke into."

Hester looked at him impatiently. "You're being silly, Harry."

"Am I? Let's have some coffee. We'll have it in the kitchen and Jack can tell us the story of his life."

Hester filled the kettle and put it on the stove.

"I haven't had what you'd call a life," Jackie said. "This is m'first chance since m'father died. I used to go round with him, see."

"What was your father's job?"

"He was a lay-about."

"How interesting," Hester said, trying to look enlightened. "What does a lay-about do?"

"He waits till people go out and leave the door unlocked, then he nips in and takes a handbag or a clock, or the change off of the mantelpiece. His idea was that he'd lay-about and I'd nip in, but I wouldn't do it."

"But of course you wouldn't," Hester said, her mind already far away, worrying about the children of burglars. Would they learn to steal? If they admired their fathers, perhaps they would.

She went out of the kitchen and stood at the bottom of the stairs, and called up softly to Morgan, who was waiting on the landing. He came down absolutely noiselessly, and went to the telephone. She stood by the kitchen door, making mental plans for the protection of burglars' children. A suppressed part of her mind was wondering what Harry had meant about the What and the Who.

"I am speaking up," she heard Morgan whispering into the telephone. "Look, I want to fly to Dublin with you on Friday. Expensive? No, I don't think that's too much. Oh, I've just taken the fancy to see the place. I'm not sure where I'll be coming from. I'll meet you at the airport... Brickford? I've never heard of it. What? What did you say the pilot said? A place called the Fairway Arms?"

He was backing steadily away from the instrument, as though it frightened him. By now he had the flex pulled out as far as it would go. In the dim light of the hall he looked like a monstrous fish tugging weakly against the pull of the line.

She was listening with a detached part of her mind to the voices from the kitchen. She had an impression that Harry had been making jokes at Jackie's expense. Morgan was beginning a discussion about the cost of a seat on the plane. She didn't want to hear his financial views. She turned her attention back to the kitchen.

"Life is made up of moments of weakness," she heard Harry saying. "History would never get anywhere at all if it wasn't."

She stopped with her hand on the door. She was too tired to listen to Harry's interminable theories.

"Just in case you're as weak as the rest of us, would you

like to take off the dainty gun you have strapped under your shirt?"

Hester was appalled. It was impossible that a mere boy like Jackie should carry a gun.

"You know there's no reason to fire it at me," Harry said in a coaxing voice. "You'd only be destroying innocence. I'm not trying to turn you in. You'll get in bad trouble if you're found with a gun on you now. Old Bailey trouble."

"I'll do you in, you slimy bastard," Jackie said.

"If you pull that gun on me, I'll run for my life, screaming," Harry said. "That's a threat."

Hester tried to open the door. Someone was standing against it. She thought of Harry, bravely waiting to be shot, defending her.

"Let me in," she said desperately.

She pushed. The door opened suddenly. Harry, with one hand in his pocket, stood smiling at her. Jackie was turning back to the sink.

"Jackie's going to be very happy here," Harry said blandly. "He looks happier already, don't you think?"

"I thought I heard—some kind of argument," Hester said.

"We were only getting to know each other. What are you going to do when you've dried the dishes, Jackie? Cosh your benefactor with a bicycle chain? Or do you mean to stay?"

"Stay."

Hester looked at them both uncertainly. It was impossible that they should be so calm if they had just been fighting over a gun. She looked at Jackie's flowered shirt. It had no menacing bulges, but it was unbuttoned down the front.

"It's hot tonight," Jackie said apologetically. "Excuse me, Miss." He buttoned the shirt up to the neck again.

"What brought you this way?" Harry asked.

"Just walking about. Haven't been in the country since I was a kid, see. Then I wanted a place to spend the night. I thought I'd doss down in that bedroom."

"Like Goldilocks," Harry said approvingly.

Hester was suddenly so tired of the conversation that she turned and left the room. Morgan had finished his telephoning. There was no one in the hall. She thought she heard her father's voice. He was probably talking to Maurice about money.

She was anxious to avoid all of them. She didn't want to be confronted with another problem that night. She needed time to think of herself, to let her mind move slowly out of the climate of anxiety. She went out into the garden, and along the path to where the roses grew. They sprawled and twisted in a riot of neglect; in the dusk of the faintly star-lit night they had no colour, but their scent proclaimed them. She bent and picked a rose that dropped under the weight of its unfurled petals. She sat down on the grass and held the rose to her face, while the petals fell silently, like shadows, on her lap. She wondered what it would be like to go to Ireland alone, to charter a plane and leave and stay on the plane for months, like a hermit in his hut, only flying free, with no old problems to solve and no new problems to meet.

She sat for ten minutes or more, with the scent of the rose in her head, her mind slowly emptying, then filling again with languid dreams, imprecise and enchanting. Then she stood up and strolled across the grass towards the trees that were black shadows floating into the nearly black sky. She heard someone move.

"Harry?" she asked uncertainly.

"I'm not Harry," a man's voice replied.

She turned to run.

"Don't be frightened," he said. "I'll go away. Look, I'm walking back towards the gate."

Hester stopped. It was a sign of hysteria, to run away from strangers in the dark.

"What are you doing here?" she asked. She could see him now, dimly. He turned towards her. "Don't come near me," she said quickly.

"I won't come near. I've been watching you in the garden. I know I've no right to be here."

"Then why are you here?"

"I saw a man climb up a drainpipe."

"Are you a policeman?"

"No, but I've been watching your house. He didn't climb down again. Are you interested?"

"He's in the kitchen. He's going to work for us."

"Do your servants always arrive by drainpipe?" he asked, and Hester laughed.

"Why were you in the garden?" she asked.

He didn't answer the question immediately. "Tell me something? What's the name of the man who came here to dinner—who came by car?"

"Reid. Maurice Reid."

"Reid." He sounded satisfied. "Have you known him long?"

"I don't see why I should discuss—"

"Oh, you're getting in a weak position," he said. "Now you've told me his name, you'll have to justify yourself. I don't mind how long it takes you, I like your voice. In gratitude for the name, I'll tell you why I'm here. I saw him in an underground in London, and I've followed him all day. But I didn't know if it was the right man."

"And is it?"

"Yes."

"I'll tell him you're following him," she said.

"Yes, I wish you would."

"Why?"

"It will give him something to think about."

"If you mean to do him harm, I'll ring the police."

"If I leave your garden, you'll have no reason to ring the police. I'll go now. Don't forget to tell him he's being followed. What's your name?"

"Wade."

"That can't be all of it."

"Miss Wade," she suggested.

"Miss Wade, good night."

"Wait," she called, but he went away.

She went back into the house. Her father and Maurice were still talking. She knew it was possible to interrupt, to tell Maurice he was being followed, but he would look at her in amazement, he would think she was mad, there would be more questions and answers. The stranger had wanted her to tell Maurice—it was surely better not to act on the advice of strangers. The arguments swirled round in her head, then cleared away, leaving her to see that doubts of some kind were forming in her mind about Maurice. She watched his face carefully while she said:

"Maurice, there was a man in the garden. I spoke to him. He said he was there to follow you."

She saw Maurice's eyes drop swiftly with the effort of concentrated thought, then he looked up, still smiling.

"Some madman, I suppose," he said. It seemed to her he spoke with great effort. "Perhaps we should search the garden?" he suggested slowly.

"He's gone," Hester said quickly. "He didn't know your name at first. He may have been making it all up."

"You told him my name?" Maurice asked sharply.

"What does it matter?" she said wearily. "It's not as though you had anything to hide. I told him my name, too."

"Hester! What—how could you come to talk to a strange man in the dark? He—might have been dangerous," Wade said.

"Here I am," she said impatiently, "so he wasn't. As a matter of fact, I rather liked the sound of his voice. No, Father, don't be upset. I'm not really as silly as I sound." She crossed the room and kissed him. "He seemed very safe. And he's gone now. I promise you."

Maurice stood up. He looked less confident than usual. "Did you tell this safe young man where I lived?" he asked drily.

"I don't think he was interested."

Maurice walked round the room, and then said it was time for him to go. Wade accompanied him to his car, and then looked around the garden with a torch. As Hester had said, there was no stranger in the garden now.

Investigation (5)

The story, as they remembered it, was like a damaged fossil found in the rocks: the story they offered was a handful of broken stone. Inspector Lewis sat now, patiently assembling the fragments.

"That's all, absolutely all, about Wednesday?" he asked. "What happened about this Jackie?"

"We gave him a camp bed in the attic, in the room over Morgan's."

"This man in the garden—he said he was following Maurice Reid?"

"Yes, I told you."

"Is that all you can tell me about him?"

They watched Hester gliding into the shelter of her secret thoughts.

"His name is Marryatt," Wade explained. The words sounded like the prelude to a statement, but the statement didn't follow.

"Do you know where we can find him?"

Hester shook her head.

Moira Ferguson leant forward. "Is he that dark young man who has been staying in the pub? The Australian?"

"Very possibly," Hester said.

"Because if he is, he's still there. I know about him, because we heard him come back in the middle of the night."

"What night?" Lewis asked.

"Thursday night."

"Let's leave Thursday until we come to it," Hester suggested.

"I don't know what he'd been doing. It must have been one o'clock."

"Hardly the middle of the night," Hester said contemptuously.

"We heard him, because we live next the pub, and old Barnes was leaning out of the window, shouting. Harry said he, the Australian, Marryatt I mean, had probably been murdering Maurice. And something about murdering sleep."

"*Macbeth*, sir," Sergeant Young said in his low, explanatory voice to the inspector, while Hester stared at Moira as if she was looking for a place to insert a knife.

"Harry said Marryatt was staying there just to get his hands on Maurice, and it was lucky for Maurice he was going to Dublin on that plane. But it wasn't lucky for him after all," Moira said.

"Can you tell us more about this Marryatt?" Lewis asked Hester stolidly.

"I can't. Not like that. One thing is always bound up with another. I don't want to say any more about him. Give him a chance to explain his own actions. If he's at The Running Fox, why not see him there? Or bring him here, and let him hear her repeat what she has to say," Hester said.

"I think we'll have to get hold of this Marryatt," Lewis said. He looked at his watch. "We mustn't keep you people from your lunch," he said in a hungry voice. "Suppose we ask this Marryatt to come here after lunch, for a friendly discussion? Or do you object? Would you sooner I saw him alone, at the station?"

"I'd sooner he was here and heard what Mrs Ferguson has to say against him," Hester said.

Lewis levered himself out of his chair. "Then we'll see you all after lunch. You were awake at one o'clock on Thursday night, on Friday morning, that is, Mrs Ferguson?"

"I had to be," she said shortly. "Harry came back with us when we left here, and somehow, I don't know how it happened, we all began to play Donegal Poker."

"Oh," said Hester, with so much pain in her voice that Prudence stood up protectively.

"Let's get on with Thursday," she said wildly. "It's mostly Morgan, I think. Let's not stop for lunch. Oh, there's the phone."

They all listened to the telephone.

"Answer it, please, Prudence," Hester said.

"Newspapermen again," Prudence said wisely. "Leave them to me. I'll think of some falsehood."

They heard her lift the receiver and answer, and protest, and then she came back in the room.

"It's for you," she said to Inspector Lewis. "Don't let it worry you. We like you to use our telephone. I told them you didn't want to be interrupted, but they said you did."

"Sergeant Young, please," Lewis said, and the sergeant went out to the telephone. Everyone waited with a feeling that some revelation was imminent, that the man who had missed the plane had been discovered at last.

The sergeant returned with his face stiff with excitement.

"Sir, the landlady, Mrs Crewe at Brickford I mean, has found the two bitters. They are on their way to the station now."

"Lunch-time," Lewis said jovially. "We must be off. Just get in touch with this Running Fox place first, Sergeant. Ask them if they have a visitor by the name of Marryatt. If you can get him on the phone and arrange for him to meet us here in about two hours, then that's so much time saved."

Sergeant Young seeped out of the room.

"Poor Harry," Moira said. "He was so happy that night. He won five pounds at Donegal Poker. Then suddenly he said he had other things to do, and left. I'm sorry for him. It's not like Maurice or Morgan. As for Joe—he didn't fly. I'm sure. Don't ask me to explain. I'm just certain he didn't fly." She dabbed her eyes.

"Your husband had no business worries, Mrs Ferguson?"

"It depends what you call business worries," she said. "He was ruined, if that's what you mean. He said he was going to be bankrupt, or taken over any day. But he wasn't worried."

"No?"

"No. I was the one who did the worrying. I always wanted to sell one of the cars, live in an hotel instead of the flat, you know, economise," she said, making a wide gesture. "But Joe believed in expansion. He said the creditors did too."

"Is there any possibility that your husband's affairs were in such—such confusion, that he might have wanted to disappear?"

"Do you mean he didn't go on that plane? That he's only hiding?" she asked, her soft face hardening in thought.

"I'm asking you."

"Oh, Joe wouldn't do that. He'd much sooner pay sixpence in the pound than nothing. Joe was so—so honest," she said, groping for the right word and finding it.

"On Friday morning you drove him into Cheltenham, early. Did you see anyone you knew, there, when you were together?"

"I don't believe we did," she said absently. "They'd know at the station. Why don't you ask them at the station?"

"We'd thought of that," Inspector Lewis said ironically. "They didn't know. They sell a lot of tickets, in Cheltenham."

Moira took a mirror from her handbag and studied her face.

"I'm so ignorant of police methods," she said apologetically. "I'm a child in the affairs of this world. That's what Joe said about me, always. But even though I'm ignorant, it does sound to me as though you're suggesting I didn't drive Joe to Cheltenham—or perhaps all you mean is that he didn't take the train from Cheltenham to Brickford? If you're really, seriously, suggesting one of these things then… I wonder what Joe would have said? I know. He'd have told me to get hold of a lawyer before I said another word. And I think that's what I'll do. So please don't expect me to tell you another thing about Thursday, about Harry or Joe or Maurice or the Australian, until I have a lawyer sitting by my side. I know Hester's sitting there thinking that only guilty people want lawyers. I will relieve your mind, Hester. I drove Joe to Cheltenham, and I saw him buy a ticket for Brickford." She pushed the mirror back in her handbag and looked defiantly round the room.

"Wait till you see that Australian, Marryatt. He's someone who really does need a lawyer," she said maliciously, her voice accepting everyone in the room as an enemy. "Doesn't he, Hester?"

Sergeant Young came back from the telephone, and for the next two hours the Wades were left in peace.

Investigation (6)

Inspector Lewis dropped the file of letters on his desk. "Nothing here, Sergeant Young. The public, anxious as ever to help, has seen one or all of the missing men in the Channel Isles, Edinburgh, Penzance, and a great many spots between. Next thing, we'll have a newspaper offering a prize. There's a letter about that old, reliable friend of the family, Maurice Reid. Here you are."

The sergeant picked up the letter and read:

"Dear Sir: I see from the papers you want information about Maurice Reid. He was the most vile and loathsome creature that ever polluted the earth. I won't be the only one to say so. You'll find out soon enough. If he was killed in that plane I believe at last that there is justice in heaven. There will be others to come forward. I've no need to expose my name."

"Anonymous, you see," the inspector said. "No need to pay any attention to that. When are those two bitters coming in? If they don't turn up, we're wasting our time here, eating dry sandwiches, giving the Wades the chance to plot out the next sequence. What do you think of the Wades anyway? The father looks to me as though he'd assassinated the Archbishop of York and was working round to a confession."

"Miss Wade, Miss Wade looked—looked very upset," Sergeant Young said, flushing.

"She's a pretty girl. Don't be taken in by looks, Sergeant," Lewis said sharply. "Here they are, at last."

The two bitters were ushered in; they gave the impression they were trying to hide behind each other. One was a dark, earthy man in his middle years; the other was old and dusty.

The sergeant took their names. The younger was called Benson; the older, Smith. Benson stared at his feet; Smith's wavering glance explored the corners of the room, as though he expected to find a guillotine somewhere. He was a grocer, and his appearance suggested that his shop was very small, and that the articles wanted by customers could only be reached by ladder. Benson was a nursery gardener.

"You were in the Fairway Arms around half-past ten on Friday morning?" the inspector suggested.

They looked at each other, and nodded.

"And there were three men having a drink," Benson muttered.

"We've talked it over. We can't describe them," Smith said in a voice that whined on a high note, like the wind in the chimney.

"You see, we go out to have a drink," Benson said.

"We'd no reason to think they were anyone special," Smith said.

"They weren't anyone special if they hadn't got killed," Benson said. "Who is?" he added sombrely.

"We were talking. You don't think of other people in the bar when you're talking."

"Nor when you're being talked at," Benson said.

"And why did they get killed?" Smith asked. "I'll tell you, because they hadn't taken trouble with their horoscopes.

Ten to one, their horoscopes would have told them to keep their feet on the ground that day. You want to find the one that wasn't there, don't you, Officer, don't you now? You get, their horoscopes, get the horoscopes of the four of them, and you'll find the one who's still got two feet to walk on."

"Their birthdays..." Lewis began, but was interrupted.

"Don't talk to me about birthdays," Smith said. "You've got to have it right, to the hour and the minute. It isn't child's play, you know, astrology's a serious thing."

"Do you believe in astrology, too, Mr Benson?" Lewis asked despairingly.

"Astrology," Benson repeated contemptuously. "I've no time for that nonsense. I'm a numerologist."

"And can you plant potatoes, by numerology. Can you tell when night frosts will end, by numerology?" Smith asked wearily.

Benson scowled sideways at the policemen. "It was this kind of talk he was at, in the pub that morning. Just let him run on. You'll get the idea."

"You're in the habit of having a drink together in the morning?"

"The habit's arisen," Benson agreed. "Gets on my nerves," he added viciously.

"Have you an arrangement to meet?"

"When things are propitious and trade's slack, I leave the shop to my daughter. Then if walking past I see him on his knees among his spindly plants, I invite him to have a drink. An invitation he's always seemed glad enough to accept, although if there's one thing he wants more than another, it's to be taken for a tee-totaller. Fear. That's his daily diet. With astrology a man knows his place and what he can do. Astrology lets a man walk through the world without fear.

Witness my presence in this place," he added, wiping his pink eyes with a tea-coloured handkerchief.

"You didn't observe the appearance of the three men. You didn't hear anything they said?" Lewis asked Benson, who seemed more like an average man.

Benson shook his head.

"And you, Mr Smith?"

"Ah," Smith said, "I've been thinking. Not having had time since he rushed me here at the bidding of Mrs Crewe."

"And what have you been thinking about, Mr Smith?"

"Astrology," Smith said.

They waited.

"You know, Friday morning, it was the last time I was in that pub until today. So it's not that my thoughts are confused, but they're distant. Now I went in talking to him, and he said he'd buy the drinks, and I sat down. He stood at the bar until old Crewe had served the drink." He stopped and looked defiantly at Benson.

"Which he did in as nice and friendly a manner as a prison warder waiting on table at Wormwood Scrubs," Benson said.

"So he stood at the bar. I waited at the corner table. Now there was these other men, but my back was to them. If anyone was to see them, it was Benson here, who was facing."

"I hadn't a thought in my head but to swallow my drink and get back to work," Benson said. "I'm not interested in drinking."

"But while I was waiting for the drink, and with my mind running on the unhappy hour of Benson's birth, and before I was deafened by his talk of numbers, I may have heard a word from these men behind me I couldn't see."

"Who were three, which was all I saw," Benson said.

"And from the time I sat down with him there wasn't a gap in his conversation. So what could I hear but him and his conversation?"

"If it hadn't been for my interest in astrology, what would I be able to say now?" Smith demanded. "And the word caught my ear because I'm an astrologist."

Lewis began to fidget with a ruler.

"Are you trying to tell me, Mr Smith, that these men were discussing astrology?"

"They must have been," Smith said. "They used a term that brought me up short in my tracks. Astrology, I thought, and I'll turn round and see what they look like, but then he came back with the drinks."

"And what was the word?" Lewis asked in a voice of grinding patience.

"Now, it was on the tip of my tongue. I was about to say it when you interrupted me. But it's gone."

"Gone?"

"It was a term, as they might have said in opposition, or ascendancy, or constellation. Or azimuth? Now I wonder if it was azimuth?" he asked infuriatingly. "I was just going to bring it out, when you spoke."

"Would it have been a name?" Sergeant Young asked encouragingly. "Like Gemini, or Mars?"

"Might have been, might have been, might not have been." Smith smiled through the gaps in his teeth, and sat back to enjoy the privileges of age.

"Taurus? Aquarius?" the sergeant suggested.

"I see you're a man of education," Smith smiled approvingly while Benson sneered.

"Virgo? Pisces?"

"Pisces? Now, that's a strange thing. It might have been

something about Pisces, but it wasn't. Pisces? No. That was before, I've got it."

"Yes!"

"They were talking about fishing."

"Fishing?"

"That's it."

"But you said astrology?"

"That's a different thing again."

"What kind of fishing?" Lewis asked. His face was impassive, but his voice was beginning to show the strain.

"Not salmon fishing. Not trout. Fishing in one of them far-off places. India was it?"

"Well, was it?"

"No. It wasn't India."

"They were smoking," Benson suddenly volunteered. "One of them had some cigarettes, and as I walked over with the drinks he offered cigarettes to the others."

"A packet or a case?"

"Now you mention it, I—" He closed his eyes. "I'm sure it was a case. Yes, I'd take my oath it was a case. I couldn't tell you what kind of case. It wouldn't have been gold, anyway. I'd have noticed that. Now I see it. It was a long, silver case. He opened it at both of them, and one of them took a cigarette. Or did they both? Now, I can't remember. Anyway, someone lit the two cigarettes with a lighter. I remember it was a lighter, but I don't know if it was the first man who used it. One man didn't smoke. Now, it's queer I noticed that, except that I'm trying to give up smoking myself, so I saw that this man didn't smoke." He licked his lips and began to fidget with his hands. "It's not to say he was a non-smoker. He might not have wanted one at the time."

"You may smoke, if you like, Mr Benson."

Benson took out a packet and lit a stub. "It's got so I can't smoke a whole cigarette," he said apologetically. "It's keeping it down to twenty a day, does it."

"If you've finished," Smith said, "I'll go back to thinking. You'd like a pinch of snuff, Inspector?" He took out a little tin, and it opened with a flurry of snuff that drifted across the desk to the inspector.

"I'll sit here and think," Smith said, applying the snuff to each nostril. "And what do you suppose I'll think about? It will be my daughter doesn't know the price of oatmeal, or she'll be giving them icing instead of caster sugar. I've got responsibilities, you know."

"The stars will protect her," Benson suggested.

"It's that type of remark takes my mind off everything else. That's what happened on Friday morning. The moment he came back with the beer he knocked everything out of my head. Before he came back, as I sat down, I heard this word about astrology, not sinking in at once, but pulling my attention, and I became conscious one of them was saying to the other this thing about fishing. 'My curiosity's satisfied,' he says, 'and I didn't like it.' Then another says about not having had the opportunity until the beginning of last season and the first says who has in this country? And the second says it has merit." He paused to wipe another rheumy drop from his old eyes.

"But how did the conversation go from astrology to fishing?" Lewis asked.

"Now that I can't answer, except to be sure they began with astrology. It might have been one word, you know, it might have been only one word, but it caught my ear. I'm very keen, very keen indeed, at hearing. Then Benson comes back and spoils it all."

Benson suddenly grunted. "Woolworth's. That's it. I was once an under-manager at Woolworth's," he explained.

"Yes?" Lewis encouraged.

"I'm not now. I'm a nursery gardener for my health. But I was sitting there quietly drinking my beer, which is not good for my health any more than smoking, when I heard that name again. Woolworth's! If ever I drown I'll see the red front and gold letters come up before my eyes. Even through Smith's babbling I heard the name. Then one of these men addressed the other by name." He stopped to light his cigarette stub again.

There was a battle of silence. Inspector Lewis lost.

"The name. What was it?"

"It began with an M. It was the thirteenth letter of the alphabet. Was it Morrison? Martin? Morley? If I'd been concentrating, I'd have known, being interested in names."

"Morgan, Morton, Maurice," Lewis suggested.

"It's gone," Benson said in regret. "I'll swear to the M, but to nothing else. 'Woolworth's, what do you think about that?' one of them said. 'I'm afraid I can't think anything. I didn't see it,' says the second. And the third says: 'Woolworth's? What's all this? When did it happen?' And that's all. I'd have heard none of it if Smith hadn't been dragging out his old chart, and from the time he began talking about his horoscope, everyone else in the world might have been dead, for all I could hear."

Smith began to cackle. "Now I've got it," he said. "They'd been fishing in a strange place. It was Ceylon they talked about. Now what would you think if you heard the word 'Ceylon'?"

"Snake-charmers and elephants," Sergeant Young suggested romantically.

"Tea," Smith said. "Even my daughter knows Ceylon is tea. So first it was astrology, then it was Ceylon to make me think of tea, and then something about being depressed but what that was about I don't know, then the fishing I've told you."

"They'd been fishing in Ceylon?" the inspector asked with justifiable amazement. "Let's go back over this again."

They went back over it again, but without enlightenment. Both men stuck to what they had said, and refused to add to it. With all their peculiarities, they were honest.

Investigation (7)

The policemen returned to the Wades' house expecting to find Marryatt there before them. They had not much idea of the kind of man he was, but they naturally supposed he would have enough social sense to be disturbed by their summons. They felt the normal official irritation at being kept waiting; they were prepared to put him in his place.

When he finally arrived, half-an-hour late, there was no hint of apology in his bearing. He was a young man, with heavy shoulders; a strong, dark face; black eyebrows. He had an air of independence, almost of insolence. His face carried the odd, uneasy familiarity of something that had been seen before. Perhaps it had been seen before, in a painting; a painting not of any contemporary; but of some aristocrat who had believed he owned the world; just as an Australian might believe it.

"You sent for me?" he said to Inspector Lewis, in a voice that rejected all respect for authority. He turned on Hester. "And I believe you told him to send for me."

She looked at him as angrily as he had looked at her. "I did.

People seemed to be accusing you of something. I thought, being what you are, you wouldn't like anyone else to speak for you."

"And what am I accused of?"

"You are not accused of anything. You are being asked to help," Lewis said coldly. "In the first place, I tell you quite openly we'd have seen you anyway. We have a report from a Mrs Lightfoot—isn't that the name, Sergeant Young?—yes, a Mrs Lightfoot, who breeds dogs, bull terriers, I think—a report of what she thought a peculiar incident on the road, about half-a-mile from this house. She took the number of the car. It happens to be the number of the car that Maurice Reid hired from the local garage. She made this report quite independently. She hadn't heard of the aeroplane disaster. It was very easy to trace the car. Then when this question, the question of which man didn't fly in the aeroplane, came up, we went into the matter a little more carefully. She described Maurice Reid quite well. At first she thought he was drunk. Then she thought he'd been assaulted, or that he'd been in a fight with someone. She had a glimpse of the other man; later, she saw someone in the village whom she thought was the same man. Well, sir, what we've been looking for all the time is a lead into any peculiarity in the lives of any of those four men who were supposed to fly in that aeroplane. What Sergeant Young here has always said is that if we can find the man among these four who had some urgent reason for vanishing, then we'll know the man who took the chance to disappear when the plane crashed."

"That's not logical," Prudence said sternly. "If one of them wanted to disappear he probably would go to Ireland and dig peat or something. He wouldn't want to miss the plane. He might miss it by accident, but that wouldn't happen to him more than anyone else. Unless they all wanted to disappear, I think it's a stupid theory."

"Perhaps they did all want to disappear," Moira intervened coldly. "Except Joe, of course."

"And Harry," Hester murmured.

"But, my dear, Harry always wanted to get out of his commitments. Surely you know that?" Moira said.

Marryatt, seeing, like everyone else, how Hester's already pale face turned paler still, spoke quickly.

"Get on with the questions. I'll answer them."

"No," Hester said. "It's not fair to put everything on to you. Particularly after what you said to me. You've accused me of enough, you know. And this isn't just a question of Maurice. It might be anyone. We don't know it was Maurice. But Father and I have talked it over, in the last hour, and we're going to tell the truth. The whole truth about the whole of Thursday. You can tell your part too, if you wish. Please remember," she said coldly, "we are going to conceal nothing, and there's no reason why you should."

They looked at each other in mutual animosity.

"It makes no difference to me who knows my private affairs, now," Marryatt said significantly. "Go ahead, I'll listen and put my hand up when the time comes."

"Don't expect me to join in this soul-searching," Moira said.

Hester looked sadly at the downcast roses on the table.

"Thursday…" she said.

Thursday (1)

It rained on Wednesday night, and on Thursday morning the sky looked as if it had been washed blue for a coloured advertisement. When Hester woke, the birds were celebrating. She looked out of the window with her usual morning happiness. She was amazed to hear a tap on her door. Prudence always charged through doors without knocking, and no one but Prudence ever came to her room in the morning.

"Come in," she said, and Jackie appeared. He was carrying a cup of tea, and looked serious and dedicated.

"Good morning," he said in a reverent voice. He put down the tea and tiptoed out of the room again.

Hester looked at the tea in dismay. She didn't like to drink anything before she had brushed her teeth and washed and dressed; she liked even less to have the anxieties of the day appear embodied in her room while she was still in bed. She was remembering already that Harry had accused Jackie of carrying a gun. She wasn't particularly nervous, but she didn't want to be given morning tea by gunmen. She made up her mind that Jackie must go. She threw the blankets off and stepped out of bed. She washed and dressed quickly, mentally preparing her interview with Jackie.

She ignored the tea and forgot that the sky was blue. It was too late to send for the police. All that could be done now was to tell Jackie to go, in the most tactful terms. It would be better not to offend him. Perhaps he carried a gun only to help him in his robberies; it was equally possible that he loved his gun and longed to use it. As she brushed her hair she remembered that Harry had asked for the gun, but she wasn't sure what had happened in the minute before she entered the kitchen. Harry had asked for the gun; she didn't know if Jackie had given it to him. If Harry had the gun there was nothing to worry about, except that Jackie might be equally ready to use a bread-knife, or a poker. In any case, Harry would never shoot anyone; he was too good-natured.

She thought tenderly of Harry, and then with a rush of anger remembered how unfairly everyone treated him. She thought of the poets who had died of starvation, drink, drugs, neglect, tuberculosis, and drowning. She would save Harry from all of these. She put down the hairbrush and went to her bookcase. There was an issue of the *Poets' Journal* devoted to Harry.

> *"The old earth groans and splits,*
> *Out streams the fury of her bright-burning breasts."*

She sat down on the bed to read more comfortably.

Prudence came in, with the violence and speed of someone being pursued by the police. It was her usual method of entry in the morning.

"Reading?" she asked suspiciously.

Hester stood up, and slipped the magazine back into the bookcase. Prudence watched carefully, then examined the bookcase.

"Reading poetry at this time in the morning!" she exclaimed in wonder. "You're a bit nuts, aren't you?"

"Is that all you wanted to say?"

"No. I'm going to that tennis club dance thing tonight. Terribly dull, I expect, and the only one who asked me was that loutish boy Baron. You know, he's going to be an accountant. He talks all the time about maths and the Pony Club. It's going to be absolutely hideous, but I thought I'd go. So I was wondering if I could borrow that blue-and-white thing of yours."

"I thought you despised all my clothes."

"I've got practically none of my own. Father thinks when he's bought me a gym blouse and hockey shorts that I'm provided with clothes till next summer."

"Of course you can borrow it, Prudence. It would be nice to have a few more clothes," Hester said, sighing.

"I told you I was going to take up dress-making. I'll be able to make myself super things for next to nothing," Prudence said cheerfully.

"You'll still have to buy the material."

"I'll take it out of the housekeeping money. We cook in margarine from now on. And I believe you can live terribly cheaply on lentil soup and potatoes. It's a healthy diet, too, if we take a little cod liver oil now and then."

"It seems a bit hot today for lentil soup. Do you want to try on the blue-and-white?"

"Please." She went to the wardrobe and looked in. "I must say you haven't got very many clothes, either. Have you been reading all those articles about how to dress well on ten pounds a year? They're awfully good so long as you don't mind wearing a sleeveless cotton frock and sandals at Christmas and you have a rain-coat already. Oh, Hester, aren't you excited? Father's going to make piles of money. Maurice is helping him, and we'll all be rich and have special clothes for looking at football matches."

Hester sat down on the bed again. "I wish you wouldn't believe in fairy stories, Prudence. The only talent Father has with money is for losing it. You must have noticed. I'm not going to let him have anything to do with this scheme of Maurice's. I'm going to stop him."

"I won't let you," Prudence said, from the heart of the blue-and-white dress. "It's our only chance. Otherwise we'll moulder away for years, drinking lentil soup and making petticoats out of old flour bags." Her head came out of the top of the dress. "Do you think it's too tight?"

Hester looked at it critically. "No, really not. It shows you up a bit, but you have quite a decent figure to show. I wish you wouldn't think about money all the time, Prudence. It's not right. There are lots of things in life more important than money."

Prudence looked at herself in the mirror. "If I can't get on the stage I might be a model," she said appreciatively. "You get paid lots of money, marry a millionaire, and have your photograph in the papers nearly every day. In fact, you get far more publicity than Florence Nightingale ever had. How many people ever pinned her up over the dressing-table?"

"You have to learn to walk and wear clothes first."

"Walking and wearing clothes are things that practically the entire human race can do, so I suppose I could learn."

There was another tap at the door. "Breakfast is served, Miss," said a solemn voice.

They went down to breakfast, which consisted of strong tea and fried bread. "Still, it's nice not having to cook it," Prudence said.

Hester looked at the fried bread with hatred and began again to rehearse her scene with Jackie.

Her father was filling a notebook with small, neat figures. "Maurice is coming over early," he said. "We have business to consider."

Hester postponed the discussion with Jackie, and began to make plans for the interception of Maurice.

Thursday (2)

Maurice stepped out of the car. His square, clean face was good-humoured, happy, and appreciative, as it so often was. He looked up at the trees and the sky, participating in the beauty of the summer morning. He seemed as solid and dependable as a pewter mug. Hester, coming through the garden to meet him, found his appearance infinitely reassuring.

"Good morning, Maurice. Have you the time—could I talk to you for a few minutes?" Although she knew that she trusted him, her voice was less cordial than usual.

"Of course, Hester," he said readily, and she wondered if she heard wariness behind the warmth.

They walked through the garden towards the roses which were rashly opening their hearts to the sun.

"It's so hard to say what I want to say," she murmured in confusion.

"Am I wrong, Hester, in thinking you want to ask my advice about Harry?" he asked her quietly.

"Yes, Maurice, you're wrong, absolutely wrong. The last thing I want to hear is more advice about Harry."

"I don't want to be a bore, Hester, but you won't marry him, will you?"

"So you think that would be a mistake?"

"I do."

"Everyone thinks it would be a mistake. They keep trying to see what it would do to me. They never think at all what it might do to Harry. They don't stop to consider that Harry may be more important than me."

"But, my dear Hester, he isn't."

"Keats was more important than Fanny Brawne. Shakespeare was more important than Ann Hathaway."

"Hester, you're not seriously comparing Harry to Shakespeare," he protested with a humorous under-tone that she deeply resented.

"You're not even trying to be serious, Maurice, and I don't want to discuss Harry. Don't look so anxious, Maurice. If I decide to marry him that's my business. I may even wait until he asks me before I make up my mind."

"If you don't want to discuss Harry, what do you want to discuss?" he asked patiently.

"Oh, nothing," she said in a wretched voice, and turned away from him, knowing that the easy mood of confidence had been kicked out of shape like a battered football.

"You can talk to me, Hester, even if you do think of me as an ageing idiot," he said in an avuncular manner. "Or you can march off indignantly, then I'll have to cut the grass to reinstate myself. Shall I get the lawn mower? I'd much sooner talk."

"It's too hot for cutting the grass," she admitted. "I'll tell you what I want to say." She looked away from him. She didn't want it to seem that she was accusing him. "Don't let Father take any of his money out of securities. He's got so little. He can't afford to lose it." She looked round anxiously, searching for something that might ornament the bald request. "It's such a lovely morning. I do apologise for talking about money."

"Money is my business, but I don't want to bring business into the garden. Hester, surely you know me well enough to trust me. I've spent the last three months persuading your father not to join in my wild affairs."

"But, Maurice, of course you have. Would you like a button-hole? Here's a lovely rosebud." She bent to pick it, admiring its undeveloped curves, preparing her next remark. She stood up, offering the rosebud. "Father seems so determined this time."

"Thank you, Hester, it's very pretty." He put the rosebud in his button-hole. "You wouldn't approve of his turning three shillings into a pound?" he asked her, smiling.

"Not if there's any chance at all of his losing the three shillings. It's time that these overblown roses were cut. I must do it today. And I should cut some buds for the house."

"Hester, your father has set his heart on making money. He's decided the quickest way to do it is by gambling on the Stock Exchange. Do you think it better that I should handle the business for him, or would you sooner he went into the jungle alone? Tell me honestly, Hester, what you think." He stood smiling at her, both hands in his pockets, his brown face serious behind the smile.

She hesitated. "I'd sooner he didn't gamble at all."

"But if he means to?"

"Then—then I suppose it would be better if you helped him," she said in a troubled voice.

"I'm glad you say that, Hester, because if you didn't trust me I—well, I couldn't bear to come here. Now, I'll tell you the truth, Hester. When people set out to make money quickly, there is no absolute certainty. High returns are only a reward for being prepared to risk your capital. If you have private information, as I have in this case, the risk is very much less, but it does exist. I'm risking everything I have on this project, but you are quite right to dissuade your father."

Hester considered this. It sounded a very reassuring statement, until she remembered that she hadn't managed to influence her father in any way.

"But I was counting on you to dissuade him, Maurice."

"I haven't encouraged him," he pointed out. "And I'm bound to tell him that if he's determined to risk his capital this is a smaller risk than most."

"I leave it to you, then, Maurice," she said, sighing. "I do trust your judgment—but remember I'm equally bound to advise Father not to speculate."

"Naturally you are, and I'll be happy if he takes your advice—although we'll all be grinding our teeth if the thing comes off."

"I hate money," she said, exhausted. "I think I'll slash away at those roses now. Oh, Maurice—are you worried about that man—who was in the garden and said he was following you?"

"Naturally I'm not." His face was fixed in good-humour, but she thought she saw a tremor pass across it. "No one has any reason to follow me. He must be some kind of lunatic. Harmless, evidently, or I might have seen more of him last night."

She nodded smiling agreement, while contradictions ran through her head. "I must do something about the roses," she said. Maurice lingered for a moment, then went to the house to find her father.

Thursday (3)

Prudence was tidying up the sitting-room when Hester came in.

"I've emptied the ash-trays," she said in a resigned voice. "If only people didn't smoke we shouldn't have to do anything in here for weeks but draw the curtains and throw out the newspapers. Even that makes me feel like Cinderella," she added pointedly. "Have you been enjoying your walk in the garden?"

Hester didn't answer. She took a cushion and shook it viciously, then turned it torn side down.

"The other side's torn too," Prudence said. She looked at her sister with an objective interest. "What's wrong, Hester? You're looking old."

"It's Maurice."

"Maurice? What on earth's wrong with Maurice? I should have thought he was the only one round here not to worry about. After all, we have Morgan, and Jackie, and Harry."

"Harry keeps saying he's trying to get Father's money."

"I've listened to them and it always sounds as if he's trying not to get Father's money."

"Harry says that's how all the best confidence men behave."

"Harry seems to know a lot about crime. Let me try curling my lip. Do you suppose when people curl their lips it's convex or concave?" She went to the glass over the mantelpiece. "It looks queer both ways. If I curl it up towards my nose it's worse, don't you think? People in those books must look odd, most of the time. 'She curled her lip. Her lip twitched.' Oh, I twitch better than I curl. I'll practise that one. Do you really think I should be twitching and curling at Maurice?"

"Stop trying to be funny," Hester begged. "I don't think innocent people get followed. Oh, I forgot, you don't know about that. There was a man hiding in the garden last night. I had a long talk with him and he told me he was following Maurice."

"Action at last," Prudence said with satisfaction. "Things have been getting a bit boring round here. Won't it be wonderful if Maurice is really an international criminal? Do you think he has anything to do with atom bombs?"

"I don't think it's funny. He may be hiding in the garden now, or the wood, waiting for Maurice."

"I'll look," Prudence said eagerly. "Anything rather than make the beds."

She rushed out of the room. She didn't want to be stopped to listen to interminable discussions about caution and

correct behaviour. She was still armed in complete innocence, and was afraid of no one.

She walked round the garden. There was no one to be
seen. She lost interest in the search, and stopped to look
across the valley to the dry brown hill on the other side. She
knew suddenly that everything was empty and boring and
that nothing would ever happen. The place was dead. It was
only in cities that life went on. She stood dreaming of a thousand faces rushing past, every one alight with secret passions.
She moved unrecognised through them all, understanding,
but aloof. In the theatre elegant women were slipping out of
their wraps; insolent, sophisticated men were preparing to be
bored. Behind stage, in the little dressing-rooms, everything
was frantic and expectant. It was a first night. She had only a
small part, but in a way the play hinged upon it. She sighed,
and shook her head, and looked angrily across the valley
again. She meant to get out of this place, or die.

She remembered she was supposed to be looking for a
lurking stranger. She turned into the woods, and became
again a little excited at the thought that a murderer might
be hiding behind the trees. She walked cautiously under the
deep green ceiling of leaves until she came within sight of the
ruined chapel. A man was sitting in one corner, apparently
slumped in sleep. He might be dead, she thought, and was
carried towards him on a wave of fear.

"Hello, Prudence," Harry said, opening his eyes.

"Harry, what on earth are you doing here so early?" she
said in exasperation.

"I've been walking around for a long time, brushing the
dew with urgent feet."

"You weren't. You were sleeping."

"I wasn't sleeping. I was composing a poem."

"I don't believe it. Tell me it, if you were."

"Then carrying my incredible maps,
I knocked at the strange king's door,
And asked now for only one ship
To drive through the unwaked sea
To that half-predicted shore,"

Harry said promptly.

Prudence tried twitching her lip. "Is it something to do with history?" she asked, backing away.

"No, it's about me," Harry said, grinning. "Practically all my poetry is about me."

"If it's about you what does it mean?"

"It means I want you to ask me to lunch," he said in a serious voice.

"Well, I shan't," Prudence said irritably. "I don't know why you want to write poetry anyway, even if it was good. There are lots of things that pay better and you don't have to know anything. You could be an M.P. or an editor or something."

"Or a tinker or a tailor. I like the idea of manual work, but my hands won't co-operate."

"They co-operated all right when you were tearing up that floor."

"Shall I tell you why you're so aggressive towards me, Prudence?"

Prudence sighed and raised her eyes to the tops of the trees, a monument to patience, preparing to be incredulous.

"It's because you're too young. When you're older, you'll find that most men are as monotonous as steam-hammers. When you've been battered by a hundred thousand soporific words from jolly decent chaps, you'll yearn for my company. But I shan't be there. I believe in moving on."

"Anyway, you've stayed here a long time."

"Only a few weeks. Your family's been here for hundreds of years. It's time you moved on, too."

For a startled second, Prudence looked at him as though she had encountered a friend. Of all the adults she knew, he was the only one who occasionally recognised an obvious truth. She was in this vulnerable state when they heard someone coming towards them through the woods.

Harry caught her hand. "Let's hide," he whispered. His face was bright and serious; he was like a soldier who enjoys war and has sighted the enemy at last. Prudence, to her surprise, found herself kneeling behind a bush, watching the man who came furtively through the trees to the chapel.

It was Morgan. He stopped by one of the broken walls, and waited, listening. Then he moved on to the ruined stone floor and knelt down. He was half sheltered by the wall, and they could no longer see him.

Prudence, hiding behind the bush, took a minute to realise how childishly she and Harry were behaving. Hiding behind bushes, watching people who thought they were alone, was too much like the games she had played long ago, when she was twelve or thirteen. She pulled her hand away from Harry's and stood up.

"I'm going home now," she said clearly.

She walked towards the chapel. "Good morning, Morgan," she said.

He jumped up.

"Hello, Prudence. Hello. Hello, Prudence," he said in an agitated voice. "I—came here—I can't stand the house when that little crook's in it. He's still there, is he, Prudence? Has your father sent for the police?" He was talking wildly, and it was evident to Prudence that he had no idea what he was saying.

"Jackie's very useful. I don't think it would be fair to send for the police," she said sternly.

"It's the only way to treat people like that," Morgan gasped. He was in a state of such agitation that Prudence wondered if he was ill, but as he was always pretending to be ill it followed that he must be in perfect health.

Harry came through the trees, said Good morning to them both with an air of gravity, and sat down on one of the walls.

Morgan turned to him, with the hatred a hunchback might feel for a jeering boy.

"What are you doing here?" he demanded passionately.

"I was wondering if I'd take up archaeology. Some of those old wool merchants may have been buried in a golden fleece," Harry said, looking speculatively at the stone floor.

Morgan was suddenly transformed. He dropped his shoulders and lowered his head. He looked much smaller, and as malevolent as a weasel about to spring on a rabbit.

"Stay away from here. Stay out of the wood and away from the house. Get out of my reach," he advised.

"Why don't you have the law on me?" Harry said.

Prudence began to back away.

"Harry, come on," she said in an urgent voice.

Neither paid her any attention.

"Get away. Quickly," Morgan said in a flat voice.

Harry, with apparent difficulty, began to fumble at his pocket, Prudence and Morgan watched him. The article, whatever it was, stuck in his pocket. In the end it took him two hands to produce it.

"Now," he said to Morgan with satisfaction, and held

out the small, polished gun, as though he was offering it for inspection. He withdrew it quickly, and balanced it on his knee.

"Don't be so violent, Morgan," he said in a reproving voice.

Morgan seemed to ignore the gun. "Are you going?" he asked.

Harry looked at Prudence, and smiled, like a performer who has finished his act and waits for the applause.

"Certainly," he said, and rose, tossing the gun from hand to hand, and walked away.

Morgan sank down on the wall and wiped his brow. Once again, he looked like a sick man.

"You see what it's like, Prudence," he said in a broken voice. "He's dangerous." He felt in all his pockets and finally discovered some cigarettes. He took one, the last, and threw the empty packet on the stone floor. He lit the cigarette with a match, and then looked up.

"Don't worry your father with any of this," he advised. "Tomorrow I'm flying to Ireland. By the time I come back Harry will have gone away. There will be no more trouble. I'll be glad when I'm on that plane."

Prudence continued to look at him with her candid, suspicious stare.

"Let's get back to the house," he said irritably.

Prudence stood waiting for him like a wardress. He jumped up, and they went back through the woods together, not talking at all.

Thursday (4)

Harry found Hester beside the rose garden. She wore gloves, and carried a basket and scissors.

"You look deliciously Edwardian," he told her lazily. "Are you sure you're not going to begin trilling 'Today I'm gathering posies of roses, roses And all the other flowers That fill the happy hours?' Enter chorus, pursued by bevy of young peers. If we'd lived fifty years ago, Hester, I'd have pelted you with the family jewels. I'll find diamonds for you still. I promise you. Now sit down, and I'll cut the flowers."

He took the scissors from her.

"Here's a pure white rosebud, for the first year of your life, when you crawled about in waterproof pants, with not an impure thought in your head, apart from a deep Freudian desire to murder your parents. And here's one with a tinge of pink—that's when you were two, and smeared your frock with jam. Then we'll have some red ones, for the dark ages up to seven, when infant feet stamp and infant faces turn dark with fury. Then we proceed in a pale rose and cream through the years of fantasy. Roses don't come in purple. I can't do you as a brooding adolescent. I shall have to take the deepest red I can find. Now we'll have the white coffee roses, and the very pale cream, for tenderness and delicacy and all the charms combined. That's twenty. Am I right?"

"Harry, I didn't mean you to take so many. You've left none at all. The garden will be bare."

"Accept the rosebuds while ye may. One for each year of your life, to emphasise the moral."

She took them from him gravely, trying to conceal the sudden surging expectation she felt in her veins.

"I'll take them in," she said in a low voice.

"If we're together when you're twenty-one, I'll pick you another then."

"I'll take them in," she repeated.

"And then?"

"I'm going to the village," she said, over her shoulder.

"May I come with you?" he asked, looking at her with his eager, pathetic smile.

"Oh, yes."

She went quickly to the house with the flowers and arranged them in the wide, blue vase. She put them on a low table by the window, and drew one curtain, so that the sun shouldn't blight her twenty years too quickly.

She went into the garden again. Harry was waiting by the gate.

"You mustn't talk to me about Maurice," she warned him.

"I'm not interested in Maurice at all. It's Morgan that fills my thoughts."

"Why? Why do you think so much about Morgan? Have you met him somewhere before?"

"No."

"I wish you wouldn't be so mysterious. You know something about Morgan. I wish I did. He said last night he'd been in South Africa, and I think that's the first thing I've heard about his past life. Did you meet him in South Africa?"

"I've never set foot in any part of Africa. I'll tell you about Morgan when the time comes."

She looked at him with deep uneasiness.

"Don't do anything—rash. I feel—I keep feeling something terrible's going to happen."

"Perhaps it is," he suggested. "Has your father parted with his money yet?"

She was so sad and angry she was afraid she was going to cry. She caught one hand in the other, and dug her nails into her own flesh, trying to think of the pain instead of her emotions.

"If you think it's funny," she said over her shoulder.

"Don't walk so fast. I think it's serious. But if it wasn't your father, I'd stand back and enjoy the comedy."

She was outraged. "Comedy!"

"Yes, comedy. The man with money who's determined to lose it in order to get more. It's one of the classic situations. The newspapers thrive on it, and there must be thousands of people whose vanity keeps them out of court."

"So you enjoy the ruin of innocent people?"

"Well, innocent of what?" he enquired reasonably. "Greed? Covetousness? A desire to enjoy the benefits of money they've never worked for? No confidence man ever got a penny out of anyone who wasn't dreaming of easy money."

"I won't listen. You're insulting my father. And you always look at things upside down."

"You're angry because you suspect it may be the right way to look at them. Hester, you're making me run to keep up with you."

"Go away."

"Don't you see anything funny in the fact that ruin doesn't mean anything more now than the loss of money?"

She didn't answer, and he walked quickly until he was alongside her again.

"Hester, you're crying."

"Go away."

"I have a handkerchief," he said eagerly, pulling one from his pocket. He looked at it reminiscently. "No, perhaps this one won't do. I have another handkerchief." He felt in his pockets, and finally produced a blue handkerchief, still in its virgin folds.

She began to laugh. "It isn't like you, Harry, to have two handkerchiefs."

"I've had my laundry done," he said, dabbing tenderly at

her cheeks. "But I suppose you want to blow your nose? Oh, well, clean handkerchiefs can't last for ever."

"Harry, why are you so horrid about Father."

"I'm not. It's just that I see him as a natural victim. How did Maurice get on to him in the first place? Who told him your father was waiting there, tied to a tree by the drinking pool? Was it Morgan?"

"No. He just met Father in the ordinary way. When we had the antique shop. Maurice came in and bought something—I think it was a table. And Father brought him home to lunch."

"That's how it would be," Harry said with satisfaction. "Your father not only attracts calamities, he asks them home to lunch. Talking about lunch..."

"I wasn't talking about lunch," Hester interrupted angrily. "When I came out I didn't want to talk about anything."

"Then don't let's talk," Harry said in a strained voice. "It will get us nowhere. Nothing will. We're on a ball, being bowled through emptiness to eternal silence. We're only pieces of animated dust. Why should we try to hurl our squeaking voices through the universe?"

Hester was frightened. His face was vacant and his eyes looked blind. She felt he was sinking away from her into blackness: she wasn't prepared to let him go. She caught his head to her and kissed him, and after a second of isolation he responded. They held on to each other for a moment, and then, by a common impulse of self-preservation, separated again.

Hester was exhilarated. She felt like a driver whose brakes had failed at a point of danger and who had miraculously survived. She would proceed more carefully now.

"Harry, how can you talk like that on a beautiful morning?" she said gaily.

The slight but distinct relief on his face vanished. "But I love you, Hester," he said resentfully. "And of course that makes me particularly miserable when the sun shines," he added, beginning to grin.

They walked on towards the village, closer in their thoughts than most people, but each still utterly confused by the behaviour of the other.

Hester looked at her watch.

"Is there something I could do to help you?" Harry asked. "What do you have to buy?"

"Some buttons and some white silk."

"These be feminine mysteries. Anything else?"

"And some coffee from Mad Meg's. That's all."

"Give me the money and I'll get the coffee."

"Here you are. A pound note and a pound of coffee," Hester said.

When they came to the village Hester went into the threatening darkness of the draper's shop. Harry went on to the grocer's. It was a good shop, smelling of incompatible foods.

"Delicious," he said approvingly, while the old woman behind the counter snuffled and mewed.

"A pound of coffee, if you please," he barked suddenly, like a bad-tempered squire.

"What kind?" she shrilled back, like one of the dangerous democrats of the village.

"How should I know what kind? It's for Miss Wade, of Tower House. Surely you know what your own customers buy."

"A pound of best coffee," she muttered.

"Well, naturally."

He walked round the shop, examining. "Cheese?" he said absently. "What kind of cheese do they like? I'd better take something in a box. Any Brie? Of course not. No Camembert? Well, really! I suppose I'd better take one of those things wrapped in silver paper. Do you know," he added more genially, "I'm sure you'd find it worth your while to keep real cheese. Throw in a pound of tomatoes, and some plain biscuits. And charge it all up."

"Miss Wade always pays," she croaked.

"Well, today she wants it charged up," Harry said.

He met Hester in the street.

"Here's your coffee," he said. "Six shillings—or was it seven? Anyway, I can't give you the change at this very moment. I should have paid with your pound instead of my own money. So either I give you back the pound and you owe me seven shillings, or you come into the pub for a drink and I'll get the pound changed and give you back—what did I say—thirteen shillings."

Hester looked confused. "But I don't want a drink, Harry."

"No drink, no change. Be a good girl. A sherry before lunch will set you up." He took hold of her elbow and steered her into The Running Fox.

"Harry, I know you're short of money. You don't have to buy me a drink."

"I want to give you the change from the coffee."

"But, Harry, there are other ways of changing a pound."

"I can't imagine what they are," he said. "Sit down by that table and I'll bring the drinks. What do you want? Sherry? Beer?"

"Ginger beer shandy," she said, and he walked over to the bar. He looked happy and relaxed. He liked having enough money to buy a girl a drink.

In the corner, dark against the dark panelling, a young man was sitting, with a glass of beer and a newspaper in front of him. Hester looked at him idly. He had a dark, strong face that could have been called menacing. He looked like a man to whom the idea of subservience had never occurred. She studied him, thinking not so much of him as of Harry, realising with pain that Harry was soft where this man and others were hard; that Harry had no pride while this man probably had too much; that Harry was weak, unpredictable, and perhaps even dishonest.

When Harry came back with the drinks she turned to him with a loving, protective smile; and accepted the shandy from him as though it had been a gift of orchids.

"I like this pub," Harry said. "Four hundred years old, and only three landlords in all that time, if the present one hits the average. Take a look at him—do you suppose he's more than a hundred and thirty-three and a third years old? Your health, Hester!" The last words were spoken with a desperate sincerity that seemed to give the act of drinking a unique importance.

He put down his empty glass, sighing. "I think I'll get another," he said. "What about you?"

"I've hardly touched this, and I don't want another."

"Or you might have high blood pressure at the age of seventy-three. That's the girl!" Harry said approvingly. "You're depriving yourself, Hester. The only bad habit you ever give yourself a chance to develop is me."

He went to the bar, and she looked after him, trying to estimate how bad a habit he could be. She felt she had no illusions about his moral strength. He was as weak as a flower that had been blown down by the wind, she thought, while the instinct of the good gardener rose in her.

"Drink up that shandy, Hester," he said. "I shall love you even when you're an old woman with dropsy. Don't look frightened. It's not true. You'll grow old like someone out of Yeats. A few minutes of lovely memories, then a graceful death with epitaphs in every anthology. But you must love me if you want to be sure of getting in the anthologies. Hester, love me and I'll write you a book of poems all to yourself. And I'll do breathing exercises before the window every morning. What a life we'll have." He began to breathe deeply, then bent down to lift imaginary weights and heave them above his head. The dark young man looked up from his newspaper, and the old landlord leant across the bar and gave an amazed, yelping laugh. Harry, as usual, was failing to be inconspicuous.

Hester didn't notice the others. She had begun to laugh. Harry was the only person who could make her forget the serious problems of life.

"Would you be the ideal husband?" she asked teasingly.

"You would have no pleasure then in reforming me. Would you like to try?"

"I'll think about it," she said lightly. She stood up, frightened by the realisation that she was thinking about it very seriously. Life with Harry would have its compensations, and she saw with absolute clarity that if no one helped him his talent would dissolve in easy words and idleness. By asking for her help he was making her responsible for his own irresponsibility. She didn't want to marry; like a young fish, she needed all the ocean to swim in before she returned to the small pools of the river. Harry was lost, bewildered, drifting. She wanted to lead him out of the darkness.

"Harry, I must go. I must go now. Goodbye."

She walked out. She had forgotten to ask for the change from the coffee.

Thursday (5)

The young man in the corner watched Hester go, then walked over to Harry.

"Do you mind if I sit down?" he asked.

"No."

"Will you have a drink with me?"

"Bitter, please."

The stranger went to the bar and came back with the drinks.

"I thought I heard a note in your voice that suggested you'd been in Australia," he explained.

"You're not accusing me of anything? Here's your health. And Australia's, to be on the safe side."

"I should keep on the safe side," the stranger advised. "You liked Australia?"

"I found it ravishing," Harry said solemnly. "But I had to leave. It wasn't the place for my profession."

"Which is?"

"I'm a poet."

"I'll be damned!" the Australian said. He looked intently at Harry, as though he was memorising him for an examination.

"You may photograph me, if you wish," Harry said modestly.

"Do you make much money out of poetry?" the Australian said, looking now at Harry's shabby coat, whose cuffs were so unsuitably bound with leather.

"Only decimal points," Harry said. "Do you make much money out of Australia?"

"In good years, yes. I'm in the farm-machinery business."

"Have you been buying many combine-harvesters here?"

Harry asked, waving his already empty glass at the empty pub. "Or is it culture that brings you to the Cotswolds?"

"I was watching you and your sister," the stranger said in level tones.

"It must have been with the inward eye," Harry said. "I haven't got a sister."

"The girl who was here with you. I thought I recognised her voice."

"You're good at voices, aren't you?" Harry said approvingly. "But you couldn't help recognising her voice. She's an English middle-class girl. They all speak alike. When you've heard one of them being Cleopatra or Juliet, you've heard the lot. Will you have a drink?"

"Yes."

Harry went to the bar. When he came back, his round face was screwed up in pleasure.

"It's a happy circumstance, drinking with strangers in bars," he explained. "My mind's moving now like a circular saw. I'm not sure now what I'm cutting. It might be monotony. It might be the branch I'm sitting on."

The stranger wasn't easily diverted. "I said I thought I recognised her voice. Does she live at the Tower House?"

"Yes."

"Who is she?"

"Her name is Hester Wade. She's the girl I'm going to marry, eventually," Harry said, making up his mind. Drink was clearing his head.

"Oh. Have you bought your house yet?"

"I hadn't thought of buying a house. I suppose if someone gave us a house, we'd accept it. We'll live with her father. He wants to go into the hotel business. He'd be glad to have us as his guests."

"Is a man called Maurice Reid going to be one of the guests?"

"In a way, I like being pumped," Harry said. "It makes me feel important, like a spy being interviewed by the secret police. But there's another side of me, longing to discuss astronomy, or bird-watching. Suppose you tell me, without what you may believe to be elaborate finesse, exactly what you want to know. Roll all your questions up into one ball and tear the answers with rough strife through the iron gates of life."

"Are you trying to be funny?" the stranger asked truculently. "No, I see, it rhymed. Did you make it up?"

"I adapted it to the needs of the moment. Adapt or die, my friend, that's the rule."

The stranger looked grimly at Harry, then made a quick decision. "I'll tell you what I want to know. Have the Wades much money? Do they trust Maurice Reid? Is he planning to swindle them? If he is, when's he going to do it?"

"The Wades have very little money. They once had more. The sooner they lose what they have, the better, then the long agony of parting will be over. Hester's father thinks he has the Midas touch, but what he has is the reverse. All his gold turns into porridge and roses. Maurice has spent six months displaying his gilt edges to him and is now going to sell him some kind of illuminated address to Australian oil, before melting into the trees and never being heard of again. That's my estimate of the situation," Harry said cheerfully.

"And you haven't tried to interfere?" the stranger asked contemptuously.

"I've told them what I think. But he's an angel! they say. They're weak on ornithology, or they'd know that vultures have wings, too."

"Oh, skip all that. There's not much doing in Australian oil, just now. If this man Reid sells them shares in an imaginary company, would it be a crime, by English law?"

"I'm just about the opposite of a lawyer," Harry admitted. "But it might."

"So if we let Reid go ahead, and then jump, we could get him into jail."

"It would be better if we stopped him. How am I to get married if my father-in-law's lost all his money?" Harry asked, bursting into laughter.

"Then suppose the company isn't imaginary. Suppose he bought up some bankrupt stock for a penny a piece and is going to sell it at a thousand per cent profit. That's a possibility. You—what's your name?"

"Harry Walters, sir," Harry said meekly.

"Keep your mouth shut, Walters. I think I'll have to deal with Reid direct."

"What have you got against Maurice?" Harry asked.

The Australian stood up. His face was dark and desperate, like a man trapped in the mountains in a thunderstorm.

"I'd sooner shake a snake by the hand than come within speaking distance of him," he said. "If I get a chance I'll twist him till his back breaks."

Harry looked at him with bright, excited eyes. "Have another drink, you—what's your name?"

"Marryatt. I'll eat before I drink any more. You ought to do the same," he said, without interest.

"I'm eating under a haystack today. Cheese, biscuits, and the beauties of nature. Where are you staying—if I want to get in touch with you?"

"I'm staying in the pub here. And I'm staying just as long as it takes me to get my hands on Reid."

"I'll have to arrange a meeting between you two boys,"

Harry said. "I've got my own business, of course," he said vaguely. He closed his eyes. The beer had made him very tired. "Morgan—if I could put a red-hot poker under Morgan's nose I'd be a rich man. It's for Hester, you see. I've got to get the money for Hester. I'll do it without the red-hot poker—and there will be no more worrying about money then."

"Who's Morgan?" Marryatt asked.

"That would take too long to explain," Harry said. "Goodbye." He turned to leave the pub. At the door he stopped.

"I carry a gun," he said. "So there's nothing to worry about at all."

Thursday (6)

Throughout the afternoon the sun blazed down until the flowers buckled in the heat and all the dogs walked with their tongues hanging out. The cows stood quite still except for the tails they swished against the flies; the bees worked against time, allowing rather less than a second to each flower, and the butterflies, the true creatures of the sun, abandoned themselves to an aimless happiness.

Hester lay down in the shade. The long grass of the lawn smelt like hay. It was one of many reminders of the work that waited in the garden. She lay in idleness, dimly aware of a shepherd shouting to his dogs on the other side of the valley; the voice of command was thinned by distance to a grumbling bird-call. In the valley below, a tractor muttered; the bees that worked beside her in the flowers made a more important noise; she had no troubles and no worries; she fell asleep.

When she woke Jackie was standing beside her, looking underfed and overworked.

"I've polished the silver, Miss. Would you want me to help in the garden?" he asked accusingly.

She sat up, remembering guiltily that she had meant to send for the police. He looked very young to go to prison.

"Yes, Jackie, you could begin to weed that flower bed over there," she said sharply.

He drooped away from her. She watched him unhappily, trying to believe that work was an infallible reformer, and that if criminals could be exposed to its pleasures, they would soon become honest men.

She stood up, looking at Jackie with a regenerative eye. He turned back towards her, holding out a great sheaf of uprooted delphiniums.

"Big weeds you've got in this garden," he said. "What do I do with them now?"

"Oh, Jackie, what have you done? You must try to plant them again."

She heard the phone ring, and wavered for a moment between the garden and the house.

"Leave the garden alone. Don't touch a thing till I come back," she said, and ran into the house.

Morgan was creeping through the hall, looking nervously at the telephone.

"Where's that little crook?" he asked.

"He's in the garden, the back garden."

Morgan turned and went quickly through the front door. Hester picked up the telephone.

"Miss Wade? Are you the girl I talked to in the garden last night?"

"Yes. Are you—I don't know your name."

"My name's Tom Marryatt. Now, look, I don't want to interfere in anyone's business, and you can tell me where to go, if you like. I'm trying to do the straight thing. I should have done it last night. I've been talking to your friend."

"You've been what?"

"I've been talking to the man you're going to marry. What's his name—Harry Walters."

"But—who said I was going to marry him?" Hester asked. She could feel herself getting hot with anger.

"He did. That's nothing to do with me. Understand?"

"I understand you're being extremely rude."

"I'm what? You listen to me. I know this Maurice Reid. If he's trying to get any money out of your family don't let him get away with it. That's all I have to say and I'll say it in any way I choose. Goodbye."

"How do you know? Wait, wait!" Hester said, but he had rung off.

She put back the receiver, and went listlessly out into the garden. The lush hot afternoon was only oppressive now. She knew she must have a discussion with her father, and that he would treat her like an importunate child who had come to ask him to draw cows and horses on the backs of envelopes.

Jackie wasn't in the garden. The only sign that he had ever been there was the ruined flower bed.

She thought of going to Prudence for support, but Prudence was too young and superior. Harry—Harry would never be any kind of help about money. She had to manage this interview alone, without help from anyone.

She found her father in the little room that was fictitiously described as his study. He had a notebook in his hand, and was consulting it with apparent satisfaction.

"I want to speak to you about money, Father," she said sadly.

"Money, Hester?" he said, assuming surprise. He shut the notebook and put it in his pocket.

"Father, please don't invest any money in this scheme of Maurice's," Hester said in a distressed voice.

"My dear Hester, you must know that Maurice and I wouldn't make any arrangement without considering it very, very carefully beforehand. If we decide that my money is to be invested in this concern, you may be sure it's ninety-nine per cent certain that the money will be safe. In fact, you may be certain that the sterling cast upon the waters will come back quadrupled," he said with a smile of innocent delight that would have touched the heart of any woman who was not a member of his family.

"I'm convinced you shouldn't do it, Father."

"Hester, you're too young to know anything about money," he said impatiently. "You mustn't trouble your head about the things you can't understand. Now, don't look at me like that, Hester. I repeat that you know nothing about money. What are equity shares?" he asked. He waited, holding back his triumph.

"I don't know. But I don't believe it's difficult to know. I could find out in five minutes."

"How?"

"By telephoning Uncle Joe."

"Don't bring Joe into it, whatever you do." He jumped up, looking as though he were going to pace the room. "Joe would be on to this thing like a rabbit trap. He would buy every share in sight. There would be nothing, nothing, left for the small man like me. Hester, promise me you won't talk to Joe!" He looked at her appealingly, putting all his considerable charm into his smile, then sat down again on the edge of the desk, looking sulky.

"Of course you won't talk to Joe," he said. "I apologise if I sounded heated, but really, Hester, to have money, actual money, almost within my grasp, and then think it might be lost by a careless word from my own daughter, naturally—no, I'll forget it. I apologise. We mustn't quarrel, Hester."

"I hate quarrelling," she said. "But a quarrel might be better than ruin."

"Ruin is a strong word."

"Not too strong for what we're discussing."

"Hester, I will try to forgive you, because you are young, and, as I have already demonstrated, know nothing about money. But this discussion is over. Do you understand? Over. Now run along like a good girl before we really quarrel."

"Father, I won't run along. If you give this money to Maurice you may not get it back."

"Hester, are you trying to tell me that you distrust Maurice? Maurice!" he repeated, with a dramatic blend of pain and incredulity.

She closed her eyes, trying not to be irritated by his affectations, reminding herself that he was a good and a kind man.

"I don't know what I feel about Maurice," she said unhappily. "Harry's always saying that Maurice—that Maurice means to have your money."

"Harry! You mean that you are prepared to take the word of that—that worthless loafer, that parasite, against Maurice!" He stood up, and walked irresolutely to the door.

"He's not a worthless loafer, he's a poet!" Hester said angrily.

"A poet!" He turned back, and looked at her sorrowfully. "My poor, deluded little girl," he said heavily. "If only your mother were alive."

"She died when I was four," Hester reminded him. "I think

we can leave her out of this discussion. Neither of us knows what she would have said."

"She certainly wouldn't have allowed you to associate with Harry. She would have known how to stop that. It's hard for me, alone," he said pathetically. He slumped into a chair. "I've been alone for sixteen years. Some of them have been very difficult. Do you think I don't know that my little daughters would like new clothes, a car, a chance to meet the best people?"

"I'm not worried about the best people," Hester said irritably. "Do learn to stick to the point, Father."

He sat up again. "Yes, Father. You don't sometimes feel that you owe me a little respect?"

"Father, I do respect you, but please—we were talking about Maurice."

"Maurice, whatever his faults may be, is a man. That is not how I describe Harry."

"Please, please, please don't talk about Harry any more."

"It's my duty, Hester. It's my duty to save you from Harry. If you'd had a brother—yes, if only I'd had a son," he said, sighing.

Hester didn't fail to observe that she was being blamed for her sex.

"If you'd had a son he might have been able to prevent your throwing your money away. I don't see why I should let you be rash and foolish just because I'm female."

"Rash and foolish! Hester, remember you are speaking to your father."

"Oh, I'm sorry, Father. But please let's be reasonable. And it's not just Harry. There's this man I met in the garden last night. And now he's telephoned to warn me against Maurice."

"A man you met in the garden? A stranger, trespassing in our garden, has telephoned. Hester, are you mad?"

"I'm not mad. He telephoned."

"Who is this man?"

"I don't know. He sounds like an Australian, or something. He's called Marryatt."

"An Australian. And where, may I ask, does this stranger from Australia—this man from our garden—where does he live?"

"I don't know. Perhaps Harry could tell us. He's been talking to Harry," Hester said incautiously.

"Talking to Harry! Well, that certainly explains everything. Talking to Harry! And I suppose he gets his facts about Maurice from Harry. Oh, this is very convincing. Where can I get hold of this stranger!"

"I don't know."

"That's just as well for him," he said, almost shouting. "Because if I could meet him I would knock him down. Let me tell you, I trust Maurice. I trust him absolutely. And trust him all the more because spongers and troublemakers and lunatics from Australia maliciously interfere in my business. Now will you listen to me, Hester. You are not to see or speak to Harry again. He is a wastrel. And I forbid, I positively forbid you to speak to strangers in the garden. If I find a stranger in the garden I will shoot him. Do you understand? Now please leave the room. I'm expecting Maurice."

"Oh, I'll be glad when it's time to go back to London," Hester said, beginning to cry. She rushed out of the room and through the hall. At the bottom of the stairs she met Harry.

"Hester! Crying!" he said in dismay. "Oh, Hester!" He caught her by the hands and pulled her into the sitting-room. He kissed her wet cheeks tenderly, then stopped to find a handkerchief. He found two, and looked at them dubiously.

"Now which was yours?" he wondered aloud. "Have I

another one anywhere, or would you like to use the back of your hand?"

Hester began to laugh. "I was crying because of the things you said about Maurice."

"I'll take them all back. He's a fine fellow to meet on a winter's night over a drink, if the thought makes you happy. I've no trouble in telling you a lie if it makes you smile again."

"And Father said I wasn't to see you again."

"Your father's a very sensible man. It's a crime a monster like myself should make love to you."

"But you are a poet, Harry."

"Certainly I'm a poet. On the last morning when the non-commissioned angels come down from heaven to organise the other ranks, I'll be lying still in the grave while the other poets are lining up for the long march. When the solid miles of them are filing up into the sky I'll be stumbling on behind, trying to catch McGonagall's coat tails, or even one of Ella Wheeler Wilcox's floating ribbons, while Shakespeare and Homer and the head of the column are so far away that they look no bigger than split peas."

Hester laughed, but looked at him with the patient air of the school teacher who is determined to persevere. "Harry, you're better than that. You must be. Don't you think if you had a place to work, and someone who believed in your work..."

"These things have ruined many a prosaic man. If you can't write poetry against every kind of handicap, you can't write it at all. I'm like a lot of other people, Hester. I'm a genius with four or five pieces left out. Do you love me, Hester?" he asked sadly.

"I think perhaps I do, Harry," she said dubiously, the determination fading from her voice as she began to consider her own position instead of his.

"No, you don't love me. You love the four or five missing pieces. You think I've only mislaid them."

"Very well. You're determined to believe you're no good and that I don't love you. It must be hard work, being so hopeless."

"But I'm not hopeless," he said, looking suddenly happy and excited. "Everything's going to be fine, soon. I have some easy money coming."

"Easy money!" she said furiously. "I'm sick of the sound of it. Go away, Harry. Father said I wasn't to speak to you, and Maurice is coming. Go away!" She ran out of the room and upstairs to her bedroom. She needed a few minutes out of earshot of all the discussions about money and love.

Thursday (7)

The gate that led to Tower House was unpainted and had the same derelict, sagging appearance as the house itself. The young man who waited beside the gate had been examining the house for half-an-hour. As he had nothing else to do while he waited, he had made imaginary arrangements for the reconstruction of the house, scraping away the ivy from the walls; cutting down the trees that grew too close; rebuilding the mildewed north wall; extending the sloping roof to cover a new garage; modernising the tangle of drain-pipes. On the south side the ground-floor windows and most of the wall could be cut away, and replaced by sliding glass doors leading on to a sun balcony.

"Hell, it would be better to tear the whole place down and begin again," he said contemptuously to himself, and felt in his pocket for another cigarette. He heard the car coming, and took his hand slowly from his pocket. He stepped back into the cover of the trees and waited until the car drew up before the gate. Then he stepped forward.

"Don't bother, I'll open the gate," he said. He looked into the car. "Well, if it isn't Maurice Reid, my old friend," he said with enormous satisfaction.

Maurice looked at him, with a humorous, apologetic lift of the eyebrows. He took his hands from the wheel, and tucked the rosebud that was slipping from his button-hole back into place.

"I'm afraid I don't know you. I think you've made a mistake."

"A mistake? I've seen your face over my bed every night for years. Sometimes I see it very small and dream of stamping on it until the filthy grin is squashed as flat as a frog under a tractor; and sometimes I see it very big, springing backwards and forwards like a punching ball every time I hit it."

Maurice looked at the gate, then back quickly over his shoulder. There was no room to turn. He couldn't get back on the road without reversing.

"Open the door," the young man said. "We're going for a drive."

"I'm afraid—I'm in a hurry—you can't get in my car."

"Take your hands away from the wheel or I'll break your arm. Open the door."

Maurice dropped his hands. "I don't know you," he repeated hopelessly.

"Open the door."

Maurice leant across and opened the door. "If you insist," he said, smiling.

The stranger stepped in quickly, and slammed the door. "Now we'll go for our ride. Somewhere quiet. Back into the road again, turn right, keep going for about half-a-mile then you'll find a lane to pull into. You can stop there. Get on with it now. I'll talk."

Maurice put the car in reverse and wavered backwards away from the gate. He looked once at the other man and smiled with a kind of humorous resignation.

"I haven't made up my mind if I'm going to break your neck or only beat you up," the stranger said. "Turn right, now. I don't know what satisfaction there would be in beating you up. I've thought about it a lot. You wouldn't fight back. It would be like hitting a woman. But I may do it."

"I think you're mad," Maurice said. "Before God, I swear I don't know you."

"My name is Marryatt."

"I've never known anyone called Marryatt."

"My mother married twice."

Maurice stopped the car and leant back in his seat. "I can't drive on," he said in an exhausted voice.

"Ask what my mother's name was."

"No."

"Don't you want to hear it?"

"Why should I know your mother?"

"You were going to marry her once. Now tell me her name."

"I don't know it."

"Surely you know the name of the woman you were going to marry?"

"I don't know it. I don't know it. Leave me alone."

"Tell me her name. You were going to marry her, but first you took all her money, to invest for her. You took her money and went away. Now tell me her name?"

"For God's sake, I don't know it. You're mad."

"Then tell me the names of all the women you've been going to marry."

Maurice didn't answer.

"Have there been too many?"

Maurice shook his head.

"Get out of the car. I said get out of the car."

Maurice sat still.

The other man hit him on the face with the back of his hand. Maurice got out of the car.

"Now tell me my mother's name."

"I don't know it." He looked down at his feet, where his long, sunset shadow started across the road, and the other shadow bent grotesquely and swung its gibbon arm. He turned to run and was hit on the side of the head as he turned. He fell and was picked up again.

"My mother's name."

"Evans," he whispered hopelessly. "Was it Evans?"

"Did she have a son?"

"I don't know. I can't remember. No, she hadn't."

"Then I'll have to take on his duties and hit you."

"No," Maurice said. He began to walk backwards. "No, no, don't hit me. Help!" he shouted. "Help!" He looked round over his shoulder. The pale smoke from a cottage chimney drifted towards the pale sky. In the field beside the road a sheep raised its head, appeared to give Maurice its critical attention, then turned and jogged away across the grass. The other man drew back, and Maurice put his arms over his face. He was hit on the side, just above the heart. He took a step backwards with his feet crossing, then collapsed.

"Get up."

He groaned and didn't move.

"Tell me my mother's name."

"Was she—was she an Australian?"

Marryatt put out one hand and hauled Maurice to his feet.

"Now, or I'll kick you till you can't speak," he said.

"She was called Fletcher, was she?" Maurice asked, choking. "Yes. She had a son."

"Go on."

"She had a son at school. It was a long time ago. Ten, twelve years ago. I don't think I ever met him."

"Oh, yes you did. It was twelve years ago. I was fifteen. I only saw you twice. You took every pound she had. Do you think I'd forget you? Then she was ill, and a year later she died. Did you know that? Did you know you were a murderer? What did you do with the money?"

"Let me go," Maurice said, gasping. "I'll pay. I'll give it back."

"What did you do with the money? You left Australia. Where did you go?"

"I went—I went to Mexico."

"How long did you stay there?"

"A year. No, six months."

"Just for a holiday?"

"No. No. Yes, for a holiday," he said hopelessly.

"You killed her so that you could have a year's holiday in Mexico?" He stopped, listening. They heard the grunt and the whine of an old car tackling the hill.

"Someone's coming," Maurice said, in gratitude.

"Get in the car and drive on."

Maurice swayed on his feet, then he threw himself down on the grass verge, with his hands under his face.

Marryatt listened, then looked at Maurice's car, where it stood, in the middle of the narrow road. The other car was already in sight.

"You'll have to move that car of yours," he said roughly to Maurice. "We'll continue this conversation later. I'll have decided by then what I'm going to do with you."

He picked Maurice up, pushed him over to the car, and seated him on the running-board. The other car coughed towards them and stopped. The fat woman who drove it looked angrily at the obstructing car, then curiously at the two men. Maurice was still white and trembling and his clothes were powdered with dust. The man who stood over him turned round to glare at her, then vaulted the fence and walked quickly across the field through the scattering sheep.

The fat woman opened her handbag, took out a compact, and began to powder her hot, heavy face with ill-tempered jabs of the powder-puff.

"Could you please move your car?" she shouted to Maurice. "Or can't you move it? Have you had an accident?"

Maurice stood up wearily. "Oh, go to Hell, will you?" he said to her.

She began to tremble, like a dislodged rock on the edge of a precipice. She dragged her handbag for a weapon, found a pencil, and scored the number XAW5116 on paper.

Maurice's wavering hand at last succeeded in opening the door of his car. He toppled into the seat like a wounded man levering himself into a moving ambulance, then began to make futile gestures of apology to the fat woman. He started the engine: when he had moved the car to the side of the road he was able to give her his charming, deprecatory smile.

"I apologise," he called to her, "I wasn't feeling well."

She snapped her bag shut. "I know your kind," she shouted as she drove away.

Maurice arrived at the Tower House twenty minutes later. There was no dust on his clothes. His hair was brushed, and he looked once again clean, shrewd, quizzical; like a sober ship's doctor.

Wade went down the steps from the door to meet him.

"Maurice," he said in relief. "I was beginning to be afraid you weren't coming."

Thursday (8)

Prudence was in the kitchen, staring grimly at a cookery book. She looked up without interest when Jackie came in.

"We have the fillets of cod. Now all we need is the white wine to poach them in. Then there's the sauce. Butter melted very slowly over warm water, yolks of four eggs beaten in, continue beating over warm water until mixture thickens. This may take half-an-hour, but with perseverance… That's a nice job for a hot night. You can do that, Jackie. A few drops of Armagnac—that's another thing we don't have in the larder."

"What's Armagnac?" Jackie asked suspiciously.

"It's a drink," Prudence said uncertainly.

"Then put in some beer."

"We couldn't do that," she said in a shocked voice. "You'd better go to the pub and get some Armagnac. That means I'll have to start on October's housekeeping money."

"I found this on the floor, Miss," Jackie said virtuously. He groped in his pocket and produced sixpence. "Where shall I put it?"

"Up on that shelf. We'd better get a move on. Dinner's going to be terribly complicated tonight, and I'm going out afterwards."

"Aw, give them baked beans on toast. What's wrong with that? And stewed apples if you want to follow with something fancy. Then we can sit down and put our feet up."

"Baked beans?"

"Yes. Open a tin. Two tins if you like. I'll make some toast."

"It wouldn't do," Prudence said. She looked with distaste at the oil stove. "Or perhaps it would. No, it wouldn't be right."

"Then I'll fry the cod nice and brown and make some chips. That's right. I said chips. You've heard of them, haven't you?"

"Yes. Do you mean I could leave you to do that while I go and change for the tennis club dance? Jackie, what a good idea!" Prudence said, abandoning all her ideas about cookery as a fine art. "Do the baked beans, if it's easier."

"Here, wait a minute, Miss. I got something for you," Jackie said. He plunged in his pocket again, and brought out a silver-coloured brooch with some shining stones in the middle. "Here, have this," he said casually.

Prudence stopped and took it from his hand.

"Where did you get it?"

"I bought it at Woolworth's. Do you think it's pretty? Anyway, you have it. I don't want it." He turned his back on her and began to whistle.

"It looks quite decent," Prudence said. "Jackie, how much did it cost?"

"I don't know."

"If you bought it at Woolworth's it wouldn't be more than half-a-crown, would it? Will it be O.K. if I give you half-a-crown?"

"I don't want any money for it," Jackie said, his face glowing with the sweet radiance of generosity.

"Then I can't have it," Prudence said regretfully. "There's a thing in our school about not accepting presents until you've passed the Advanced Level Certificate."

"The what? It makes no odds. If you won't have it, you won't," Jackie said. He looked abject and bewildered, like a waif who had been thrown out of a churchyard where he had come to lay flowers on a grave.

"I've hurt your feelings, Jackie," Prudence said.

"You haven't hurt m'feelings. I've no feelings. I had them kicked out of me before I was twelve."

"The same thing happens at our school," Prudence said. She walked about the kitchen, picking up saucepans and putting them down again, looking occasionally at Jackie, who was stabbing with a tin-opener at the baked beans in a kind of frenzy, as though he was having his revenge on an enemy.

"Jackie, I'm going to a party tonight. Could I borrow that brooch? I'd be terribly grateful, and I promise to give it back in the morning."

"In the morning?" Jackie said. He laughed satirically. "You borrow it, Miss. It makes no odds to me."

Prudence took the brooch and went upstairs to get ready for the party.

Morgan came out of his bedroom door as she walked across the landing.

"Who's that?" he called.

"It's me. Prudence."

"I thought it might be Harry," he said, beginning to retreat into his bedroom again. "He's always creeping around, spying on me. Is he in the house, Prudence? Is Harry in the house?"

"I don't know," she said impatiently.

"You don't believe he's spying on me, do you?"

"Morgan, please, I have to get ready for a party. I'll be late."

He came out of his room, advancing with small, shaking steps, like a patient who is trying to walk after an operation.

"You know he's spying on me, don't you? Tell me something, Prudence. Has he been in my room?"

"Let me pass," Prudence said desperately. She rejected the idea that the time had come to tell a lie.

"Has he been in my room?"

"What if he has?" she asked brutally. "He was looking for death watch beetles anyway."

"Tell me what he did in my room?"

"Morgan, I have to get ready for a party." She ran past him and into Hester's bedroom.

Hester was sitting on the bed, doing nothing.

"There's something wrong with Morgan. Go and shut him up, Hester."

Hester went over to the dressing-table and began to brush her hair.

"Please, Hester, don't bother about your hair now. Please do something about Morgan. I want you to help me get ready and I think Morgan's mad. I'm sure this doesn't happen to other people getting ready for parties. I'll bet Rosemary and Jane are just getting dressed quietly. They'd go mad themselves if they had something like Morgan in the house. I'd sooner keep a couple of werewolves and a poltergeist as paying guests than Morgan," Prudence said, her face changing shape as she tried not to let the tears out.

Hester put down the hairbrush and went to the door.

"And Jackie's making baked beans for dinner," Prudence called after her.

Hester tapped on Morgan's door.

"Are you coming down to dinner, Morgan?"

"No."

"But you didn't have any lunch, Morgan."

"Come in, Hester, if you're alone."

Hester opened the door and looked in. Morgan was sitting in his outdoor coat, holding a briefcase on his knees. In the diminished daylight, he looked very pale.

"I wondered if you were all right," Hester said weakly.

"Is Harry in the house?" he asked.

"I'm not quite sure," she said apologetically.

"I'm not leaving my room while he is in the house."

"But Harry won't do you any harm."

"Oh, won't he?"

"I'm sure he won't," Hester said with spirit.

"You be a good girl and get him out of the house for me. And keep him out. He's getting on my nerves. And I'll tell you someone else who's on my nerves," he said, suddenly beginning to shout. "That little crook who came last night. Why didn't you send for the police? Can you tell me that? Is your father in this too?"

"Morgan!"

"Oh, it's terrible," he said, putting a cigarette in his mouth and lighting it from the half-smoked one in his shaking hand. "I'm being spied on by everyone, Hester. You're the only one I trust. You wouldn't steal anything from me, would you, Hester? You wouldn't steal anything from anyone, would you?"

"No, I wouldn't, Morgan," she said in a soothing voice.

"Do you know why that little crook came here? This isn't the kind of house where he'd expect rocks and mink. He came for me. Now what am I to do? What would you advise me to do, Hester?"

"Don't you think you'd feel better if you went out more?" she suggested timidly. "It's depressing to be in one room, always."

"I'm not depressed," he said angrily. "Who said I was

depressed? Harry? Was it Harry? Has he been talking about me?"

She retreated towards the door. "Of course he hasn't."

"Oh, Hester, don't go," he said, watching her in terror.

She stopped, in compunction. "Morgan, you're not well."

"I'm all right," he muttered.

"You'll come down to dinner, won't you? It isn't good to be alone too much."

"Alone," he said, and sighed in relief as the word escaped him, as though he had managed at last to make his confession. "I'll tell you something, now. I've been alone for two years and two months. All that time I've been hiding from them. Now there's Harry, and there's this little crook, and tomorrow there will be more. Perhaps they'll be here tonight. I've been frightened to leave the country, but I'm going to do it at last, Hester. Tomorrow I'll be in Ireland, if I have the luck. But I don't feel lucky, Hester. I'm telling you these things because I trust you, not because I've been drinking. I can drink twice as much as I've had tonight and still keep my mouth shut. Hester, if I gave you something, you'd look after it? Would you? You wouldn't let anyone know about it?"

"I don't know," she said reluctantly.

"Just take it and hide it for me?"

"It would depend what it was."

"I thought so. You'd try to find out what it was. There's no one I can trust, you see."

"I think I hear Maurice's car."

"It was bad enough before, but now they'll all be after me. He'll send for them all. If I try to go, they'll stop me. If I stay here, they'll come. Hester, you'll do one thing for me?" He felt in his pockets and brought out a wallet. "Take this money and give it to Ferguson." He offered her a bundle of notes.

"To Uncle Joe?"

"Yes, for my seat in that plane tomorrow. I don't want there to be any doubt about that. You give him the money. Give it to him tonight. Do you promise?"

Hester took the money. "I promise," she said. She was glad to be able to do something for him.

She went out of the room and stood quietly on the stairs. She wondered if it was too late to help Prudence dress for the party. She had decided to turn back to her own room when she heard Maurice's voice, low and easy, speaking into the telephone in the hall below.

"Joe? About this plane you've chartered for Ireland? What do you mean by a stiff price? Oh, I see. Is it too late to get a fourth passenger?... Someone interested in drinking and horses. Why not Harry? Oh, I didn't know you felt like that. Where shall we meet? Oh, you're coming over tonight. Here, to the Wades'? I'll see you then. Goodbye."

Hester went downstairs slowly. It was her duty to be polite to Maurice over the baked beans.

Thursday (9)

"Baked beans!" Maurice said. "By Jove, that takes me back! When I was a boy being starved at school I used to nip into a little place in the town and fill up on baked beans. I've loved them ever since!" He caressed them with his fork, and then looked at Hester, his eyes begging her to admit that he was behaving very well.

Hester smiled as though her face was being worked by electricity, while she wondered if real people ever said By Jove. The feeling that Maurice was not real, that he was only someone she had read about in a book, was increasing. She looked at her father, who was examining the baked beans with genuine distress. He pushed his plate away.

"What comes next?" he asked in a voice that quivered with self-pity. "Something made with suet and jam, I suppose?"

Hester murmured that Prudence had gone to a party, and then sat in an oppressed silence until the segments of apple, floating in an ocean of sweetened water, had been borne triumphantly to the table by Jackie. She was worn-out by the weight of too much emotion; she had no energy to examine Maurice's socially admirable reactions, or to smile maliciously at her father, who was displaying astonishment at his daughters' failure to support him with adequate food. She waited listlessly until they had finished, and then went quickly out of the room, out of the house, and into the garden.

She sat down in the shadow of the trees, and remained there while the world turned her slowly under the dark sky, and she let all thoughts of people drift away behind her.

A long time afterwards, she heard her father calling to her. She didn't answer.

He walked across the lawn towards the trees.

"Hester!" he called again.

"Yes, Father," she said, and came slowly towards him, not seen at all except as a pale flicker of a summer dress moving through the black trees.

"Hester, Uncle Joe is here. Will you come in?"

"Yes, Father."

"Hester, I hope you don't think I spoke too harshly to you this afternoon?"

"It doesn't matter now, does it?"

"Don't hold it against me if I was a little hasty," he said, preparing to redefine his hastiness as logical and excusable conduct.

"I said it doesn't matter now. Does it?"

"There are times when the older generation must think it's wiser."

"Father, does it matter now?"

He sighed, and admitted the question at last.

"I've fixed things up with Maurice," he said, his voice suddenly full of doubt.

"You don't sound elated," she said coldly.

"But I am, Hester. It's a wonderful thing for me, Hester, to think that at last I'll be able to do things for you and Prudence. It's for the sake of you girls that I've taken the risk," he said pathetically.

"I thought there was no risk." She began to move away, impatiently.

"Hester, do you think I've done the right thing?"

"I've told you what I think. Nothing's happened to make me change my mind."

He looked at her unhappily. It was too dark for him to see the expression on her face, and it is difficult for an indulged parent to realise when he has said something that his children will not forgive.

"You sound so hard. Not like my little girl Hester."

"I'm twenty. I can't go back to being a little girl." They were moving out of the shadows into the lights from the house. For the first time she saw his face.

"Don't look so sad, Father," she said impulsively, and his expression changed to gratitude. She caught his hand and squeezed it. He seemed overcome by an almost excessive emotion, but she suppressed the slightly irritable thought that older people yielded too readily to sentiment, and smiled at him affectionately, although she herself felt the hardness beneath her smile.

They went in the house together. Wade was so relieved to have captured her again that it was impossible for him to show instantly what he felt when he found Harry in the sitting-room.

"Harry! How nice!" Hester said ironically. "Good evening, Moira, Uncle Joe!"

She sat down to listen.

"What I don't understand, Uncle Joe," Harry was saying in the confident voice of easy friendship, "is exactly why you are going to Dublin in Horse Show week. If you mean to buy a horse I can put you in touch with a man. He's a genius at the game. He'll sell you a horse with an Irish brogue, if that's what you want."

Joe looked at the carpet for strength.

"No, Harry, I do not mean to buy a horse. It would interfere with business. It would run in races. My friends would telephone. We've backed your horse today, Joe, they would say. And I would know if it didn't win they would be angry with me. Don't, I would tell them. The horse is rheumatic. In its stables it groaned all last night. They take my advice. They leave it alone. The horse wins, and they are very cross."

Harry shook his head. "It's a great step up in the world when a man owns a horse. There's no better way of keeping up appearances than a horse. A tractor doesn't serve the same ends at all. To make a good showing in the eyes of the world, you need something useless as well as expensive—and there's nothing in England today that's half as useless as a horse."

"That's what?" Wade said in an outraged voice.

"You have patriotism mixed up with loyalty to horses," Harry explained to him. "It's the fault of your old regiment."

"Why are you going to Ireland, Uncle Joe?" Hester asked quickly.

"Business. There's a man over there; he owns some cinemas, and he's looking under the fauteuils every night for television sets, so now he wants to have a nervous breakdown in Jamaica and I buy his cinemas. I have to go quickly because already he begins to draw television aerials by accident when he tries to sign his name. But Aer Lingus is booked up. Then I remember meeting a pilot with a plane to charter. In fact, it was you, Harry, who made me buy this pilot a drink at The Sheaf of Wheat."

"What, are you flying with old Lee?" Harry asked. "Why, I know him. Suppose I come along for the trip, as cabin boy or something?"

"When I met him with Harry," Joe explained to the others, "he gave me his card. If you ever want to charter a plane, he says, remember me. So I remember him. Then my directors are very annoying, and don't come. But the plane has only four seats, and now Morgan and Maurice come with me."

"Morgan!" Harry repeated.

"Maurice!" Hester said. "Oh, yes, I heard you on the phone."

"Maurice! I thought you had to be in London tomorrow?" Wade said uneasily.

"I had a sudden idea I'd like to see Dublin again," Maurice said lightly. "And there's nothing I have to do myself in London. I must give instructions to my broker. That's all." He glanced at his watch. "I know his home number. I'll go out and make a London call now, with your permission."

He walked out of the room. Hester saw her father watching him with anxious eyes. People had once been afraid of their lives in this way; they had gone banqueting with their enemies; laying aside their swords; waiting, vulnerable, for the entrance of the murderous retainers. Her father, now, was beginning to suspect betrayal, but it was only his money that was in danger. It was monstrous that money should mean so much, she thought, while the tension in the room mounted until it was felt as a physical force, like the pressure of the water fifty feet below the surface of the sea.

Moira was speaking in a languid, petulant voice. Hester, not listening, looked speculatively at the flesh that hung like the rich fruit of autumn from her chin; at the built-up, dewy complexion and the lines that showed heavily through it like pencil marks. She was a woman who could have no enthusiasms apart from the preservation of her exterior, but when Harry smiled at her tenderly, her face became animated. Hester was shocked by the realisation that a woman of Moira's age could still be interested in love. Harry must see her for what she was.

Hester jumped up. "Morgan—Morgan gave me some money for you. I must get it." She hurried from the room, brushing past Maurice as he returned.

"I've telephoned London," he said, "that's fixed."

Harry followed her, and stood beside her in the dark hall.

She turned on him. "He's going away with Father's money. He won't come back. He'll go to Ireland, we'll never hear of him again. Be quiet. I don't want comfort. I want Father's money back again."

"There's a lot of worry about money. It may be easier in the end to have no money at all. It's a rash thing I'm doing, to try to change my manner of living just because I love you, Hester. It's for you I'm grossly interfering with things that would be better left alone. We'll have money to last a time," Harry said confidently.

Hester didn't listen. "I don't believe Maurice was telephoning his broker. I'd like to find out whom he was telephoning," she said fiercely, looking at Harry, trying to force the thought from her head to his.

"You could ask the Exchange."

"Oh, no," she protested in a shocked voice, still looking at him intently.

"Your standards are too high," he said ironically, and she saw that he understood that she was begging him to do what she wouldn't do herself. "It seems that by having no moral qualities at all I'm just the man you want. A little spying will leave my self-respect quite intact."

He went to the telephone. "Hello, Operator? I want to find out how much that call to London cost? All right, I'll hang on." He turned back to Hester, still holding the telephone. "You didn't tell me Morgan was going to Ireland. I'm not sure, Hester, but will you mind if I leave you for a couple of days? I think I'll have to be on that plane myself. There's the money question, again. Do you suppose your father would like to lend me fifteen pounds?"

"No, Harry, I'm sure he wouldn't."

"Well, I can hardly borrow it from Morgan. I want it to be a surprise for him to find I'm on that plane too. I want to stick as close to him as the hairs on the back of his neck."

"Why are you so interested in Morgan? Everyone in this house is mad," she said despairingly.

Harry swung back to the phone. "Hello, Operator. What? No calls to London, no trunk calls from this number. You're certain? Well, thanks."

He hung the receiver back. "Got that?" he asked Hester. "Now things are heating up. I'll ring old Lee and tell him I'm flying with him tomorrow. I might as well get that bit fixed before I begin to worry about how to raise the money."

Hester was lost in a labyrinth of futile plans. She decided

that she must attack Maurice at once, in front of them all; that it would be better to wait by his car and confront him alone. She heard Harry's voice explaining to someone at the other end of the line that he was flying in the plane tomorrow, but she didn't stay to listen. She fetched the money Morgan had given her and went back to the sitting-room with it. Harry had finished his phone call, and was sitting now in a chair close to Moira's.

"Cheltenham is a fine monument to the limited liability company," Joe was saying. "Moira wants to spend the day there. She's driving me in early tomorrow, and then I take the train to Brickford."

"Shall I come with you for the ride?" Harry asked. "Or will you lend me one of your other cars? To get to the airport."

"The other cars are in London. Did you say airport, Harry?"

"Yes. I was thinking of flying with you, when I get the money."

"Yes, Harry, when you get the money you shall fly with me," Joe agreed quickly. "But this trip is business. I should like you to come, Harry, but when I make up my accounts it is necessary they should be exact. So if you give me the money tonight, you shall come tomorrow."

"You mean that?" Harry asked, grinning.

"Of course. When you have paid the money, I shall be so happy to have your company," Joe said heavily. He looked at his wife, who began to polish her fingernails by rubbing them together. She studied the result, then yawned.

There was a tap at the door, and Jackie's voice was heard to ask meekly if anything else was wanted.

"Come in, Jackie, and show your shirt," Harry called, taking on himself readily, as usual, the duties of the head of the household.

Jackie came in meekly, and stood with his eyes downcast. Hester thought for a moment she saw triumph in his face.

"That's a wonderful shirt," Harry said. He stood up lazily and went to the blue vase that stood on the table. He took out two roses and tucked them into one of Jackie's button-holes. Jackie stood meekly, like a child being prepared for the Sunday school play in the church hall.

"Flowers to add to the garden of your shirt," Harry said.

Jackie's face became very pinched. "I heard you had a sense of humour," he said. He looked humbly at Hester. "They're very pretty, Miss," he said. He peered down at the roses. "I never had a chance to have a garden. Never saw nothing but parks and don't touch the flowers before. I'll keep these," he said, touching the roses with one of his thick fingers. He walked softly out of the room.

Hester looked at Harry. This was the time to conceal absolutely the depths of her pain and disillusionment. She smiled fixedly, as though she was being photographed, while the memory of the morning in the garden blackened and withered. She saw that Harry's agile mind had danced away from the rose garden.

"You've given away two years of my life," she said to him, in a voice that was meant to be light, but that sounded instead hard and glittering, like granite.

Joe looked at her quickly. "I have a new rose, Hester. Do you like it? See, it is snow-white, tipped with this angry red. I put it in my button-hole to show you. My gardener is very proud. I want to name it for Senator McCarthy, but he wants to call it Mabel Spick, after his aunt. Maurice has a button-hole too. We are very festive, except your father, and Harry." As always, he appeared to wince when he mentioned Harry's name.

Maurice looked up, smiling. "Hester gave it to me this morning. Roses mean England to me," he said, touching his rose with a gesture of affection that seemed to expose an inner man, untarnished by the bitter air of cities. "They grow them in other places," he added, in a tone that carefully mocked his own display of sentiment. "Have you ever been in Australia, Joe?"

"Never. And now you will tell me of the hanging gardens of Wagga Wagga," Joe said in a resigned voice. "I have never been in New Zealand, America, any part of Asia or Africa. In all these places you will tell me about the roses. You are a travelled man. I am at your mercy. How can I answer you? I have nothing to tell. I come of a family that travels only when it is forced to."

"I hope you're not being forced to go to Dublin," Maurice said easily.

"I am going for business," Joe said, watching Harry, who sat now on the arm of Moira's chair, with his hand an imperceptible inch from hers. "I'd give you a lift to Brickford, Maurice," Joe said, looking smoothly away again, "but I've told you I'm going to Cheltenham first with Moira," he said, speaking her name so loudly that she started up, with a movement that carried her fingers away from Harry's. "It would be too early for you," Joe said. "You probably prefer to drive yourself."

Maurice shook his head. "I shan't drive," he said. "You know the car isn't mine. I have a standing arrangement with Ames at the garage here to hire it when I'm down this way. I've always found it pays to hire a car on the spot. But now I'm thinking of settling down at last I'll have to buy a reconditioned taxi or a jeep or something humble."

"Don't you own a car at all?" Moira asked in a voice of horrified sympathy, as though she had discovered he had no legs.

Maurice smiled denial. "Taxis in London, hired cars everywhere else. I travel a lot," he apologised, looking gravely at Hester, asking her to appreciate the exaggerated importance of owning a car. She smiled back at him, wondering what he would do, what they would all do, if she stood up and screamed accusations to his face.

"I suppose you'll go by bus?" she enquired pleasantly.

"Yes," Maurice said. "If you'll excuse me for a moment I think I should telephone Ames at the garage—he lives above it. I'd better get him before he goes to bed. I'll ask him to pick up the car at my cottage tomorrow."

Hester considered the certainty that there was nothing to hold Maurice, not even a car, while she listened with an air of intelligent interest to Joe's instructions. "Ten-fifteen at the Fairway Arms by the airport. The plane leaves at ten-forty-five."

Harry followed Maurice out of the room, and she sat, watching her father's face. It wore his devout missionary aspect, as it usually did when he was thinking about money. She jumped up, saying something wild and inconsequential about Prudence, and ran out of the room.

In the dark hall she could barely see the two men.

"If there was a pawnshop in this delightful village," Harry said. "Hello, who's that?"

"It's only me. Hester."

"Oh, all right, Hester, don't go away. I was explaining to Maurice if there was a pawnshop in the village my worries would be over. I have a natural suspicion that he doesn't want to lend me fifteen pounds."

"Correct," Maurice said easily.

"So I was going to offer him this splendid gun as security." Harry felt around his pockets and dragged out the gun.

"Come into the light," Maurice said. They moved across the hall into the dining-room.

"It's a nice little gun. Loaded, too, if you're thinking of murder," Harry said cheerfully.

"But a gun is no use to me, Harry," Maurice protested. "Still… Do you need that fifteen pounds desperately?"

"You heard me. I want to fly with you tomorrow."

Maurice grinned across Harry at Hester. "I won't buy it. I'll lend you fifteen pounds, and keep the gun as security." He took the gun, weighing it in his hand, looking suddenly cautious and a little frightened, as though he wasn't used to guns. "I'm always afraid of those things," he explained. He put the gun in his pocket, took out his wallet, and counted out fifteen notes. He gave them to Harry.

"We don't need to sign any documents," he said. "Hester can be the witness. You can have the gun back if you ever have any money."

"I'll have the money all right," Harry said, speaking not to Maurice but to Hester.

Maurice smiled at them both indulgently and left them alone together, like a kindly uncle who sympathises with calf love.

"I'm flying tomorrow," Harry said with the satisfaction of someone who visualises a changing scene. "I'm coming back, Hester. I'm not going to miss the train this time. This is something I'm going through with, tonight, if I can. Everything's fixed. Cross my heart with diamonds, choke me with pearls, your worries are nearly over. Have you any food in the house? I've had practically nothing to eat all day." He put his arm round her; he seemed to think it was a natural gesture. She remembered the roses, and shook him off.

He followed her to the sitting-room.

"Simple Simon brings his penny," he said, bowing to Uncle Joe.

Joe made an involuntary movement with his hands, like a woodcutter trying to ward off a falling tree.

"Thank you, Harry," he said in a low voice. He took the money. "I should have known," he said humbly. "Old Joe is not so smart. Harry, I shall see you tomorrow between ten and half past at the Fairway Arms, Brickford. Until then we shall not meet."

"But tonight—I'll come back with you now and pack," Harry said, with an air of decision.

Moira began to laugh. "Yes, Harry, that would be best. You mustn't go without your shirt."

Prudence came in, talking fast, cutting through all the tensions like a pneumatic drill going through rock, preparing the way for the dynamite.

"Hello everyone the tennis dance was absolutely stinking you should have come Hester you could have mooned about under the trees holding hands I really think these old people are terrible I hope I don't behave that way in ten years' time. The people I danced with their conversation was absolutely asinine. But if you don't mind terribly Father I'm going to a dance in Campden next week the first time I was asked I was expected to go on a pillion. Can you imagine me on a pillion? But it's all right now I'm going with that ghastly Peters boy in his mother's car."

"But doesn't school start next week, Prudence?" Wade asked.

"Oh, that! The irregular verb and the war of the Austrian Succession? I'm not worried about that. Rosemary and I have decided not to wear our brains out when we're too young," Prudence said airily, but it was obvious she had been humiliated by the reference to school. "Talking about wearing things out, Maurice, I suppose you're aware that you've left the lights of your car blazing away?"

Maurice hurried out of the room.

"How odd of Maurice the motorist to have the wrong reflex action. Has he had a shock?" Harry asked, with his usual lazy insight. "I wonder if he'd like to give me a lift tomorrow? But he's turning his car in, isn't he? Do you suppose he's giving up that cottage, too, as from Saturday? On to fresh friends and problems new? How do I get to Brickford tomorrow?"

"There are two bus routes and a railway line," Joe said.

Harry felt in his pockets, brought out one coin and an empty cigarette packet. "I wonder if Maurice would like a game of Donegal Poker?"

Prudence was working her way towards the door, moving spasmodically, as though she was being washed out of the room by small waves. She hadn't yet solved the problem of how to say a collective Good night.

Moira looked at her, concentrating, trying to remember where she had last seen the blue-and-white dress.

"I do like your dress. And what a pretty brooch," she said.

Prudence, brought to a stop, flushed. "It's only Woolworth's."

"But it's lovely. Do let me see."

Prudence took off the brooch.

"Woolworth's!" Moira repeated.

Joe bent over her shoulder and peered at the brooch, like a man whose profession was always to know a bad thing when he saw it.

"Woolworth's is in the high-class trade now. These stones don't look like Woolworth's. They look like real paste to me."

Harry looked at the brooch. "Are you sure you haven't

been heaving a brick in Bond Street?" he asked. "Where did you get it, Prudence? Did Morgan give it to you?"

"I got it in Woolworth's," Prudence repeated angrily. "May I have it back? I'm going to have a glass of milk and go to bed." This time she swept out of the room like a surf-board rider.

Harry looked as though he would follow her, then stopped. "I'm not an expert," he said, irresolute. He sat down again, as Moira began to make the social noises that precede departure.

"Do stay," Hester said. "We were going to play some Bach on the gramophone, weren't we, Father?"

Wade didn't hear her. He was waiting. Then he heard Maurice's step, and his face began to relax. He listened in relief as Maurice came in, explaining that he had moved his car, in case Joe wanted to leave first.

"Bach," Hester repeated.

"Bach?" Joe asked. He shuddered. "I'm sorry, Hester, but I must make an early start tomorrow."

"So must I," said Maurice. "But it's hard to resist Bach. You'll let me stay for just half-an-hour?" he asked Hester. "Perhaps you'll post this for me, Joe, then I needn't go through the village?"

He held out an envelope.

Hester went to the door with Joe and Moira, looking wistfully at the letter.

"I am sorry I am too polite to stay. If you have trouble, Hester, don't be too polite to telephone me," Joe said.

She looked at him, rejecting him, because he was leaving when he must know there would be trouble. He was too shrewd not to see that her father and Maurice had been playing a money-game. Then another thought returned to her head.

"That letter. Uncle Joe, I'd like to know what that letter said."

He looked at her with the sympathy wiped off his face.

"It's not like you to suggest that, Hester. It wouldn't do, to interfere in business."

"Even if the business is a swindle?"

"It's still business, until the swindle is proved."

"Well, good night. Have a nice trip to Ireland," Hester said wearily.

Joe walked down the steps.

"Harry!" Moira called from the car.

Harry bolted out of the house. "I'm not staying the night with them," he said reassuringly. "Hester, you're going to marry me, aren't you?"

Hester turned to look at him. The light shone down on him from above, gilding his hair, shadowing his desperate face, darkening his cheekbones, hiding his eyes. He looked wild, exalted and afraid, like a young paratrooper who has jumped and doesn't know if his parachute will open.

"I'm not ashamed to beg. You'll marry me, won't you, Hester?" he repeated in a trembling voice.

"Harry!" Moira called again from the car. The muttering engine began to roar.

"Wait, I'm coming," Harry shouted. He caught her hand and held it for a second, then ran down the steps to the car. Hester stayed alone by the door, crushing down whatever emotions had arisen.

Thursday (10)

When Hester came into the house again, it was Maurice who decided to move in to the attack.

"Hester has been looking at me suspiciously all evening. What's wrong, Hester? Something about my tie? Straighten it for me."

He stood up, looking at her with the old, friendly, direct smile, so that her hands moved spontaneously towards his tie. Distrust was in the air all around him, but monstrous suspicions are difficult to voice to the person monstrously suspected.

"Shall we have this Bach now?" Maurice suggested. Hester, moving towards the gramophone, became faintly doubtful. If Maurice was what she supposed him to be, surely he would be in a hurry to leave with his gains, instead of behaving as though he was reluctant to leave at all?

"Bach," Wade repeated in a voice of exaggerated relief. "You don't want arias from one of those operas Hester's always raving about."

"I took Hester to an opera one night in London. It wasn't long after we first met. But I told you about that? Yes, of course I did." He looked at her with a reminiscent smile, a man who had thrown bread upon the waters and felt justified now in asking for its return. "Yes, Bach, please. There's no one like him for soothing the spirit," he said gravely.

Hester went to the record cupboard. "The Goldberg Variations?" She spoke in a tired, relaxed voice. It was impossible for her to believe that a man who liked Bach could be a criminal. Her father seemed to be equally deceived by this cultural fallacy. He smiled at Maurice in full companionship, then settled down to listen. All the doubt had fallen away from his face, and he looked like a man who had survived a period of religious persecution and emerged with his spirit strengthened.

Maurice sat with his eyes half-closed, and an expression on

his face that might have been noble content. The music had set its question and was developing its magnificent answers. Hester felt her mind rising in a spiral of hope. Then she thought of Harry, and slipped back into uncertainties. She looked at her father and Maurice, the one perhaps cheated and the other cheating, Maurice with her father's money in his pocket and his plans for escape already complete, and both of them sitting with their eyes half-shut, looking as though their only concern was the nobility of the music.

"You look like twin monuments to culture," she said, so quietly that they didn't hear. She was trying to say what Harry would have said. He would see it still as a comedy.

She jumped up, and turned off the gramophone.

"It's not a comedy," she said loudly.

Her father turned to her, and the room, bereft of music, seemed to sway under the weight of his alarm.

"I won't wait for the record to finish," Hester said. "I—I—Maurice, I want to say something…" Her voice trailed into a whisper and dissolved.

Maurice didn't look up. His eyelids dropped a fraction of an inch. He felt in his pocket, brought out his cigarette case, took one cigarette, and put the case back in his pocket, while Hester and her father watched, as though his actions were of tremendous importance, and that he might expose himself by his manner of holding a cigarette. Hester waited long enough to let him use his cigarette lighter, and then she tried to speak again, but her voice wouldn't come strongly enough.

"What is it, Hester?" her father demanded, in a threatening tone.

"How can I say it, Father? You must know what I want to say?"

"Hester, you're tired. I think you ought to go to bed."

She ignored him. "Maurice," she said in a frightened voice. "Maurice. I rang the Exchange. At least Harry did. You didn't make a call to London. You didn't telephone your broker."

Maurice's cigarette finished its interrupted journey to his mouth.

"So you trust me as little as that, Hester?" he asked.

"I—how could you do it, Maurice?" she said miserably.

"Do what, Hester?"

"Well, you didn't telephone your broker. You didn't. You know you didn't. But you came in here and said you did. And now you're going to Dublin tomorrow."

"Why shouldn't I go to Ireland for a couple of days?" he asked impatiently.

"Are you coming back, Maurice? Can you look at me and tell me you're coming back?" she demanded.

He looked at her steadily. "I am coming back, Hester," he said.

Her father turned on her angrily.

"Are you satisfied now, Hester? Have you put enough poison into our relations with Maurice?"

"Father, are you satisfied? He didn't telephone London."

Her father looked quickly at Maurice.

"It's perfectly simple," Maurice said in a tired voice. "My broker—Johnson he's called, doesn't happen to live in London. A lot of stockbrokers don't. You must know that. He lives in a village called Boston Tracy that happens to be in the area of this exchange. So there was no trunk call to record."

"You said you'd telephoned London," Hester repeated. "I know I'm saying all the wrong things. I know I'm not doing this the right way. But, Maurice, you did say you'd telephoned London."

"And I wrote to my broker as well. I gave the letter to Joe to post. I assure you everything is in good order," Maurice said patiently.

"You said you'd telephoned London. London. Why did you say London when you knew it wasn't true?"

"He'll be in London tomorrow morning, so it was true in a sense."

"Father, can't you see he's not telling the truth? And what about the Australian? The man who was in the garden last night, following you. He telephoned today to warn me against you."

"The Australian?" Maurice said. His eyes flickered down. "Hester, you're mad. I don't know what she's talking about." He appealed weakly to Wade. He stood up. "I think it's time for me to go home anyway."

"You're not going home, Maurice. Father, don't let him go home. Don't you believe me now? Father, why don't you go and phone this Johnson who lives in Boston Tracy? Just ring him and ask if he's a broker."

"I have the number in my notebook," Maurice said. He took the notebook from his pocket, and began to turn over the pages. "Here it is."

"Tell me the number, Maurice," Hester said.

Maurice closed the notebook.

"He'll have gone to bed. It's too late. It's nearly twelve," he said.

Wade turned very pale.

"Let me have the number, Maurice."

"He'll have gone to bed," Maurice repeated stubbornly.

"What am I to believe?" Wade shouted. "Hester, what am I to believe?"

Hester looked steadily at Maurice.

"Please, Maurice, give the money back while you can do it decently."

He looked at her father. "You're prepared to lose the chance of a fortune on the advice of an ignorant girl—you know what she wants, of course—she wants the money in her own hands so that she can spend it with her precious Harry."

Hester began to tremble. She stepped away from Maurice and leant back against the wall.

"You filthy swine!" Wade shouted. He jumped forward and caught Maurice by the throat and, groaning and shouting, shook him backwards and forwards.

"Father, don't. Father, let him go," Hester cried.

She ran towards them and pulled at her father's wrists, trying to make him loosen his grip. He flung Maurice away from him.

Hester saw Maurice staggering back, turning, and falling, his head directed with a dreadful precision towards the projecting corner of the fireside curb. Wade's arms were still extended, Hester still clutched in futility at his wrists, when they heard the head strike. There was no other sound, and for a moment, no other movement, then Hester dropped her hands with a sigh and turned to her father.

He was standing with his hands held before him, as though he was preparing to defend himself against some violence from the man on the floor.

"Have I killed him, Hester? Tell me, Hester."

"Quiet, Father," she said urgently. She was bending down towards the fallen man when she heard a step on the stairs.

She straightened, and moved quickly, like a criminal, to the door. Morgan, his face mushroom-pale, was creeping along the hall.

"What is it, Morgan?" she asked in a voice of excessive calm.

"I saw them from the window, Hester. I know I saw them. I'm not imagining it this time. They're round the house, Hester. They've been coming since we saw them on the road yesterday. I wonder—suppose I ring the police," he said hopelessly.

"The police! Oh, no, Morgan. These people aren't there. It's only that—that you're tired. Not the police, Morgan!"

He was bending slightly forward, listening with the concentration of a man who believes that an effort of will can intensify his hearing.

"What is it, Morgan? What are you listening to?" she asked in terror, thinking of her father.

"Can't you hear? There's someone in the garden. They're coming for me," he said, looking past her to the door. "I ought to ring the police—but if I ring them..." He looked at her pathetically, and stopped, waiting for the word of advice that would resolve all his problems.

"Morgan, it's so easy to imagine things. Please go up to bed. Please, Morgan. In the morning..."

"If only they'd wait till the morning. In the morning I'm going to Ireland. Only till the morning. Nine hours!" he said, shaking like a frightened traveller at the prospect of the long voyage through the night.

"Morgan, what are you afraid of?" She looked back desperately at the room she had just left. She took his arm and tried to lead him to the stairs. "If you go back to bed I'll give you a sleeping tablet."

"A sleeping tablet!" he said in consternation.

"Then ring the police," she said desperately.

"You don't mean that. You don't want me to ring the police. You know more than you pretend. You know what will happen if I ring the police, don't you? Have you been discussing me with Harry, Hester? Is that it?"

"I haven't discussed you with anyone."

"I know what I want. I want someone to search the garden. Perhaps you're right. They may not be there. So if someone— your father, Maurice—could go into the garden, into the wood, even as far as the chapel," he said, beginning to falter.

"My father. Maurice. I'll speak to them. Go to bed, Morgan. I'll ask them. But go to bed. You'll be safer upstairs."

"I'll be safer upstairs," he agreed, looking at the closed door of the sitting-room. "So I won't ring the police. But don't let anyone else in the house. You wouldn't, would you?"

"No, I wouldn't," she said. She waited until he had walked heavily up the stairs, holding the rail and staring at the dimly-lit landing above as though he was examining the night sky.

She went back to the sitting-room. Her father was leaning against the table, trying to light a cigarette. She watched the little match-flame circle jerkily around the end of the cigarette, then she turned again to Maurice.

She knelt beside him, opened his coat, put one hand against his chest, then touched the side of his head with reluctant fingers. Her father, waiting, struck another match, then held it to his cigarette and stared at Maurice's head through it, so that the patch of blood on the temple was lost in the little flame.

"I think it's only concussion," she said. Still kneeling, she turned and rested her head on the chair beside her. "Concussion, Father," she said into the cushion. "I—should we ring for the doctor? Or perhaps he's all right. I'll bathe his head."

She went to the kitchen for warm water, rehearsing the words. 'He stumbled and fell, Dr Nelson.' 'He tripped over the rug and fell quite suddenly, I can't understand how it happened.' Or: 'He and Father were having a discussion. Father pushed him in self-defence.' She wondered if there were marks on Maurice's throat.

She went back and bathed the thick blood from the side of his head, and cleaned the wound: it was only a small, triangular hole in the temple. She thought that he was beginning to stir, and then that he was dead. She stood up. There was a black pressure inside her brain, struggling to compress every part of her mind to the point of explosion. Sweat was being crushed out of her on to her forehead.

"Feel his heart, Father," she said. She dropped into a chair, and freed herself from the intolerable strain of balancing.

Her father was sitting with his face in his hands.

"Am I a murderer?" he asked in a whisper. "Is that what you're trying to tell me?"

"He's very still," she said, shaking.

"It would have been better to let him keep the money," Wade muttered.

"The money," Hester repeated in surprise. She had forgotten that money was part of the affair. "We must get a doctor, Father. But before we do, listen. If they don't know about the money, they won't know about anything. No one would suppose you'd any reason for quarrelling with Maurice."

"It was only a cheque. That was all. Only a cheque."

"I'll look in his pocket-book. A minute, perhaps half-a-minute, then we can telephone the doctor."

She knelt again, and put her hand slowly into the breast-pocket of his coat, trying to reach the pocket-book without letting her hand rest near his heart. She took out the pocket-book and looked quickly through it. Money, driving-licence, passport, cheque-book, stamps. She flicked the pound notes, shook the cheque-book, opened the pages of the passport. Her father's cheque was not in the pocket-book. She slipped the wallet back again.

"It must be in another pocket," she whispered.

She began to feel in all his pockets, turning out the contents wildly and ramming them back again: pencils, notebook, cigarette case, lighter, handkerchief, small change. To reach the pockets on his left side she had to turn him a little. She drew back sharply as she saw the rosebud she had put in his button-hole that morning; felt quickly in the pockets, and found keys, and the gun Harry had sold him. She dropped the gun, and stood up.

"Oh, I can't find it," she said. She wondered when she was going to scream.

"It's of no importance. I can stop the cheque," her father muttered.

"Oh, won't you understand. The cheque must have been in that letter he gave to Uncle Joe. You can't stop it if he's dead. They'd know at once you'd killed him for the money. Father, it's not the money. It's the cheque. It mustn't be found. Stopping it doesn't help. Can't you see?" Her voice was rising. All that she could see was her father accused of murder, perhaps sent to prison, perhaps… She tried to imagine herself disposing of the body, taking it to the woods. She shook her head wildly.

"Hester, if I've killed him I'll tell the truth."

"Father, leave this to me. I must find that cheque."

Her father looked up.

"There's someone outside," he said.

She ran to the door and switched off the light. She waited, hearing the step on the path outside, not hearing her own heart, but feeling it rise and fall like the water inside a sea-cave in rough weather.

When the door-bell rang she thought she would not answer it, but Morgan was upstairs, and might come down.

"Stay there, Father," she whispered back into the darkened room, and went along the hall to the door.

She turned the handle, and stood in the half-light, looking in terror at the hatless man on the doorstep, having only the impression of someone dark and aggressive.

"Good evening," he said. "I want to see Maurice Reid."

She recognised his voice at once. He was the man who had spoken to her in the garden.

"Maurice. He's not here. He's gone home," she said hopelessly.

"He's left his car," the man observed. "I want to see him. My name's Marryatt. I've spoken to you before."

"Yes."

"So you know I want to see him."

"You can't. He's gone home."

"Would you tell him I want to see him?"

Her father came along the hall towards them.

"What is it, Hester?" he asked in a flat voice.

"It's a man to see Maurice. I've told him Maurice has gone home," she warned him.

"Nothing could be clearer than that," the stranger said. "Do you mind if I come in?" He came in, quickly.

"I do mind. It's late. We were going to bed."

He looked past her at her father. "Excuse me, but I want to see Maurice Reid."

"You can't see him now," Wade said, uttering every word like a separate sigh. "The truth is—"

"No, it isn't. Go to bed, Father. Go to bed. Oh, go!" Hester cried.

"If I can't see him, I can't. But I want to warn you directly, you—Wade. I was talking to a friend of yours, to Harry. I told you on the telephone, Miss Wade. I don't think I made it strong enough. I don't want to stand back, now. I saw him in London by accident and I came down here to get my hands on him. He robbed and ruined my mother. I saw him in London and I followed him down here, for my own purposes. Now I thought I'd put it as straight as I can, in case—in case he gets anything out of you."

"Now you've told me. Thank you. Good night," Hester said.

"But I still want to speak to him. If you don't believe what I say, that's the end of that. But I'm going to see him now."

"Get out, please," Hester said.

"I know he's in the house. I'll wait."

"Make him go, Father."

"I won't do him any harm. I want to give him twelve hours to get out of the country. I want to tell him in front of you, so he can't go with your money. Not because I care about you and your money. I want to see there's no more easy money for him."

"Tell him the truth, Hester," Wade said. He groped for a chair, there was no chair, so he swayed against the wall. "Tell him the truth. Tell everyone the truth. There's nothing else."

"Maurice isn't here. I've told you," she cried.

"I've killed him," Wade muttered into his chest.

Hester put her hands against Marryatt's chest and tried to push him out of the door.

"I've killed him," Wade repeated loudly, like a deaf man struggling to hear his own words.

The silence gathered for a moment, then Marryatt sighed, and Hester spoke wildly, crying that her father was ill and Maurice had gone home.

Marryatt ignored her. "You're sure?" he asked Wade.

"I don't know. I think I've killed him. All I want to do now is ring the police and tell them." He still leant against the wall, not moving towards the telephone.

"Would you like me to see him? Before you ring the police?" Marryatt asked, looking at Hester.

"Do what you want," Hester said.

"Don't let yourself get worried," Marryatt advised. "Hell, there might be nothing at all to get worried about."

"He hit his head on the curb," Hester said. "He attacked Father. There was a struggle, an accident."

"No, Hester, I attacked him," her father said.

"It was an accident," Hester said.

"No, I was trying to hurt him."

"In there." Hester stopped at the door. She didn't want to go in the room again, but he held her by the arm and she went with him, keeping her eyes from the spot where Maurice lay.

The Australian looked down, bent over him, picked up one of the slack arms with his fingers on the wrist. He dropped the arm again.

"He's not dead," he said. The relief on his face struggled weakly and then succumbed to hatred. "You'd better tell your father."

He stood over Maurice, staring curiously at the square, solid face, with its wooden look of reliability now intensified by its absolute stillness. "In about ten minutes he'll be fit to rob the first orphan he meets. Do you know what I'd like to do with this imitation corpse? I'd like to stamp on his face until I'd changed its shape so much that women would run away from him, screaming. I don't want to see him dead. I want him alive, and suffering; working for a living until his back's bent; turned out of mean lodgings because he can't pay the bill; jailed for begging in the streets."

"No. No," Hester said. She turned and ran from the room, along the hall to where her father sat.

"He's not dead. He's all right, Father," she said, bending over him and kissing him. "Father, you've nothing to worry about now. It's all over."

She caught hold of him, trying to make him stand up. His hands were cold and trembling.

"Father, you've had a shock. You must go to bed now."

He shook his head.

"We can forget about it," she insisted.

"No, we can't. I'm glad, I'm thankful you and Prudence have been spared," he muttered.

"But it's finished. We've escaped. Maurice has escaped."

"I tried to kill him. It wasn't right," he mumbled, his voice trailing away and losing itself in a fog of bewilderment.

"You must go to bed. When he wakes up I'll send him away."

"I can't leave you with him alone. I tried to kill him."

"I shan't be alone. I'll get that Australian to stay."

"Hester, it wasn't right. I—I shouldn't escape. I should be punished for this."

She helped him to his feet and guided him up the stairs. The power to control the physical processes of movement was deserting him, he walked slowly, like a wounded soldier lost in enemy territory. He didn't speak while she took off his shoes and coat and laid him down on his bed. She put some blankets over him and then hurried downstairs again.

The Australian sat in a chair, smoking, his eyes on Maurice.

"What are you going to do with it?" he asked roughly. "You want me to stay?"

"Yes, but…"

"Well?"

"I can't, I just can't have anything to do with what you feel about him. I don't think it's right to hate anyone like that."

"Bravely spoken," he said contemptuously. "Have a cigarette."

"I don't want to stay in the room with you when you hate him like this."

"Should I go? Or would you like to leave me alone in the room with him? For God's sake don't begin to cry. I'm not trying to be rude," he added brusquely.

"You're horrible," she said. She sat down. Tears of exhaustion were running from her eyes: she couldn't stop them. "You're just eaten up with hatred and I thought Father had killed him."

"He's moving. Look at him. He's moving."

"And I had to go through his pockets when I thought he was dead."

"That's enough," he said angrily. "Have a drink. Do you keep drink in this house? Crusted port or Napoleon brandy or something elegant and English?"

"I don't want a drink."

"I do," he said. "All right, cry away. Cry as much as you like." He kept his eyes on Maurice.

"Life can't be the same, after this."

"Who wants life to be the same?" he asked. "I hate that man there." He jerked his head at Maurice. "But if he hadn't taken my mother's money I'd have lived a softer life: I wouldn't have been forced to turn out at sixteen and fight for a living."

She went on crying hopelessly.

"Why are women always so soft?" he demanded angrily.

"I'm not soft. It's just you have no imagination and no human feelings and I hate you."

"I thought English girls were quiet and reserved. I thought you wouldn't stay in the same room with anyone who hated anyone else. If you're going to hate me, you're building up a problem for yourself."

She put her head in her hands, trying to hide her tears.

"I apologise. I certainly don't know what I've done wrong, but I apologise. If you'd stop crying, we could talk like human beings," he said.

She didn't answer him.

"You look absolutely terrible when you cry. All women do," Marryatt said deliberately.

Maurice moved and groaned, and Hester stopped crying instantly.

"What are we to do? How can we explain to him?" she asked.

"Look, what's your name, Hester, get out of this apologetic attitude. It's that rat who's got to do the apologising." He walked across to Maurice, who was turning his head uneasily.

"Get up!" he said.

Maurice opened his eyes, stared at the face above him, and closed his eyes again.

"Get up!"

"Let me help you, Maurice," Hester said. She ran forward and put an arm under his head. "Are you all right, Maurice?" she asked anxiously.

"I—what—I don't know," he sighed.

"Help me to lift him. Quick!" she said in a peremptory voice to Marryatt. He jerked her out of the way, and dragged Maurice on to a chair.

"You can open your eyes," he said. "Time to wake up. You've been having a little instalment of what you're going to get. Life's turning against you, Maurice. You're moving into hard times. Don't look so frightened. I'm going to take you home now."

Maurice moaned. "My head."

"Shall I get a doctor?" Hester asked.

"He doesn't need a doctor. I'll take him home. You don't want him here, do you?"

"I can't move," Maurice groaned. "What happened?"

"Well, what do you think happened?" Marryatt asked.

"I don't know."

"Maybe you never will. When a man's been hit on the head, he sometimes forgets what happened before. Perhaps I hit you. Do you know? I might hit harder next time."

"Hester, I want to stay here," Maurice whispered.

Marryatt looked at her, and then back at Maurice. The gun she had taken from Maurice's pocket lay in the fireplace, she saw him bend and pick it up.

"Please, Hester," Maurice repeated.

"I'm taking you home."

"Hester, he's a murderer. He wants to kill me."

The Australian flicked Maurice on the cheek with the back of his hand. "Get moving!" he said.

"How dare you, how dare you hit him when he's like this. Of course you can stay, Maurice," Hester cried.

"I'm taking him home," the Australian said. "You needn't worry. All I want is a chance to moralise. I'm picking the habit up from you," he said insolently.

"Please go away."

"Not without him."

"You're not a civilised being."

"I give up," Marryatt said violently. "I give up the whole damned business. Keep your rotten little swindler. Bathe his head and stroke his hair and give him breakfast in bed. Let him fill his pockets with your father's money until the whole family's bankrupt. So long as you do it politely in the English manner, you'll be able to admire yourself at the end of it. I don't understand how your father forgot his social position long enough to let him knock the little rat down."

"It was because—because of something he said." Hester stopped, looking at Maurice, remembering, while both the men watched her. "If he's strong enough to move, I wish you'd take him home," she said to Marryatt. "You can't stay here," she said to Maurice. "You can't come here again."

"I'm not well, I want a doctor," Maurice said. His eyes were closed. He seemed to be making a brave effort to speak. "Sorry to be a nuisance," he said, whispering.

"You'd be wasting your time, seeing a doctor," Marryatt said. "He'd tell you to spend a couple of days in bed. But I'm telling you to get out of this country by tomorrow. The two things don't match."

"It's my head," Maurice explained. "If I could go to sleep now, if only I could go to sleep. I'm going to Ireland tomorrow, sleep..."

Hester looked at him uncertainly.

"You can sleep at home," Marryatt said quickly. "I'll take you there. I've a few things I'd like to say to you on the way. Now get going."

"Be quiet," Hester said furiously. "I won't have you in this house giving orders."

The Australian turned away from Maurice and looked at her. "Good night!" he shouted. "If you can look after yourself so well, get on with it!"

He went out of the room in a rush, and she waited until he had slammed the door. Then she turned to Maurice.

"You must leave early in the morning. I needn't see you. I don't want to see you again, ever."

She left him quickly, and went upstairs.

She stopped outside her father's room. She could hear no sound: she didn't want to disturb him, so she went on to her own room, and undressed, and lay down. The grinding anxieties that filled her mind destroyed all sense of time; she didn't know how much later it was when she heard the car. Perhaps Maurice was leaving? It was safe now, the Australian had gone away. Someone was moving in the house; it was easy to imagine these things. She listened in terror, but there was no one moving. It must be nearly dawn. If Maurice had escaped, there was still the question of the cheque. She should go down and ask him, but she had heard the car. A grey light was coming now, and the birds were singing hoarsely as though their voices were breaking. The stairs creaked again, it was cowardly not to get up, not to shout 'Who's there?' It might only be Morgan. She was sure that someone passed her door. It was nearly daylight, and then everything was black as she fell into sleep at last.

Friday (1)

Prudence woke at eight in the morning. She lay still for a few minutes, thinking of the tennis dance, and luxuriating in the memory of her partners, how some of them had been enthralled by her conversation, and how Peter, who was already up at Cambridge and very experienced, had asked her for a second dance. She remembered Neville, and his oafish looks of adoration, and began to giggle. Rosemary knew all about Neville; she must telephone Rosemary, or was it too early? She began to dress, but when she had washed and brushed her hair, life seemed too dreary to be endured. The truth was, she simply couldn't tango properly: Marion had noticed, even if Neville hadn't: Marion had looked at her in a very bitchy way, and said, "You are learning quickly, considering." Marion was coming to the dance next week. If she couldn't tango perfectly by next week she would die. She threw the brush on the floor, and looked in the mirror. Her frock was too short, good enough for the house, Hester would say, but it wasn't good enough for anything. If she bought some material she could make herself a new frock over the week-end and the family could starve. She remembered that Jackie was there to do the cooking; she was suddenly very hungry. She ran downstairs.

Jackie wasn't in the kitchen. There was no burnt toast, no strong tea. She went to the sitting-room, and looked in.

Jackie was standing in the middle of the room, holding a duster. His flowered shirt looked shockingly bright beneath his drawn, exhausted face. Two limp rosebuds sagged from his button-hole.

"Good morning, Jackie. Going gay—the roses, I mean."

Jackie's hand went up to the roses. "He—he put them there, last night."

"He?"

"Harry," Jackie muttered.

"You mean Mr Walters," Prudence said severely.

"I've always been fond of flowers. I'll get the breakfast, Miss."

Prudence suddenly remembered. "Morgan's flying to Ireland today. I'd better get him up."

She went back upstairs and knocked on Morgan's door.

"Are you going to have some breakfast before you go, Morgan?" she called.

She opened the door cautiously. The room was heavy with cigarette smoke. Morgan sat in the middle of it, dressed in his usual dark clothes, holding his briefcase.

She looked at his face, and was frightened by the despair she saw on it. She took refuge in a breezy refusal to see that anything was wrong.

"Is that all you're taking?" she asked, indicating the briefcase.

He shook his head. "Nothing more. Everything's gone. Two years and two months. The end's worse than the beginning. The end's the worst. Do you think I can go, Prudence? Will they stop me? Brickford's a long way. Ten-forty-five the plane goes. It's only half past eight. Prudence, when they say it, don't believe them." He jumped up, and stood staring into her face.

"Don't believe them. I'm telling you."

"Morgan, have some breakfast," she said in a frightened voice.

"I'm going. The plane's my only chance."

He pushed past her. She heard him running down the stairs. She was so glad that he had gone that she forgot she couldn't tango, although the memory soon returned, so that she was curt and abstracted all through breakfast, while she waited for an opportunity to ask Hester for a secret lesson. Hester seemed scarcely aware of her presence, and spoke only once throughout the meal.

"You're still wearing the roses in your button-hole, Jackie. Didn't you go to bed last night?"

"Slept better'n I've ever done on Brighton beach," Jackie assured her.

When he had left the room Hester stood up.

"How do you feel about dancing?" Prudence asked quickly.

"Just what I feel about singing, laughter, and love," Hester said.

"Are you quoting someone?" Prudence asked suspiciously. "I mean someone like Harry?"

Hester looked at her watch. "He may be in Brickford now. In just over an hour he'll be in the plane for Ireland. I don't suppose he'll ever come back," she said in a low voice that acknowledged the humiliation of being deserted. "Prudence, don't worry me today. I must go to Father. He's not well."

Prudence was left alone to contemplate the endless horrors of a day in which no one would help her to tango.

Friday (2)

At eleven o'clock Prudence was kneeling on a green sward of cotton, looking hopelessly at the instructions which were supposed to map her course around the strange peninsulas of the human form.

"Bring Fold to meet perforations at F, gathering lower back to meet notches. Leave open at G," she read in despair. "Who's that? Oh, Jackie. There's no G, and I've lost all the notches. Attach collar to waist? It can't mean anything."

"It's eleven o'clock, Miss. The plane will have gone."

"The plane? To Ireland, you mean. I wish I'd gone too. I've just had about enough of dress-making. But I don't want to go to Ireland. I'd like to go to Italy, or Spain. Somewhere hot, some country where people had feelings, and did things, and weren't so dull as they are here. I go back to school in ten days, Jackie. Oh, it's going to be so boring. What would you really like to be, Jackie, if you had the chance? I'm just going to go ahead and cut this, even if it's all wrong."

"I always wanted to be in a dance band," Jackie said dreamily.

Prudence slashed at the material. "Can you play anything, Jackie?"

"No, Miss, I never had the chance."

Prudence stood up, looking in amazement at what she had cut out.

"They're flying now. I wouldn't care if they stayed in Ireland for ever. Except Harry. Who's quite funny sometimes."

Jackie pulled the roses out of his shirt and dropped them in the wastepaper basket.

"Salmon for lunch, Miss?" he said, beginning to back out of the room. "You could have it straight from the tin, and no cooking."

"Can you tango, Jackie?" she called after him. He didn't hear. "Well, it was only a policy of desperation," she muttered, kneeling down again with the scissors.

Quarter of an hour later she looked out of the window. Jackie, wearing his yellow pullover, now, was hurrying through the garden. He was carrying a bulging brown paper shopping bag by its string handle. Prudence assumed he was going to the village to buy some food for lunch. She wondered where he had found the money.

When she went into the kitchen, the housekeeping money, a meagre enough remnant, was intact. Underneath the opened tin of salmon was a sheet of paper, stained with the dismal grey oil of the dark, repellent fish.

"Dear Miss," it said.

"I have gone to see my Mother in Hospital. (Being visiting Day) Love Jackie."

Jackie didn't come back. Hester and Prudence ate the tinned salmon alone. Later, when they heard the news about the aeroplane, they had no thoughts to spare for Jackie, or to wonder why he had gone away.

Explanation (1)

"That's all," Hester said. "It's the whole story. So you see…"

"What do I see?" Inspector Lewis demanded, not yet aware how much he ought to see.

"I don't know what you see. But it's the whole story," Hester repeated. "Isn't it, Father?"

He looked at her with a stricken smile, guilty as a man who has survived a disaster but has seen his friends drown. She crossed the room quickly and sat on the arm of his chair.

"Father, we've told all the truth. There's nothing more we can do now."

"You can answer a few questions, Miss Wade," Inspector Lewis said. "There's some information I'd like. About Maurice Reid, for instance. Now, Mr Wade. You gave him a cheque. Was it a sizeable cheque?"

"It was for all I've got. No, that's not quite true. I have a very small income from a trust fund."

"The amount of the cheque?"

"It was for nine thousand, five hundred."

"You've stopped this cheque, of course?"

Wade squirmed. "Actually—I—I was going to stop it, that Friday. Then we had the news. Then, then I thought everything was over. So—so I haven't."

"But if he sent it direct to his bank, it would form part of his estate. It wouldn't revert to you."

"Stop it now, by wire, Father," Hester said.

He nodded.

"I wonder why you didn't stop it before? Was it because you thought it would still draw attention to your quarrel?"

"Don't say a word more. Don't say a word until you get a lawyer," Moira advised sharply.

Inspector Lewis hesitated. "Do you want a lawyer to be present, Mr Wade?" he asked formally.

"No. I've nothing to say except what is true. I have no complaint, if I'm judged on the truth."

"I'm not here to judge you, Mr Wade. I'm here to try, with your help, to arrive at the truth. If you wish, I'll wait until you have a lawyer to advise you. Also, if you prefer it, I'll continue this interview privately."

"No, let's continue as we are," Wade said, shivering, like a penitent who has chosen his own punishment.

"Then we'll return to Maurice Reid. He decided to fly to Ireland either because he had been assaulted by you, Mr Marryatt, and feared another attack; or because he had your cheque in his pocket, Mr Wade. It might, you know, seem to some people, although not necessarily to me, that it was in both your interests to get rid of him. If it can be proved that he is the man who didn't fly, I should very much like to know where he is now." He turned on Marryatt. "The gun," he demanded in his most formidable voice. "Where is the gun that Harry sold to Maurice Reid?"

"That's just the kind of question they're always asking at school," Prudence said sympathetically.

"School?" Lewis said incredulously.

"Miss Barker-Smith, she teaches us English, she's always appealing to our honour to make us tell the truth. Then if we're simple enough to give it to her, she flies at us with lines and detentions. Now we've told you the truth, I can see it's Dartmoor for us."

"Prudence!" Hester warned faintly.

Lewis turned away.

"The gun?" he repeated.

Marryatt looked more arrogant than ever. "I couldn't tell you. It's not my habit to carry a gun. When I came in, this gun was lying on the fireplace. I picked it up. I might have had the idea of putting it out of Maurice's reach, though I don't believe he'd ever have had the guts to use a gun. I'm not sure what I did with it, then. I put it down somewhere. On that table, I think."

Sergeant Young walked across to the table where the drooping roses stood in the blue vase. He touched them reflectively, listening still to the questions and answers.

"It wasn't here in the morning when you came in this room?" Lewis asked Prudence, speaking to her coldly, like an acknowledged enemy.

"No. Jackie was in here first, you know."

"Mr Marryatt, why did you come to this house so late on Thursday night?"

"I didn't come late. I came early, waiting for him. After I left him on the road, I thought a lot about what was the right thing to do. I mean my idea of what was right. It might not be yours," he added indifferently. "I'd hit him once or twice. It gave me no satisfaction, or not much. I didn't want to go on with it. Too much like pulping up a frog by hand. But I wasn't letting him off. I tell you, I saw him on that train in London by chance, and I thanked God for the chance. I hated him. I've often dreamt of killing him. That's why I followed him down here. You can use the information just as you like. I wouldn't be giving it to you if I'd killed him."

"So you thought of what was right—and you decided?"

"I decided I'd run him out of the country, without the Wades' money to help him. I was waiting to get hold of him, and—and put my point. Then Miss Wade there got me kind of annoyed. I walked out of the house and went back to The Running Fox. I didn't try to get in quietly. I shouted to the landlord to open up. You think that's what I'd have done if I'd just killed a man?" He turned on Hester, challenging her to answer.

Moira jumped up. "Oh, do get a lawyer," she said impatiently.

"You're putting it too directly again, Mr Marryatt. No one has accused you of anything," Inspector Lewis said.

"That's not the way it sounded to me," Marryatt said angrily.

"You're quite certain you left the gun in this room?"

Moira arranged her hair with an absent hand, while she studied Marryatt intently. "Don't answer that," she advised. "If you're not careful they'll be saying you made that noise at The Running Fox, just for an alibi. They'll be accusing you of coming out again quietly, a little later, of meeting Maurice, when you were supposed to be in bed."

"Thanks," Marryatt said. "I'll remember you tried to help me, when I'm choosing my last breakfast. Have you got any little word of encouragement, Miss Wade?"

He turned his angry glance on her. It was as though he stood alone, hating everyone in the room, and caring nothing for any of them.

"Yes. I have something to say. I don't know what all this talk of murder is about. I thought all we were trying to do was find out who didn't fly on that plane. If it's to be more than that, why shouldn't you suspect me? I'd as much cause to kill Maurice."

Sergeant Young turned away from the table and the roses.

"If you'll excuse me, sir," he said apologetically.

"Yes, Sergeant Young?" Lewis asked, not taking his eyes from Marryatt.

"There are only sixteen roses here, sir."

"Roses?" Lewis repeated in amazement.

"Why is it all Maurice? What about Morgan?" Hester demanded. "He was the kind of man who might hide instead of flying."

Moira shook a smile on to her face.

"What about Harry, while you're about it? He was a man who never finished what he'd intended to do. He said so himself," she said, smiling in a kind of triumph at Hester.

"Any minute, now, Mrs Ferguson, I'll tell you what you should do," Marryatt said. "Maybe you're not feeling too good yourself. But lay off other people. And I'll tell you something while I'm about it, Mr Inspector Lewis. Leave the Wades out of this. I saw him, Wade, crazy to ring the police and give himself up when he hadn't even killed the man. As for Miss Wade, she wouldn't have the heart to throw a stone at a rabbit. Another thing. What about giving us a bit of information? You must know something?"

"You're not on trial, Mr Marryatt. I'm not obliged to produce any evidence."

"Too right I'm not on trial. So you answer me just one question, not like a policeman, just like a man. You've been to that bar in Brickford, where they met. You've been to the airport. You've heard something. Are you telling me not one of these men has been identified? No one heard one of them call the other by name? I don't believe it."

"You'll have to believe it. Some of their conversation was overheard. One of them did call another by his name. But the man who heard isn't willing to swear to anything, except the name began with M. It might have been Maurice, it might have been Morgan, it might have been Montmorency, for all we can get out of the witness. At this point, he simply doesn't know. Being a numerologist, he observed it was the thirteenth letter of the alphabet, and then he simply turned his thoughts away. So we know that either Morgan or Maurice was at Brickford, and presumably went on the plane. But that's nothing. We know one of them went on the plane anyway. As only one man didn't fly, the other three did."

"I don't believe that's all," Marryatt said violently. "They were in a bar. What did they drink?"

"Give me those notes, Sergeant Young. No, I don't want them all, complete with the three-thirty at Lingfield. I want the extracts."

Sergeant Young left the roses with a sigh, opened his coat dreamily, and selected a few pages of typescript from his inside pocket. He glanced absently through the pages, stopped for a second to read, then walked across the room, still reading.

Lewis snatched the papers from him.

"They drank whisky. Three. Twice."

"Were they all whisky drinkers? I had some drinks with Harry. He drank beer," Marryatt said.

Moira shook herself with an angry tremble, like an old woman remembering an insult. "Oh, come," she said. "Harry would drink anything he could get free."

"But he liked beer?"

"I don't think that's in any way conclusive," Lewis said regretfully. "The others drank whisky on occasion, I suppose."

"Joe did, sometimes," Moira said. "I don't propose to answer any more questions about him," she added quickly.

"I've known Maurice to drink whisky," Wade said.

"And you should just see the bottles in Morgan's wardrobe," Prudence said. "So we still don't know what happened to Maurice." She turned her frank unembarrassed stare on Marryatt.

"Oh, yes, we do," Sergeant Young said reproachfully. "We know for a fact Maurice Reid flew in that plane."

"You know what?" Lewis asked, turning on him massively. "You know it for a fact, Sergeant Young? Tell me how you arrive at this fact?"

"You remember the evidence of this numerologist, the gardener, Benson, isn't it? You have the notes, sir. Benson said he saw one of our three men offer the others cigarettes out of his case. Here, sir. 'One of them had some cigarettes and as I walked over with the drinks he offered cigarettes to the others.' He was then asked if it was a packet or a case. 'Now you mention it, I'm sure it was a case. Yes, I'd take my oath it was a case… It was a long silver case. He opened it at both of them, and one of them took a cigarette. Or did they both— now, I can't remember. Anyway, someone lit the two cigarettes with a lighter. I remember it was a lighter, but I don't know if it was the first man who used it. One man didn't smoke. Now, it's queer I noticed that, except I'm trying to give up smoking myself, so I saw that this man didn't smoke.'"

Sergeant Young had been reading from the typed pages. Now he stopped, and looked round the room enquiringly.

"Harry smoked. He didn't have a case. Morgan didn't have a case? I thought not. But Maurice Reid did? Was it a long silver case?"

"Yes. I remember it. And Uncle Joe didn't smoke at all."

"Now just wait a minute. Not too fast," Moira said huskily, and everyone turned to look at her. "Joe didn't smoke cigarettes, but he often carried them to offer to other people.

He carried them in a silver cigarette case, and I'm quite sure he wouldn't go to Ireland without that case. So you see, all you've proved is—nothing."

"Why don't you keep quiet till you get that lawyer to think for you?" Marryatt asked unpleasantly. "It was a good try, anyway, Sergeant. Let's have some more."

Inspector Lewis made an impatient movement, and everyone was silent. He sat still for more than a minute, then stretched out his hand and took the pages from Sergeant Young. He read slowly, while they all watched him. Moira made an effort to speak, but Prudence scowled at her so fiercely that she gave up. Lewis began to smile. He looked as though he was apart from them all, enjoying some unique experience, like listening to a crystal set with the only available earphones.

"Sergeant Young was absolutely right," he said benevolently. "Maurice Reid flew on that aeroplane. There really is no doubt at all. This passage, Sergeant." He handed the pages to the sergeant, who read them in a bemused manner.

"Yes, I see," he said flatly.

Lewis smiled delightedly. "Are you sure you do, Sergeant? Read the passage aloud. Let them all see."

"'There was a word about horses and Ireland, but next thing it was accidents and Australia, or it might have been South Africa, then I lost interest.' When asked what they said about horses: 'It was only the Grand National.' When asked about Australia: 'Nothing about Australia. It might have been South Africa. It was a place like that. No it wasn't New Zealand. It was South Africa or Australia. I'll swear to one of them. I've a cousin in one and an uncle in the other, so I'm sure of my facts... One of them says to another that reminds me about something that happened to me once. I had a premonition, he says, or words to that effect, when I was in Australia, or South Africa, and you haven't been there, have you, he says to that other, crushing the opposition. No, says the other, But I have, says the third man, interrupting, Isn't it time we left?'"

Sergeant Young put the paper down slowly, and stopped to consider what he had been reading. "I'll have to look at my notes," he said doubtfully. "No I won't. I remember. It's all there. Oh, sir, that's a very nice piece of reasoning."

"I'm not sure I understand," Hester said slowly.

"I do. I do!" Prudence cried, "No, wait. I wish I had a pencil."

"I don't think I know all the facts," Marryatt said. "Harry had been in Australia. Had he been in South Africa? No?"

"No, he hadn't," Hester said. "Maurice had been in both. Morgan—"

"You told us," Inspector Lewis said happily. "You told us all of them. Morgan had been in South Africa, but not Australia. Maurice Reid had been in both. And Mr Ferguson—"

"I've told you already. Joe had never been in that part of the world," Moira admitted cautiously.

"So Maurice was one of the three men there, one of the three men on the aeroplane. I follow," Marryatt said. "So that's over." He didn't specify what he meant. He spoke in a voice that was hard and sharp, like an iron fence erected quickly to keep other people out of his private world. "I'll be getting along, then. I think I'd like some fresh air."

"No, stay," the inspector said. "We haven't finished, have we, Mr Wade?"

Wade turned his handsome, muddled face to the inspector. "Poor Maurice," he said, sighing.

"But I don't understand," Hester said. "Do you, Father?"

"I—actually, I haven't been following at all. I see something's there, but I can't see how it proves anything. Poor Maurice!"

"I'll explain," Inspector Lewis said, very glad of the opportunity. "Listen. Harry had been in Australia, but not South Africa. Morgan was the reverse. He'd been in South Africa, but not Australia. Mr Ferguson had been in neither. Maurice Reid had been in both. Now what's the evidence? One of the three men in the Fairway Arms, and these three were certainly the three who flew in the plane, one of them made a remark that showed he had been in South Africa or Australia. The second man hadn't been there. The third man stated he had been in the country referred to. Now, as we couldn't get the landlord to be more explicit, we can't know who made the remark, or even who answered it, but we can prove Maurice Reid was present."

"Please wait. Oh, if only I'd had a pencil, I'd have seen it first," Prudence said.

"One of the four men who were supposed to have travelled in the plane must have made the initial remark," Lewis continued implacably. "Joseph Ferguson had been in neither country, so he can be excluded. Any of the other three could have said it. If Harry Walters made the initial remark, saying, for instance, 'It happened when I was in Australia, have you been there?' only Maurice Reid could have said, 'Yes, I have.' So if Harry made the remark, Maurice Reid was present. If Morgan Price said: 'It happened to me in South Africa, have you been there?' only Maurice Reid could have said, 'Yes, I have.' And if Maurice made the initial remark, either Harry or Morgan could say, 'Yes, I've been there!'"

"I see. Don't tell me. I've got it," Prudence cried. "Maurice has to be there, in that Brickford pub I mean, every time.

Because Uncle Joe didn't say it, and if Harry said it Maurice was there, and if Morgan said it, Maurice was there, and if Maurice said it, he was there too. But are you sure the three men in the Brickford pub were the three men on the plane?"

"They were waiting in the Fairway Arms, together, three of them. When they got to the plane they said they'd been waiting for someone who hadn't turned up. It's a certainty."

"Oh, I'm sorry about Maurice," Hester said miserably. Marryatt stared at her, then jabbed his cigarette in the ashtray, and pressed on it until it disintegrated.

"Yes, Maurice," Prudence agreed, and dismissed the thought quickly. "I think it's terribly clever of you, Inspector Lewis. But it doesn't prove anything more, does it? I mean it shows Maurice was on the plane, but not who was off it."

Hester looked up. "Don't enjoy yourself so visibly, Prudence," she muttered.

Inspector Lewis was examining the typescript again. "I think we can work out the rest now, don't you, Sergeant Young?"

"Yes, sir."

"But first of all I need some more help from all of you. Which of these four men was interested in fishing?"

"Fishing?" Moira said. "Certainly not Joe."

"Not Harry," Hester said quickly. "He—he didn't like anything like that. I'm sure he'd never fished in all his life—not his adult life, anyway. Maurice? I'm certain I once heard him say he hadn't fished since he was a boy. Morgan—I can't be so definite about Morgan, but he wasn't the kind of man you could imagine with a fishing rod."

Lewis scowled. "But two of these men were enthusiasts!"

"But they weren't," Prudence protested. "They just simply weren't."

Lewis looked at the typescript again. "I'm exaggerating when I say enthusiasts. One of them said he'd satisfied his curiosity and he didn't like it, and another said he hadn't had an opportunity until the beginning of last season. When's the close season for fishing, Sergeant Young?"

"Well, sir, it depends on the fish, and the place. If it's coarse fishing, it's more or less in the spring, ending about the middle of June. Salmon close a bit earlier, owing to their habits. About December, say, and open again—is it March?"

"So two of these men had gone fishing, one of them at the beginning of Spring or Summer. I ask you all to think again."

They thought again, but none of them could produce a word of evidence about fishing.

Explanation (2)

Prudence was in the kitchen, making tea and cutting sandwiches, when Marryatt walked in. He looked disparagingly at the dishes that lay in the sink like an irregular monument.

"You haven't been doing much dish-washing lately, have you?"

"And you haven't been knocking on many doors, have you?" Prudence retorted. "If you'd like the information, a thing that people simply can't stand is other people to come in their kitchens to see if the bottoms of their saucepans are shining like a domestic science department."

Marryatt took off his coat. "I'll wash the dishes for you," he said. "I suppose you haven't had much time."

"We've been living on fried eggs and tea since Friday," Prudence said. "And every time I go near the sink I begin to cry. I'm getting over that, now. I can't spend my whole life crying for people who've been killed. I suppose I'm callous," she added with a certain satisfaction, her mind already racing ahead to the time when she would move, hard-hearted, disdainful, mysterious, through a wondering world.

"The kettle's boiling. Don't worry about the policemen. They've gone to The Running Fox for a meal, in their prim way, afraid of being corrupted by a sandwich. Prudence—"

"You wouldn't like to call me Miss Wade?" Prudence asked.

"No, I wouldn't. You can call me Tom. Prudence, you're getting over this. What about Hester?"

"You'd better ask her yourself. Of course, she did rather like Harry," Prudence said cautiously.

"She was going to marry him? Do you have something for drying dishes?"

"There's a clean tea towel somewhere. Oh, I'm sorry, it has a hole in it. She wasn't going to marry him. It's the kind of news people do tell their sisters. But she did in a way rather like him. Do you want cheese or some cardboard out of a tin on your sandwiches?"

"Cheese. Harry told me he was going to marry her."

"Harry was always making plans that didn't come off," Prudence said scornfully. "He didn't have real purpose in life. Only poetry, and he didn't work at that. He told me once he didn't want to be one of those people who choose the longest road they can find and sweat along it at top speed with their graves travelling beside them on oiled wheels. He said the brow was for laurel wreaths, not sweat."

"But Hester liked him?" Marryatt put the last of the cups carefully on the table.

Prudence sighed. "I know absolutely what you're getting at. Don't be so—so oblique. If Hester's given half a chance she'll spend the rest of her life with his memory, bringing out hand-printed editions of his poems. People do seem to get a bit soppy when they're twenty. But I shan't. Anyway, she hasn't made up her mind. She thinks he might be alive, she thinks he might be the man who didn't fly."

Marryatt's brows came down. He had features that lent themselves easily to the expression of anger. "If she finds that he did fly? That he's dead? She wouldn't enjoy having that proved? Whether she enjoys it or not, she's going to get it. I'm not going to have the shadow of Harry, neither dead nor alive, hanging around for the rest of my life."

Prudence's face darkened. "Kill him if you like, if it makes you feel happier. I'd sooner he was alive. I dare say I'm being sentimental," she added faintly.

"Prudence, put down that tray. You're going to help me. You know that Harry was after Morgan. He was searching for something he believed Morgan was hiding. He was doing it inefficiently and recklessly—like a boy who's looking for gulls' eggs only because he enjoys climbing a cliff," he said, going back to his own experience for the metaphor. "Now, when Jackie came here, what did Morgan do? He shut himself up in his room and didn't come down to meals. Jackie was a crook. Don't you think there's a chance Morgan was afraid of being recognised by Jackie—because he was a crook himself?"

"I think Morgan was just mad," Prudence protested.

"Keep to the point. Morgan was hiding something. Harry was looking for it. For all I know, Jackie was looking for it too. If Morgan went to Ireland, Harry went too, because he was trailing Morgan."

"They were all mad," Prudence suggested.

"People who hide something aren't necessarily mad. I'm not calling you mad, for instance," Marryatt said carefully.

Prudence's pink and brown face became entirely pink.

"You've been pretty vague about that brooch, haven't you? Jackie went away, and the brooch isn't mentioned any more."

Prudence's face was so red now that it seemed possible she might cry. "It isn't your business. None of it's your business. You're here only because of Maurice. We know what happened to Maurice, so now you can go away. Hester hates you anyway, and so do I, and if you won't go out of the kitchen I will."

She began to walk to the door. He caught her roughly by the arm and swung her round. She had no brothers: she wasn't used to physical violence: she wondered for a moment if she could kill him.

"You still have the brooch, haven't you?"

"Perhaps," she said. "Let go my arm."

He let her go. "Now fetch the brooch."

"I'm not sure if I can find it," she muttered, watching his face.

"You'd better find it. The police will want to see it. I don't know why you kept it. That's not my business. Perhaps you just wanted an expensive-looking brooch."

"It's not true. It's simply not true. I was going to give it back, then Jackie went away and everything happened and I forgot."

"Now you've remembered. Go and get it." He was quite offensively uninterested in her explanations. He treated her simply as a nonentity with an interesting brooch. "You'll have to get it sooner or later. The police will make you."

"The police would never bully me like this," she said angrily. "They have better manners. I'll go and look for the brooch. If I throw it out of the window, that's my business."

"And if the police throw you in Borstal or approved school that's your business too. Come on. So far as I'm concerned, you forgot about the brooch and you've just remembered it."

Prudence went sullenly from the room.

Marryatt picked up the tray and took it to the sitting-room, where Hester and her father sat in the kind of exhausted silence that might overtake people who have drifted too long alone, helpless, in a lifeboat in an empty ocean.

He poured the tea and offered it to both of them. Wade tasted it, and put the cup down heavily.

"It's cold," he said, with the painful resignation of a man almost totally inured to misfortune.

Explanation (3)

Inspector Lewis and Sergeant Young looked particularly out of place on the chintz sofa where they now sat side by side, menacing but professionally uncomfortable, like bailiffs.

"This fishing," Lewis said. "Everything else is fixed now, it's only the fishing. We've worked out the rest, you see, we'll get to that in a minute, but if we can't get something out of the fishing, we can't see the end of this at all. If one of those bus conductors, one of those railwaymen, would stop telling us it's August and the place is full of strangers and how can they be expected etcetera, we might get somewhere, but it's like asking a slot machine to identify a penny. So it's back to the fishing. Now this old man Smith who was drinking bitter with his mind on the stars and talking about how they might have been fishing in Ceylon or they might not, I told you he kept bringing astrology into it. We haven't any inside knowledge to explain this. You people, who knew all the men well, absolutely must try again. Did you ever hear any of those men who were to fly to Dublin discuss astrology?"

Hester looked at her father hopelessly, and shook her head. She was about to speak, when suddenly an expression of the deepest concentration, followed almost instantly by doubt and irresolution, crossed her face. She was like a novice playing chess, who sees a good move and realises almost at once that it may be a bad one.

"I had an idea," she said weakly, "then it went away. But I have thought of something. Wherever this fishing happened, if it took place last season, it can't have been in Ceylon. I knew that was ridiculous. Morgan, Maurice, Uncle Joe—none of them has been out of England for at least a year. And I don't believe people go fishing in Ceylon anyway."

"Except the people who have to earn their living by it," Marryatt said.

Wade looked up, and smiled faintly at his daughter.

"Don't forget the pearl-fishers," he said. "Bizet." He relapsed into his private agony.

"Bizet?" Lewis turned on Sergeant Young. "Have you ever heard of Bizet, Sergeant?"

"Sir, he wrote *Carmen*. Tor—eee—a—dor. You know. And an opera called *The Pearl-Fishers*. I haven't heard it."

"Yes," Hester said. "That's it. Oh, I nearly had it before, when you were talking about astrology. It has to be *The Pearl-Fishers*. The hero's called Nadir, that's your astrological term, and he falls in love with a priestess and goes away for five years and comes back and he finds she saved his life when she was a child—or was that his friend? Yes, it must have been. The friend is the chief and the other two are going to be burnt and the friend lets them escape and is burnt on the pyre instead. Why, we have some records here, if you want."

Lewis shook his head. "It sounds very confused," he said guardedly. "Opera is not my subject."

"When did you see this opera?" Sergeant Young asked quickly.

"I think it was Sadler's Wells. Covent Garden has never done it, or not for a long time. I went with—with Maurice."

"At the beginning of last season?" Young asked, knowing the answer.

"Yes. A lot of people went, because it was the first chance they'd had to hear it. Maurice liked it more than I did."

"Ceylon?" Lewis said impatiently. "Where does Ceylon come in?"

"It's set in Ceylon."

"And Maurice Reid liked it. So he was the man who said it had its merits."

"Not necessarily," Marryatt interjected. "What if the others had seen it too?"

"Morgan was tone deaf," Prudence said. "He wouldn't go to opera."

"I don't think Harry liked opera. But he couldn't have gone anyway. He was in Australia when it was put on. I know he only came back four months ago. So—" She looked at Moira and checked herself quickly. "I'm sorry, I'm terribly sorry," she said in a stricken voice.

Moira stood up. "Yes, Joe and I saw it together," she said. "Only he could have discussed it with Maurice. You're right, all of you. You've proved what you set out to prove. Joe is dead. It makes no difference to me," she said in a shuddering voice. "I knew it. He'd never hide himself from me." Her expensive pink-and-white complexion remained inexorably pink-and-white. She walked to the door, holding her hands a little before her, as though she was groping her way through the darkness.

Hester ran forward and touched her gently on the arm.

"Moira, shall I go home with you?"

Moira looked rigidly ahead. "Why should you? We never

liked each other. You've been trying to arrive at the truth: that's part of it."

Marryatt stood up. "If you've a car outside, I'll drive you home," he said impersonally. "Otherwise, we'll walk. Have you a car here?"

"Yes."

"Come on, then."

When they had left the room Hester sat, holding on to the sides of the chair as though she was afraid of being thrown out of it.

"Please, Miss Wade..." she heard the inspector say, and from far away her father's voice interrupted: "Let her alone. Don't speak to her now. I insist..."

Her head was churning into a wild clarity. She tried to think of Uncle Joe, but all she saw was Harry, standing by the door, asking her to marry him, then, not waiting for an answer, running to get in the Fergusons' car. He could have come back; instead he had remained with them for hours, cards in his hand and money on the table; innocently cunning as he always was when he gambled; reckless, gay, oblivious of her existence. That was Harry; then, now, and for ever.

"He's dead," she said weakly, struggling back into con-sciousness of the room, as though she was coming out of an anaesthetic.

Inspector Lewis made preparatory noises with his throat. "Are you feeling all right, Miss Wade?"

"Yes." She had to be all right, she had to be excessively normal; humiliation is an emotion that demands its own interment.

"Astrology isn't one of my subjects. I didn't see..."

"Nadir," she said. "That was the astrological term your witness couldn't remember. At least it means something in astronomy, so I suppose it does in astrology. It's the opposite to the zenith, I think. It also means a time of depression, like this, I suppose," she said sadly. "Nadir is the name of the hero in *The Pearl-Fishers*, but he escaped."

Lewis glanced again at his notes. "Time of depression. Yes, I see. It fits. And you're all reasonably satisfied that only Maurice Reid and Joseph Ferguson could have seen this opera—that they are the only two of these four men who could have discussed it?"

"Yes, we're satisfied," Wade said.

"Then I think there's no doubt that Ferguson was on that plane," Lewis said regretfully, feeling, perhaps, that of the four men concerned, Joe, the most reputable, should, by some moral law, have been the man to escape.

"So it's Harry or Morgan," Prudence said in a taut voice. She put her hand in her pocket again and clutched the brooch tightly. She wanted to fling it on the table and run out of the room. Explanations were rising as far as her throat and sinking again. It was a time for nonchalance; she was sure she would blush. She had an important piece of evidence; they would all be grateful. She couldn't endure the thought of being attacked as her father and Marryatt had been attacked. It was important that the brooch should be produced and the discussion finished before Marryatt came back. The door opened, and Marryatt was back already.

"Is everything finished?" he asked. "Was it Harry? Was it Morgan?"

"I'm about to explain," Lewis said, sighing.

Marryatt looked at Hester. "Let's get it over quickly," he suggested.

"I was waiting for you, Mr Marryatt. I wanted to ask you—when you met Harry Walters on Friday, he told you he was having lunch under a haystack. He wasn't more explicit? He didn't tell you where he was going to eat his lunch."

"No."

"We've interviewed the woman in the village shop," Lewis said, blinking at Hester. "She says he bought coffee, processed Stilton cheese, wrapped in silver paper, packed in a round cardboard box, with a yellow label; a pound of tomatoes; and some cream cracker biscuits in a blue paper carton. All on your account, Miss Wade. She remembers it clearly because afterwards she thought he should have said on Mr Wade's account. She also thought he should have paid cash."

"Oh, you keep nibbling away at Harry's reputation," Hester said wildly. "You don't have to do it. Everything's admitted. Harry wasn't reliable. I know all about Harry."

"But do you, Miss Wade? And I'm not here to attack his character. What I was wondering, was he a tidy kind of man?"

"He wasn't," Hester said shortly.

"Then he might have left that cardboard box and the blue paper carton lying around where he ate his lunch. It might just follow—I'm not saying necessarily it would—that we could find if there's some place, not in this house, that he had reason to be interested in."

"I think—" Prudence began.

"One minute, please, until I've finished what I have to say. I have some notes here, taken from a statement made by a man called Murray, the editor of a poetry magazine. He was a friend of Harry Walters' and his statement may add to your knowledge of that young man. What he has to say is that Harry cultivated the society of criminals. He wanted to be—where is it? What was it, Sergeant Young?"

"François Villon, sir."

Lewis looked over the papers at Hester.

"You know about this François Villon?"

"I know who he was."

Lewis looked relieved. "Then I needn't explain. You understand that your friend Harry had some idea of becoming one of these criminals. It seems he actually arranged to take part in a train mailbag robbery, but he missed the train. You know about this?"

Hester shook her head.

"Incidentally, the attempt failed, and the gang was caught, but not because he informed on them. We've checked on this. Murray came to us because he was afraid the gang had held Harry responsible and might have—retaliated. But we needn't go into that, although it's possible the men concerned may still wrongly suppose that Harry was responsible for their failure."

"And why are you telling us this, if we needn't go into it?" Hester demanded.

"I'm trying to fit your Jackie into the picture. I've already arranged to have his description sent out—we won't have much trouble in finding him. But, Miss Wade, Mr Wade, you should have known this isn't the kind of place, nor yet the kind of house, that attracts men like this Jackie. There's a chance, you know, he came here for a purpose."

"You wouldn't like to cut a straight line through all those circumlocutions?" Marryatt asked. "If you know which went on that plane, Morgan or Harry, why not tell us now?"

Lewis held up a warning hand. "There's a possibility that Jackie chose this house and place by accident. There's another that he came here deliberately, or was sent by others, to find out what he could about Harry, or Morgan. Wait. When the thoroughly confused statement made by this editor, Murray, is laid alongside Miss Wade's evidence, a most significant point emerges. Murray explains that Harry was shown a photograph of the man who got away with the Sackford diamonds. You know about that? It was one of the biggest robberies of this generation. It was a classic affair. All the jewels were out of the bank for the Sackford girl's coming-out dance. The dance of the year, the papers said it was going to be. The Duchess and her three daughters were going to shine like Blackpool on Bank Holiday night. In the middle of the afternoon, in broad daylight, when the family was playing croquet on the lawn or whatever families like that do in the afternoon, someone walked into the house, coshed a detective at one end of a corridor; gagged a housemaid, tapped a footman on the head, lifted the jewel boxes, and walked away. He had five minutes to do it in, while detective number two was downstairs getting himself a cup of tea, so we're certain that the someone was at least three men. And that was the end of the Sackford diamonds. The insurance company was offering ten thousand, but the diamonds didn't turn up through the usual fences. The first fact we've had on it is Murray's statement. One man got away with the diamonds and left his two friends out in the cold. These two have been looking for him ever since. They show everyone his photograph, and they showed Harry. Shall I tell you when that robbery took place? In June, two years ago. Two years and two months ago." He looked at Hester. "Does that make anything in your mind stir?"

"How could it? What could we have to do with a diamond robbery? You don't mean that Harry had anything to do with it?" she asked in a terrified whisper, as though she was speaking across a death-bed.

"No, he doesn't. And we've had enough of this," Marryatt said loudly. "Why don't you come right out and say what you mean? If Harry had anything to do with it, it was only because he'd seen the photograph. Two years and two months. Hester, don't you remember what you told us about Morgan? He said he'd been alone for two years and two months."

"Morgan! Do you mean that Morgan stole these jewels?"

"I told you," Marryatt said to Prudence. "I told you that he was hiding something and Harry was after it. And don't get this wrong again," he said angrily to Hester. "Harry had seen the photograph. He came down here with the Fergusons, met your lot, recognised Morgan. It's a million to one he was only after the insurance. He wanted to marry you and he'd no money, and no other chance of getting any."

"He should have come to us," Inspector Lewis said bitterly. "All he had to do was to come to the police. If he'd told us he knew the man who had the Sackford diamonds, we'd have had them within twenty-four hours, and he'd have had his reward as well. But he had to go plunging round with his idiotic stratagems, playing his infantile games with death watch beetles and guns, until he had this Morgan Price in such an alcoholic panic that he took the terrible risk of arranging to leave the country, which is what he'd have done long ago if he hadn't been afraid of being spotted at the ports. When Morgan heard that a plane was leaving from an obscure airfield for Ireland, he was driven by fear of Harry to take the chance. Remember, there are no passports needed for Ireland."

Wade began to run a hand back and forward across his forehead, quickly, like a man trying to rub out his thoughts.

"So I've been harbouring a thief in my house," he said. "Oh, this is terrible. I knew he was hiding something. No, I didn't. It's not true. I thought he was mentally ill. I thought he drank. I thought anything, but I never thought he was a thief. I wouldn't have had him here. Can't you understand what this means to me? A thief!"

"Don't, Father. It's all over. Morgan has gone. He'll never come back. It's not your fault, Father. How were you to know? And you were right. He was mentally ill. He'd been hiding for two years. Hiding from the police, hiding from the men he'd betrayed, in the end hiding from Harry."

Marryatt looked belligerently at the inspector. "Let's get on with it. You know, I suppose. Was Morgan the man who didn't fly?"

"I can answer the question," Lewis said shortly. "If we're right about the rest, it's the most obvious point of all. But first I'd like to add something to what Miss Wade has said. Morgan Price had someone else to hide from. And that was Jackie."

"Jackie!" Wade repeated numbly.

"Jackie. You've made it plain enough in your statements. From the moment Jackie came into the house, Morgan was afraid to come out of his room. He wouldn't come downstairs to telephone until Miss Wade promised to keep Jackie and Harry in the kitchen. He wouldn't come downstairs for meals."

"But he did come out," Prudence protested suddenly. "He came out to the chapel, when I was there with Harry, on Thursday morning."

"I think you'll find Jackie was busy in the kitchen at that point. Morgan took the risk and came out the front way. But if I'm right, it was a risk, or he saw it as one. But he took that risk—to get to the chapel, and Harry."

Hester made a restless movement with her hands, then forced them into stillness again, and sat rigid.

"If you're not going to get on with this, I will," Marryatt said violently. "What about that brooch, Prudence?"

"I'm so glad you reminded me," Prudence said graciously. "This is the brooch Jackie lent me, Inspector. I thought you might be interested in it." She put her hand in her pocket and held the brooch out to him, with an amused, disparaging smile, like one collector showing another a trivial piece unwisely acquired in the sale-room.

He took it, and held it in his thick, scrubbed hand, turning it a little, to let the light enter the hard heart of the stones. He stared at it, bemused and angry, like a peasant examining the countess's jewels. He took a list from his pocket, and looked at it, and nodded.

"It's not my subject," he said cautiously, "but if it's as real as it looks, then Jackie was in this up to his neck." He scowled as he spoke the last few words. "He found where Morgan Price had hidden the lot, even if Harry didn't. He wouldn't have tried to give the brooch away if he hadn't found the rest. Very generous, these crooks are, on impulse, but not to the point of giving away all they've got."

"But, Inspector Lewis, surely he wouldn't give away anything valuable," Hester said.

"It's part of the pattern. Don't ask me why they do it. I can only tell you that again and again we catch them because they do. I'll keep this brooch. Miss Prudence will perhaps be prepared to sign a statement declaring how it came into her possession."

"Oh, gladly," Prudence said, dejection spreading across her face.

"And now, Mr Marryatt, as you're so determined, we'll get on with it. If we take the evidence of this numerologist, Benson, the man who remembered someone's name began with M. He wasn't listening, he wouldn't have heard anything if he hadn't once been an under-manager at Woolworth's. But as it happens, his ear was caught by the familiar name."

He stopped, took out the sheaf of papers, and looked

through the typescript once again. "This is what he heard: 'Woolworth's! what do you think about that?' And the second man said: 'I'm afraid I can't think anything. I didn't see it.' And the third man said: 'Woolworth's! What's all this? When did it happen?' And that's all." Inspector Lewis folded the papers again carefully, and returned them to his pocket. "After that, the grocer went on with his astrology, and neither of them heard another word that could usefully be called evidence."

"And the conversation could only refer to the brooch. If you're going to take the word of a crazy numerologist as proof, I'm not," Marryatt said.

"Take it easy, Mr Marryatt. A man can be a numerologist or an astrologist and be just as sane as any member of the Stock Exchange, or any dealer in farm machinery, when it comes to that. People take up these things as a way of passing the time, or explaining the universe, two things we're all concerned with, in our own way. I'm prepared to take the word of this numerologist because he's an honest man, who was clearly not prepared to manufacture evidence to oblige. You know what it proves, do you?

"You think it proves that Morgan went on the aeroplane, because there were only two of these four men who didn't see the brooch that night, Morgan and Maurice Reid, and there were two men at Brickford who said or implied they didn't see it. You think it proves that either Harry or Joe Ferguson is the missing man, because they had both seen the brooch, but only one of the three who flew had seen it. And as you're already satisfied that Ferguson was on the plane, you're satisfied that Harry was the man who didn't fly."

"Harry? Harry alive?" Hester said faintly. "Oh, why didn't you say so before?"

"They didn't say because they're not sure. That's why,"

Marryatt said. "And I don't accept that evidence. I don't accept this reported conversation."

Lewis looked at him speculatively, searching for a vulnerable point.

"You accepted the evidence of reported conversation when it established the fact that Maurice Reid flew in the aeroplane. When it established a point that it was in your own interests to accept."

Marryatt was standing up now. His strong, challenging face dominated the room.

"Then I was wrong. But my views, right or wrong, are of no importance," he said, while the intensity of his belief in himself radiated from his face like an almost visible force. "I don't accept the fact that this Harry, who had no money, should get hold of fifteen pounds, spend it on buying a passage to Ireland, and then abandon the idea of flying and say goodbye to the only fifteen pounds he had in the world."

"Why are you so anxious Harry should be dead?" Hester asked angrily.

He glared at her. "Because I want this matter cleared up. And no one can tell me that any court will accept the mixture of parables and logical problems that's been brought up here."

Inspector Lewis heaved himself up and gathered the sergeant in with his glance.

"We must go," he said. "I am very grateful for the help you have all so freely given. You are right, you know, Mr Marryatt, but this matter isn't going to court as it stands. There is no criminal case to bring forward. There will eventually be an inquest. All we have been trying to do here is discover in a friendly way what kind of proof of identity might be offered at the inquest. Also, if one of those four men didn't fly in that aeroplane, it's obvious that he must be somewhere else.

It's easier to look for one man than four, and what has happened here has been quite enough to convince me that Harry Walters is the man to look for. I think we'll find him," he said significantly. "Where are you going to be for the next few days, Mr Marryatt?"

"I'll stay at The Running Fox," Marryatt said, looking at Hester, who was absorbed in some private calculation, and scarcely seemed to hear him.

"Then goodbye for the present. If you happen to see Jackie, don't forget we'd like to get in touch with him."

They went, and a few minutes later Prudence had the great pleasure of showing Marryatt out.

Proof (1)

For the first part of the night Hester allowed herself to think of Harry, to recreate his face and remember the few words of love he had spoken, to dream of the plans she had made to save him and believe again in his genius. She struggled with unreality, desperately injecting life into it, and won a guilty victory. She offered herself to his memory, and fell asleep believing she would dream of him.

She woke early in the morning with a shock of unhappiness and terror, convinced that she had heard an anguished voice calling to her. Desperate fancies and premonitions bred in her mind like bacteria in an open wound: she lay in agony, trying somehow to find the strength to control her own thoughts. She saw Harry's face again, and angrily pushed the picture away. He had gone, he had left her; to try to live with his memory was like nurturing corruption and decay.

She forced herself to rise and dress, to think of her father and her sister, and of the fact that they needed her. She thought bitterly that she no longer needed them. The last few days had forced her into an existence that was quite apart from theirs; she had her private life, her secret thoughts; she couldn't relapse into being a member of her father's house. She would live alone for ever.

She went downstairs and found Prudence in the kitchen.

"Hello," Prudence said. "I thought if I peeled the potatoes now you wouldn't mind if I went swimming."

"Swimming!" Hester repeated. "Oh, I'm very glad that you are able to enjoy yourself again. You're not worried about what people will think?"

"Don't say people when you mean you," Prudence advised. She threw the potatoes into the sink, viciously, as though she wanted to knock the bottom out of it. "We can't let this go on for ever, that's what I think. Why shouldn't we just behave? Let's get some pleasure before the summer's over. If Father didn't stop that cheque I'll probably have to go and be a kitchen girl among the cockroaches in some ramshackle hotel where people murder each other in the third floor back."

"He sent a wire last night. He won't know till this evening or tomorrow if the cheque has been paid in already. It's more than likely that it has—in that letter Maurice gave Uncle Joe to post. Now, Prudence, could we stop talking, just stop talking for the rest of the day? Go swimming. Do what you want. But whatever you do don't go on talking for ever and ever and ever like this making me think of everything all over again."

Prudence looked at her angrily, then, in compunction, looked away again. "Don't worry too much, Hester," she said awkwardly. "I'll take the tea up to Father. You wouldn't like to come swimming?"

Hester shook her head. She sat, drinking hot tea, considering with dull surprise the death of her emotions. She had no more capacity to feel. She didn't know how life was to be faced. She put down the tea and went to the sink and washed her face in cold water, thinking sadly there was no way of washing out her mind and making it clean and clear again. The police, she thought, could come and go for ever, asking questions, producing results, assaulting her with each question, destroying her spirit with every answer, taking a technical interest in the nature of the wounds they inflicted: she had no refuge from them, although she had committed no crime.

She went out of the house and into the garden, hurrying past the bed where the roses grew. It was less than a week since Harry had cut the rosebuds for her, one for every year of her life. She went into the woods and slowly towards the chapel. She sat down on one of the ruined walls, remembering the hour she had spent there with Harry, probing the wound, trying to make it hurt again.

When she heard a step she looked up, half-afraid that Harry had come back.

It was Marryatt.

"Hello," he said. "I've been looking for this place. And I wanted to talk to you again."

She nodded mutely. She didn't want to talk. She had no energy to tell him to go away.

He sat down in the corner where the two broken walls met, lit a cigarette, and smoked it in silence. She looked at him once or twice, impatiently.

"You wanted to say something?" she asked.

"No, not now."

"Then what are you doing here?"

"Just accustoming you to my presence..."

"Then I'll go."

"No, please. We needn't talk. I won't worry you at all."

She sat down again. She was too tired to force herself to any kind of action. She drifted slowly into a waking dream of the past. Marryatt was part of it. His presence in the corner was neither remembered nor forgotten, until he stirred and she looked round to see an increased intensity on his face. He was staring across into the far corner of the chapel, and she looked too, and saw the blue paper carton lying there.

"So this is where Harry ate his lunch," she said. "It doesn't matter, does it?"

"Not if he liked this place," Marryatt said, still looking intently at the blue paper. "Did he?"

"Oh, he might have liked it," she said angrily.

"And Morgan liked it too? This is where your sister saw Harry and Morgan quarrel, isn't it?"

"Questions again," she said wearily.

He walked over to the blue paper, looked down at it, bent, and touched it. He pulled one corner of it gently, but it was imprisoned between two stones.

He stood up again, looking dubiously at Hester, not certain how much she should be asked to hear.

She walked across to him.

"So someone's raised the stone," she said. "Don't look like that. You needn't look like that. It doesn't mean anything. If you think it does, lift the stone yourself. Go on. Lift it. I've more right than you to see."

"We'll go back to your house," he said quickly. "You'll come with me, won't you?"

She let him take her by the arm. She didn't listen to anything he said, as they walked back through the woods, but when they reached the house she shook free from him.

"There's the telephone," she said bitterly. She began to

walk upstairs, but on the landing she stopped and listened long enough to hear what he had to say to the police. Then she went in her bedroom and locked the door.

When the police came and raised the stone and descended into the six-foot deep vault, they found all that was left of Harry. He had been shot in the chest, and one hand still lay protectively over the wound.

At first they thought there was nothing in the vault but Harry and the decaying wooden coffins. When they raised him they found a few scattered flower petals; colourless, shrivelled nearly to the heart, but still with a vestige of the soft bloom of the living rose.

They searched the vault, but nowhere in the disturbed dust was any proof that the Sackford diamonds had ever lain there.

Proof (2)

Inspector Lewis, confronted with murder instead of an irritating problem about missing persons, looked like a marble statue of himself. If he had any feeling of indulgence or sympathy for interfering civilians, he calcified it instantly. He had made it known he wanted to see Hester, and he waited for Hester to be produced.

"I'm sorry," Marryatt said. "You can't see her. She's not feeling like that."

Lewis looked at Marryatt as though he was measuring him for the gallows.

"She's told you everything she knows. She can't add to it."

"I don't accept your authority," Lewis snapped. "I'm prepared to see you later. I don't want to see you now."

"Oh, come," Marryatt said gently. "I'm the man who put

you on to this. I knew there was something about that chapel. I guessed things might have worked out that way."

"What way?"

"I thought maybe Morgan might have won the battle with Harry."

"So that's your opinion. Morgan. I might have supposed you'd jump to the easy conclusion."

Marryatt's manner of careless arrogance didn't change. "He was the man who'd hidden the diamonds. He was the man who went to the chapel on Thursday morning, quarrelled with Harry, threatened him. Harry brought out the gun then: he knew about the gun. He was the man who was in such a state of despair on Friday morning that he frightened even Prudence. He told her, didn't he, that the plane was his only chance?"

"Mr Marryatt, I can do my own guessing. Your views are of no importance. You hadn't even met Morgan Price."

Marryatt made a quick step forward. His dark brows were drawn together, and his eyes were very bright. He was a bigger man than the inspector, and he looked for a moment as though he was going to ignore the immunity of office. Then he drew back again and smiled with the maximum of unfriendliness.

"I'm asking you to get this straight before you see Miss Wade, or her father. They've had enough. They've lived a sheltered life for five hundred years. Now, you listen to me. As I see it, Morgan, who'd been dithering about all night, finally came down, to this room, and found the gun lying on the table where I left it. Then he went out, found Harry in the vault, and shot him."

"Throwing a rose on the body for remembrance?" Lewis suggested coldly. "Thank you, Mr Marryatt. Now I want to see Miss Wade."

Marryatt, scowling, sat down on the arm of a chair. "I have no way of stopping you."

"It won't be necessary for you to be present, Mr Marryatt. You may wait in another room, if you wish."

Marryatt's wishes showed clearly enough in his face, but he stood up and walked out of the room.

He met Hester in the hall.

"I'm sorry," he said. "I couldn't stop it."

She passed him without listening, and went into the room where the police waited. She sat down, ignoring them entirely, maintaining the appearance of a woman who had her own reality, and would admit no other.

"Miss Wade, I've asked you to come because you are the only person concerned who can be relied on to tell us what we want to know."

She nodded, still examining her own thoughts, not interested in the police and their questions.

"Was Morgan Price wearing a rose in his button-hole, that Thursday night?"

"No."

"Could you think carefully about that?"

She closed her eyes, calling up a vision of Morgan's tortured face. She had seen him before dinner, she had seen him again when Maurice lay unconscious and she thought he was dead.

"No, he wasn't wearing a rose."

"Was he the kind of man who would wear a button-hole? Had he ever, to your knowledge, worn one?"

"Never."

"Was Harry wearing a button-hole that night?"

Her face twitched a little at the mention of Harry's name.

"No. But you had better ask Mrs Ferguson, hadn't you?" she said with sudden passion. "He saw her last, didn't he?"

"And your father didn't wear a button-hole? No, I thought not. Now Maurice Reid wore the rose you gave him in the morning in the garden, when you appealed to him not to take your father's money. He was still wearing it, when you left him here, in this room, late on Thursday night. You said so, didn't you?"

"Yes, he was still wearing it."

"And there was this scene in this room here, when Harry fixed the roses on Jackie's shirt?"

"Yes, I remember that," she said, her voice quivering. "Please, need we go on?"

"I'm afraid we must. Would you say that Jackie resented being made the butt of Harry's humour?"

"I didn't notice."

"Then Mr Ferguson drew your attention to the special type of rose he was wearing in his button-hole?"

"Yes."

"So three people, Joseph Ferguson, Maurice Reid, and this Jackie, all wore roses that night." He made the statement flatly. "This Marryatt, what about him?"

Hester looked up. "Marryatt? I can't remember. I don't think so, but I can't remember. What are you trying to find out? What have roses to do with this?"

"There were petals, quite a lot of petals, in the vault," Inspector Lewis said harshly. "I want you to try to remember if Marryatt wore a rose."

"I've had enough of this," Hester said on a note of repugnance. "I can't go on. Why should Marryatt wear a rose, just to oblige you in your search for a victim? You sit there, destroying us all, because you want to have your case tidied up, and put away in a box file. I didn't know the police were like this! And you," she said, turning on Sergeant Young, "pretending to be a pianist, to like Bach, to be a human being like everyone else. It's a lie."

"Please keep calm, Miss Wade. That's all we wish to ask you. Your sister has supplied the rest of the evidence. I'm afraid it may be necessary to see her again and to take a statement from her. If she confirms what she has already told us," he added in a kinder voice, "the case will be settled, beyond any reasonable doubt."

Hester stood up to go, her glance resting pitifully on the roses.

"Prudence is only sixteen. I can't agree that she should be left alone with you, to make a statement on murder," she said, her voice wincing away from the final word.

"You would like your father to be present?"

"Father is not well. He's suffering from shock. I'll stay."

"As you wish," Inspector Lewis said indifferently. He wasn't in any way interested in the limits of her endurance. For the present he was concerned with only one problem, and until that had been settled, no others existed for him.

Prudence came in. Her hair was still wet from swimming, and there were two damp channels on her cheeks. She looked in terror, not at the detectives, but at her sister.

"Oh, Hester, I'm sorry I said all those things. I liked him so much. I did, truly. I'm so sorry. What can I do?"

Hester walked quickly over to the table where the roses languished, and stood, fingering the fallen petals, picking them up one by one, crushing them, until her fingers were wet.

"There's nothing you can do," she said, still standing with her back to the room. "Tell them what they want to know."

"We want you to describe, in your own words, what this

man Jackie, Jackie Daw, if that's what he called himself, looked like when you saw him on Friday morning. I want you to think very carefully, because it's possible your words may be used as evidence. In fact, we want to take them down."

"All right," Prudence said. She looked guiltily at Hester's back. "I didn't see Jackie on Friday morning when I went into the kitchen. So I came in here, to the sitting-room, and he was sort of standing around, with a duster. He was wearing that dreadful flowered shirt. I don't know if you heard about it before, but it looked as though he'd bought it at a jumble sale on the Gold Coast. It was all colours of flowers, and he still had two rosebuds pushed in it, that Harry put in the night before. You know. And he was looking kind of pale and underprivileged and underfed, the way he always did. I don't know about his trousers. I don't remember what they looked like. Then I saw him again at breakfast, and he said:"

"I don't want to hear what he said," Inspector Lewis interrupted.

"Well, Hester said at breakfast, 'You're still wearing your roses, Jackie, were you up all night?'"

"I don't want to hear that either. Your sister may make a separate statement about his appearance."

"All right. Then I was in here cutting out a frock. I wanted to ask him if he could tango, but I expect that's another thing you don't want to hear again. I must say, I do think you're trying to have it both ways," she added candidly. "You've heard all this already, and now officially you're not hearing it."

"Confine yourself to what you saw," Inspector Lewis said.

"Then that's practically nothing. No, wait, I saw him take off the roses and throw them in the wastepaper basket. They are probably still there, because I haven't emptied it. And I saw him go away. He was wearing his pullover then, and carrying a paper shopping bag. I thought he was going to the village, but of course he must have been going away with his things."

"But he didn't have any things," Sergeant Young pointed out quickly. He looked down again at his notebook. "Shall I go back to the station and get this transcribed, sir?"

"No, copy it now."

While Sergeant Young wrote the statement, Lewis went to the wastepaper basket and shook out its contents. The two withered roses lay among the old papers and empty cigarette packets. He picked them up and put them away carefully, and then waited until the sergeant had handed over the statement and Prudence had signed it. He took the statement and folded it slowly, almost lovingly, as a hunter might unconsciously caress his gun.

"Then?" Hester asked.

He turned on her, smiling almost indulgently. He was a human being again. "Miss Wade, you look tired," he said in solicitous tones, that, after what had gone before, failed to convince. "We needn't trouble you any more today."

"You can't go like this. You have no right to. We are the people most concerned. Perhaps we are the only people who care at all about him. You can't leave us like this, not knowing."

"We police must be allowed our little secrets, you know," he said, beaming at her.

"You said it wasn't Morgan, because he wasn't wearing a rose. You said it couldn't be Jackie, because he still had those roses in the morning. You're leaving us to suppose that Uncle Joe or Maurice must have—have done what was done. If that's not true, then you must tell us, and not leave us to think evil thoughts of the dead." She spoke with a conviction that made her seem sadly ingenuous.

Inspector Lewis allowed his expression to slip almost to

the edge of compassion, to the slopes that are too dangerous for officialdom to tread.

"I'm issuing a warrant for Jackie's arrest," he said. "I wish I could be sure about his other name being Daw."

The rose petals that Hester still held floated softly to the ground and settled there before she spoke.

"But he—we've sworn that he still had his roses in the morning."

"That's almost the whole point, Miss Wade. He had his roses in the morning, although we think he left them, or most of them, in that vault. We shan't know exactly what happened there, until we get him. There may have been a struggle. Enough of a struggle, anyway, to make someone's button-hole, or the petals from it, fall off. He wouldn't have noticed at the time that they'd gone, but he certainly noticed it afterwards. He wouldn't want to go back there, searching for rose petals."

"But how do you know it was Jackie?" Prudence said in exasperation. "He wasn't the only one with a button-hole."

"The others were wearing only one rose. And, you see, you have the evidence in this room that it was Jackie. There are only sixteen roses in that vase, as Sergeant Young noticed earlier," he said in a voice which contained only a careful measure of approval.

The sergeant moved forward eagerly. "There were twenty, Miss Wade. You—he—I mean you watched them being picked, one for every year of your life, he said. And you noticed when he gave Jackie two of them. Eighteen left. No one else touched them, so far as you know. In the morning Jackie stayed long enough to flaunt the fact that he still had two roses. He was shrewd enough, in his way, but quite blinded by his own shrewdness, or he'd have taken his substitute roses from the garden, and not left the vase here with only sixteen."

Inspector Lewis sat still, looking as though he would like to bite his fingernails. "That's enough," he said impatiently. "There are no more facts we can give you. Only theories. It's possible that Harry found the place where Morgan Price was hiding those jewels he may have stolen. It's possible he went there late at night with the idea of getting these jewels and delivering them up to the insurance company. It's possible that this Jackie, quite independently spying on Morgan Price, also discovered the hiding-place. The brooch he produced earlier in the evening certainly suggests this. It's possible that when Jackie had made his plans he went back to this vault and found Harry there already. All that will have to wait till we get him. It won't take long. We get a lot of co-operation when we need it. The first of the Sackford diamonds that comes on that market will be the end of your Jackie."

He began to make ponderous preparations for departure. Sergeant Young looked wistfully at the two silent girls, as though they represented something he had given up, like the piano, but, whatever he felt, he attached himself hastily to his superior, like a railway carriage being impelled towards its engine.

Inspector Lewis stopped at the door.

"There's a point about a letter, the letter Maurice Reid gave Ferguson to post. He must have forgotten it. He gave it to the—to Harry Walters to post, or so it seems, for it was still in his pocket. There's no danger now that the cheque will ever be presented."

He gave them a bureaucratic nod that included in its scope a contempt for the fallible men who forget to post letters.

Then he lumbered from the room. Sergeant Young followed, smiling anxious messages over his shoulder.

The two sisters were left alone to survey the empty wastes of misery. Prudence made an effort to approach Hester, then retreated, frightened by the silence.

They were sitting nervously apart when the door opened and Marryatt came in with two cups in his hands.

"Tea's up," he said. "It's strong, the way we like it in Australia. You'll get used to it."

Conclusion

Marryatt and Hester climbed the long slopes of Furlong Hill with the rain drifting in their faces.

"I know it's the finest view in England," Marryatt said. "But it's like every other view in England: fifty yards of sodden grass, then wet invisibility."

"Doesn't it ever rain in Australia?"

"When it rains it's real rain, not this filtered drizzle. I'm going back, Hester. Did I tell you? Next week. The firm's getting jumpy. They think I'm staying here for the fun of it."

Hester walked on quickly through the wet grass.

"Don't accuse me with your back," he said. "I know the kind of time you've been having. Do you suppose I couldn't understand what you felt at the trial?"

Hester looked resolutely ahead. "We're nearly at the top. They made it as easy for me as they could."

"You're always trying to give people credit where none is due. They made it as easy for themselves as they could. He'd kept the gun: he had the diamonds. Naturally, they made their case out of that. They couldn't have got a conviction out of two rosebuds in a button-hole."

Hester turned. "Tom, I can think about these things. I won't talk about them, even to you."

"You have to talk. You have to talk and talk and get it out of your system. Root it out now or your mind will be smothered with it, like prickly pear. I don't suppose you know what that is."

"Of course I do."

"I thought you didn't know anything about Australia. We could sit down on that stone and wait for the mist to clear. If it does, we'll be able to see the valley looking just as wet as the hill."

Hester looked at the dripping stone, then sat down. He moved away from her, wiping the rain angrily from his face.

"Now you listen to me."

"I thought you wanted me to talk."

"Later. I don't want any novelettish misunderstandings. Hester, you know what I'm like. I hated Maurice Reid. I wouldn't have killed him, but I can't be sorry he's dead. That's the truth about me. You think it's bad, don't you?"

"Yes," she said simply.

"I suppose you wouldn't want to marry me, knowing what I'm like," he said defiantly.

She shut her eyes, calling up her vision of Harry.

"Harry always said I had to marry someone weak."

"Harry wasn't necessarily right. Anyway, I'm weak enough to satisfy most people. I'm weak enough to be afraid of Harry. He had a lot of faults: I know they don't count now. He was anti-social in quite an innocent way. He could make you laugh; he was in love with you, perhaps he could write poetry. I don't know. I can compete against someone alive, but not against a man who's dead. So I'd better clear off."

Hester stood up. "No, you left out one thing. I wasn't in

love with Harry. I wasn't. I wanted to change him, that's all I wanted, just to prove to myself how wonderful I was. He was wrong about me, you know. I couldn't marry anyone weak."

She kissed him, and there was nothing left of Harry, except a small handful of poems for the anthologies.

No Bath for
the Browns

Before the estate agent had time to shut his eyes and stick a
pin into the waiting list, he found he had let the house to Mrs
Brown. She took it, unseen, on a ten years' lease, and on her
way back to the basement room she dropped a pound in a
pavement artist's hat. The pound marked, for her, the end of
a year's exercise in concealing furious despair behind a façade
of untroubled, almost aristocratic, courtesy.

When she unlocked the front door she felt like Robinson
Crusoe surveying, for the first time, what was, through no
design of his own, to be his kingdom. The grim mosaic of
the hall floor would have been naked to the sunshine if it had
not been for the porch, a kind of sun baffle-wall in coarsely
stained glass. The floor of the porch was also tiled, making
it suitable for potted plants.

"A dear little house," Charles said to her, with just a hint
of a question in his voice.

Her mind was wandering on. "If we bought a carpet—
second-hand, of course—we could cover those tiles."

"And how are we to conceal the railway line which passes
under the bedroom window?" Charles asked.

She opened a buff-coloured door and peered down the stairs. "Charles," she said in excitement. "There's a bath!"

They looked at the bath. "It isn't very handy," she admitted. "No," Charles said. "But I suppose you can dive in from the top step and dry in the hall when you come out."

Greta ran upstairs. "Look!" she called. "Here's a room that isn't really good for anything. Don't you think we could move the bath up?"

"We'd never get anyone to do it."

"Nonsense!" she said briskly. "We can do it ourselves. Cut off the water, move the bath, ring the water and the gas company and say our bath's not connected. Then we'd be priority. We can do it with ropes."

"I begin to see why this house was to let," Charles said.

Greta said she'd meant to tell him about that. It belonged, she said, to a man called Smith whose wife had left him for another man, at least that was what the neighbours said, anyway, she'd disappeared, and he was so heartbroken, the neighbours said, that he couldn't bear to live there any more.

"I'm surprised he ever bore it. Do you think it has a queer-ish smell?"

"It's probably only rats," Greta said, with a flash of her old victory spirit. "Now, I'll begin to scrub the floors tomorrow. We must buy some distemper for those awful walls. You must get in touch with the storage people and the gas and electricity and water. There's the food office, and we must find a coal merchant who'll have us. Do you think we can get that broken window mended? Do try and eat well through the day—there'll be nothing but bread and marge in the evenings. And buy some rat poison."

———

Their lives for the next month might have been planned by some lunatic master mind. One part of the day was spent in making pathetic appeals to gas, electricity, telephone, food, and fuel functionaries; the other in trying to buy things that could not be bought. In the evenings they scrubbed the floors, painted the walls, and ate bread and margarine. All their friends told them how lucky they were, and asked if they had any rooms to spare.

The faintly nauseating smell they had rented with the house did not diminish. Charles said Mrs Smith had run away, not to find romance, but to escape the smell.

Charles found it was impossible to turn on the bath taps without taking off his shoes and standing in the bath. When he had done this he found that the pipes had been disconnected. He agreed that the bath must be moved.

It took them four hours to haul the bath upstairs: some of that time was spent in offering each other conflicting advice at the corners, but there was enough hard work to make Charles feel that his heart was affected. He sat trembling on the edge of the bath, while Greta went to make some tea.

She came upstairs without the tea and stood silent for so long that her husband began to feel nervous.

"I think you should have a look at the bathroom, not this bathroom, the other one," she said in a thin voice. His smothered thoughts leapt to the surface. It was Mrs Smith.

He went downstairs. When he came back, neither of them spoke for some minutes. They were thinking of estate agents, furniture stores, gas and electricity men, food and fuel offices, carpenters, builders, pots of paint, stacks of bread and margarine. They were thinking of the quiet and orderly lives they had once led, and of how they had never done anyone any harm.

Charles sat stiff and still. He hoped he would never be asked to get up, to speak, to act. Unpleasant as this moment was, he wanted it to last as long as his life and not be succeeded by any kind of future.

"Do you think the shops are shut?" Greta asked.

"We could get some cement from the builder's," she said. "Or something airtight. I think jobs like that should be done properly." She smoothed her hair and hummed a little. "I'll make some tea while you go for the cement."

That night, when the rest of the work was over, they moved the bath downstairs again. The neighbours were curious about the noise, but they never learnt what had caused it. This was just as well, for if any rumours had reached the ears of Mr Smith, he would have been most upset.

Mrs Smith was past caring.